Fallen

Martin Hyde

ANDREW

Andrew Cummings surveyed the London Docklands from his fiftieth-floor office in One Canada Square, the highest peak in London. The Thames snaked its way through the skyline, framed by the newly completed HSBC and Citigroup towers. Skeletons of future skyscrapers surrounded him at every angle.

All around him the city was rising, but he was falling.

How long would it take to hit the ground from here? Twenty seconds? Fifteen?

He tore himself away from the window and resumed his pacing.

On the wall-mounted flat screen, a BBC reporter read the details of the Queen Mother's passing - the first news story in three days to rival Apollo Pharmaceuticals' own media shitstorm.

The muted clap of his heels echoed through the fog of his thoughts.

He needed to focus. The board meeting was in - he checked his Patek Philippe - fifteen minutes.

Fuck.

He fell into his desk chair and set his Newton's cradle in

motion. The metronomic chink of the balls lulled him back to the present.

He pulled out his bottom desk drawer and fumbled for his eight ball of cocaine. He heaped the powder in the groove behind his thumb and swiped it across his nose. A cold, alpine wind stung his sinuses. Blood rushed to his head.

The monitor on his desk displayed the London Stock Exchange. In red text – *Panic!* - Apollo Pharmaceuticals (APP) showed an 11.2 percent drop before the market had closed for the Easter weekend. Worse still, they had dragged the FTSE 100 down 4.8 percent.

And there had been two more deaths since.

The morning's papers fanned across his walnut desktop. He scanned the headlines with a fresh dose of disgust.

Fourth Death in Apollo Drug Trial, cried The Guardian.

Schizophrenic Apollo Subject Murders Wife, roared The Times.

The Sun, the Independent, and the Daily Mail had been no more forgiving.

Worse than the headlines was the grainy black and white photograph in The Times of the test subject, Edward Dennis. He stared out at Andrew, the black holes of his pupils burning with ineffable horror.

The image of him biting into his wife's jugular flashed through Andrew's mind. He shuddered.

A speck of crimson blotted the man's face. And then another.

Blood dripped in perfect synchronicity with the sound of the Newton's cradle before he cupped a hand under his nose, roamed for a tissue with the other.

Finding none, he went to the bathroom and rolled off a stretch of toilet paper. He wiped up the blood and blocked his nose with cotton wool. He did not have time to sit around nursing a nosebleed with the board meeting in... Jesus, eight minutes.

He swallowed the bitter, coke-infused blood and washed

his hands and face. His shirt was stained crimson, but he could hide that with his jacket.

Two nosebleeds in a week. This was getting out of control. He needed to pump the brakes on the powder - just as soon as the dust had settled on the scandal.

Andrew returned to his desk, fastened his jacket over the blood stains.

He looked up at the sound of his name. On the TV, the BBC studio was replaced by a shot of himself walking through Canary Wharf, surrounded by a swarm of journalists.

'Do you have anything to say to the families of the deceased, Mr Cummings?' a reporter called over the din. The camera closed in on his face before Andrew swatted it away.

'Although Apollo's CEO has refused to comment,' the newsreader said, 'we have their head of media communications in the studio.' The camera cut back to reveal the man to whom Andrew had offered a substantial bonus only hours ago, on the mere condition he didn't fuck this up any further. 'So, tell us, Mr Brockbank, is there any danger of further fatalities?'

Andrew snatched the remote and killed the TV. He took deep, measured breaths, both hands splayed on the desktop. The minute hand of his Patek Philippe pointed accusingly at five-to.

He stood and cautiously withdrew the sodden cotton wool from his nostril. He poised a wad of toilet paper underneath to catch any blood but none came.

Andrew stuffed the toilet paper into his pocket and headed for the door, careful to breathe only through his mouth.

SIMBA

'Spare any change?'

The crowd flowed endlessly out of Camden tube station. A faceless mass of bodies. They didn't see him, and he didn't see them.

He saw only one thing.

'Spare any change?'

The din was white noise to his ears: individual voices and footfalls were no more human than the murmur of car engines.

The street was a grainy silent movie. The only colour was the silver and gold coins occasionally dropped into his McDonald's cup.

'Spare any change?'

A girl in a blue Card Factory polo and gold hooped earrings snapped around. 'Get a job, you junky prick,' she spat in a South London accent. Lewisham, probably.

He twisted his hips, rolled his shoulders to shift the aches, but now he was acutely aware of the cold, unyielding ground beneath him. His body was a sack of meat wrapped in skin, but soon the rough edges would soften. The tension would melt away.

'Spare any change?'

A hand emerged from the crowd, dropped some shrapnel into his cup.

Yes. There we go. Another hour or two and we'll be safe. And then I'll be quiet. You know I will.

'Hello, stranger.' A hiking bag hit the ground and Daisy slid down the wall beside him. Something was different about her. She wore eyeliner and lipstick - a rarity - but there was something else too.

'You're in a good mood.'

She shrugged. 'Just happy to see you, innit.' Her mask slipped for a moment, and he saw the eternal ache bleed into her features before she averted her eyes. She took a packet of Lambert kings out, lit one, and passed another to Simba.

'Thanks. How was Sam's?'

'Alright, actually,' she said, exhaling. 'We just linked and watched TV.'

'Sounds good,' Simba said. A well-dressed twenty-something met his eye. 'Spare any change?' he asked, but the man looked away.

'Hey, allow that, man,' Daisy said. She reached into the pocket of her Adidas jacket and produced a twenty-pound note between two fingers.

'He paid you?' Simba asked.

'No,' she said defensively. 'I swiped it.'

'Right.'

'What?' she laughed. 'Don't tell me you wouldn't.'

'No, it's just... You should be careful. You don't want to get hurt again.'

Daisy kissed her teeth, glanced up and down the street as though searching for someone who would dare try their luck. 'I can take care of myself, man.'

This was true. And there was the blade she carried; although, to his knowledge, she'd only used it on herself so far. On the nights she couldn't score.

'I know.'

She elbowed him lightly. 'Come on. Let's get out of here. Let me link K.'

'Alright.' He got to his feet, shrugged into his rucksack, and slung his sleeping bag around his neck like a giant, novelty scarf.

Daisy led the charge up Camden High Street to the nearest phone box. He waited outside as she went into the booth and used the phone.

'He'll meet us by the lock in twenty,' Daisy said when she stepped out.

'Safe. You want to go now?'

'Yeah.'

They waded up the street and down the steps to Camden Lock. A cool breeze came from the canal, caressed his hair and face. They sat by the water and shared another cigarette. Daisy leaned her head on his shoulder.

'Where we sleeping tonight?' he asked.

'I was gonna go Terry's yard. He's got a flat in Whitechapel, you know?'

'Really? Won't he mind me coming?'

'Why would he mind?'

Simba pointed to his face. He'd crossed his fair share of mindless racists in the ends.

'Nah, man. He's cool. You got money for the tube, yeah?'

'Yeah, I've got a few quid. And we can shoot there?'

'I told you, man. He's cool.' She punched him lightly on the shoulder, knocking ash from his cigarette. 'I've missed you, you know? Did you miss me?'

Simba smiled. 'Of course.' He scanned the lock. 'What time is it?'

Daisy drew back her sleeve and checked her Hello Kitty watch. 'Quarter-to. He'll be like five minutes.'

They walked under the bridge and waited in the cool dimness. Snippets of strangers' conversations echoed around the space as they passed.

'Yo, that's him,' Daisy said as a youth in a grey tracksuit rounded the corner. 'Wait here.' She walked to meet K, and they shook hands to perform the deal.

'Alright, let's go,' she said, digging her hands into her pockets. Simba imagined the plastic-wrapped powder balled in her fist.

The knot in his stomach loosened.

That's it, Simba. Feed me. We've been hungry for so long.

Soon the voice would fall silent. Just a sharp prick as the cold needle slid into his vein and the warmth drained every tension from his body.

Soon he would drift into oblivion.

KAREN

Karen fanned her thumb absentmindedly down the pages of the travel brochure in her lap - a window into a world for which she had yearned her whole adult life. She was a lonely princess and London was her tower. Where was the dragon lurking now?

Soon she would be free. Two months and six days, to be exact. Then Venice, the Himalayas, and Times Square would not just be pictures in a book, but living, breathing worlds around her.

She'd been waiting for so long. There was so much to see.

She closed her eyes as she swayed on the swing seat, imagined the smell of the sea on the faint breeze. The smell of vast, unexplored worlds.

Andrew had travelled to every continent on business trips. Even Saff had been on school trips to Paris and Milan. They had both downplayed their experiences for her benefit, but she knew what she was missing from the things they didn't say.

Two months and six days until Saff's eighteenth birthday. And then Karen would be free, and it would be Saffron resigned to the tower, to a life of dos and do nots. A life of constant surveillance.

For all her excitement concerning her imminent freedom, there was a slowly inflating balloon of apprehension pressing against the walls of her stomach. It would be a big change for Saffron, the biggest transition of her life. And it wasn't like she could talk to her friends or a therapist about it. Only Karen understood the weight of her new burden.

Congratulations, honey, you're eighteen! You can vote, watch eighteen-rated movies in the cinema, and go out drinking with your friends. But unlike all of your friends, you're also now confined to the Greater London area, you have to carry a second mobile phone everywhere you go, and you have to bear a child before you hit forty or the contract is void. Oh, and you can never tell anyone about this little arrangement except immediate family and your spouse when you marry.

Would it be the same man that had come on Karen's own eighteenth birthday? The man in the dark suit. He would be much older now, of course. She used to be able to recall his image, but the memory was scrambled now, like a chewed-up tape.

She'd sat at the desk in her father's study as the mysterious agent had opened his briefcase and slid a paper contract across the surface. He'd smoked a cigarette as Karen scanned through the contract. Her father had read it too, given her a shrug and a nod, and she'd signed it. Signed away twenty-three years of her life just like that.

Soon it would be Saff's turn.

'Mum?'

Karen jerked around. Saff stood beside the swing seat. When had she come home?

'Jesus, honey,' she laughed. 'You trying to send me to an early grave?'

'Sorry.' Saff looked at the ground like a chastised child. 'There are journalists outside,' she said.

'Oh. Did you say anything to them?'

'No.'

'Okay, good. Just leave it to your father.'

Saff had a strange look in her eyes. Had she been crying?

'Honey, are you...okay?'

'I need to tell you something,' Saff said seriously.

Karen sat up, planted both feet on the ground to stop the swing seat. 'Oh, God. You're pregnant aren't you?'

'No. It's not that.'

'You're on drugs?'

'What? No. I...' She lifted her left hand, showed Karen the diamond ring on her finger. 'Rory proposed.' A fragile, girlish laugh escaped her. 'I said yes.'

The balloon in Karen's stomach burst.

'Oh, dear.'

She knew she should say something else, but nothing came. How did she feel about this? How was she supposed to feel?

It was too soon. It was far too soon.

Rory was Saff's first love. She was seventeen. She didn't know what she was committing to.

'Are you happy for me?' Saff asked uncertainly.

'Of course I'm happy for you.' She folded Saff into her chest, tears filming over her vision. 'It's just a lot to take in. That's all.'

'I know,' breathed Saff, crying herself.

Karen regarded her daughter, a surreal composite of both the young girl whose hair she'd once brushed and the woman she was yet to be.

'Probably best we don't tell your father. Not for a week or so.'

Saff let out a breath of relief and wiped her eyes with a ball of tissue. 'Yeah. That's what I was thinking.'

'God. My daughter's getting married. Go on. Show me the ring again,' she said.

Saff gave a broken laugh as Karen took her hand and raised it to the light.

'He has taste,' she said and smiled with finality, though the questions were stacking in her head for further rumination.

Shit. Tomorrow was Sunday. Her parents were coming

at eleven. She had so much to think about and so little time to think it.

'Oh, and probably best not to say anything to my parents, either. Have you told any of the girls yet?'

'No. I wanted to tell you first.'

'Oh, honey,' she said, and hugged Saff again. 'Come with me.' Karen got to her feet, spilling the travel brochure to the lawn. 'Come on.'

She took Saff's hand and led her back through the kitchen and into the living room. She opened the drinks cabinet and searched for the Bordeaux her parents had gifted her and Andrew at their engagement party. She'd kept it for when her first child got engaged. Her only child.

'Get the glasses,' she told Saff, peeling off the wrap and turning in the corkscrew. She just needed to be careful not to leave the bottle out when Andrew was home; she didn't know if he'd remember which wine she'd reserved but she couldn't take any chances. He was under too much pressure as it was, even if he wouldn't admit it.

'Can't I just have a cider or something?' Saff asked.

Karen waved away the ridiculous notion. 'Nonsense. I've been saving this.' She poured them both a glass and handed Saff hers. 'So,' she said, raising her glass, 'to a happy marriage.'

Saff blushed, chimed her glass against Karen's. It echoed like a gong to signal the beginning of some new chapter.

Karen drank. The wine was rich, a landscape with a bittersweet history in her mouth.

She sunk into the sofa. 'So, tell me everything.'

MAC

Mac leaned against the passenger window and aimed an air-con vent at his face. If he was lucky, he'd be able to squeeze in an hour or so of sleep before his night shift.

Charlotte turned left on Seven Sisters Road, going past Luke's old school. Mac turned inquisitively to her.

'Just filling up,' she said, pulling into the Texaco garage. Despite the relative traffic, the garage was deserted besides a cluster of youths outside the shop.

Charlotte stopped outside the first pump and killed the engine.

'I'll do it,' Mac said, freeing himself from his seatbelt.

'I can manage,' Charlotte said, a little sternly. She compensated with a strained smile. 'Back in a sec.' She climbed out of the Golf and started to fill the car.

Mac glanced at Luke in the rear-view, who stared absently out of the window, and turned on the radio.

'…died in her sleep at the Royal Lodge in Windsor with the Queen by her side. At a hundred and one, she was the longest living member of the royal family in history. No decision has yet been reached as to whether the Queen and her family will attend the Easter service at St George's Chapel tomorrow.

'In other news, a fourth death has been revealed in the Apollo Pharmaceuticals scandal. Following two suicides and a murder, a man named as Edward Dennis has also killed his wife during a heated argument last night. It has been confirmed that Mr Dennis suffered from Paranoid Schizophrenia and was part of the third phase pharmaceutical trial. Apollo Pharmaceuticals, in collaboration with the World Health Organisation, have ordered an urgent recall of all antipsychotics from the trial, and all participants are urged to stop their medication and consult their pharmacist immediately.'

Mac changed the station.

In the street outside, it seemed just another day. Traffic dragged by. Charlotte returned the petrol nozzle to its cradle. If there was one thing he'd learned in the Met, it was that no matter how calm the city appeared, there was always some violence, some secret chaos unfolding somewhere.

Charlotte opened the rear-door, reached inside for her purse, and ruffled Luke's hair. Mac watched her walk into the shop. The hoodies paid her little notice.

A moped with a blue Domino's Pizza box on the back pulled up beside them.

'What do you fancy doing tonight?' Mac asked the rear-view.

Luke shrugged. 'I don't know. Can I have my egg early?'

Mac smiled. 'You wish.'

'Just the chocolate bar?' Luke countered.

'You'll have to ask your mother.' He didn't imagine it would take much for Charlotte to succumb, but who was he to deny her the opportunity to spoil Luke while she still could?

His fingers drummed on the door's arm rest, itching to hold a cigarette. He'd take Byron around the block when they got back, smoke a fag - or most likely two - make a quick oven dinner, and then crawl into bed.

The moped rider crossed the station and entered the shop. Through the glass, Mac saw the man hurry forward and duck out of sight.

Mac reached for the door handle, a weight sinking in his

abdomen.

Something had happened.

Perhaps he was panicking over nothing. It wouldn't be the first time. Had his Met years - and that one night in particular - made him paranoid? Probably, but paranoia kept you alive.

'Stay here,' Mac said, pushing open the door. He started towards the station shop at a brisk walk, then broke into a jog. Adrenaline coursed through him like electricity. Blood pulsed in his head.

The youths clocked him coming towards them. A couple shrank back against the wall, but the other two stood tall, fixing him with suspicious gazes.

Mac slipped past them into the shop.

Charlotte straightened up, supported by the moped rider and the station attendant. Packets of crisps and sweets fanned across the floor.

'I'm fine. I'm fine,' Charlotte said. 'I just slipped.'

'What happened?' Mac demanded.

'She fell down,' the attendant said, regarding him with a cautious half-smile.

Charlotte shrugged away their arms. 'I'm fine, honestly.'

She didn't look fine. She looked deathly pale and emaciated. When had she lost so much weight?

Mac drew out his wallet and handed the attendant three twenty-pound notes. 'Thank you.' He stooped to pick up the packets Charlotte had pulled down, but the man waved him away.

'I'll do that. Don't worry yourselves.'

Mac nodded his gratitude and guided Charlotte out of the shop.

'I'll drive,' he said, opening the passenger door for her.

She fixed him with a petulant stare. 'I can manage.'

'I know. But I wasn't asking.'

He got in behind the wheel and started the engine.

'What happened?' Luke asked.

'Nothing,' he said. 'We're going home.'

SAFF

A little less than two years ago - just after she'd met Rory but before they'd started seeing each other - Saff had gone to her GP for the contraceptive pill. She'd traded the threat of public enemy number one for a slew of minor side effects, one of which was the false awakenings she sometimes had around that time of the month - she became aware somehow that she was dreaming, only to wake up in another, more convincing dream world.

What if she were dreaming now?

The rain distantly lashed her window, as though the sound came from a TV, and there was an intoxicating fog in her mind. A fog that hid secrets.

It did seem too good to be true, when she thought about it. Things weren't this perfect in the real world. Just in stories.

Or dreams.

The last two days were already a distant blur, like childhood memories, but maybe that was just how these things felt. Surreal. Magical. It probably didn't help that she'd barely slept in two days. A few hours last night, and only a brief nap the day before. They'd had no time to sleep, with all the talking and planning. And the sex, of course. Lots of that. Slow and romantic, like in the movies. And quiet as to not wake up his mother next door.

God, how would she take it when he told her? How would her own father take it?

No. She was not dreaming. If she were dreaming, she wouldn't feel the sober anxiety that chased behind her joy. She was just tired, and suffering a dopamine lag. It was only natural that she would experience a come-down of sorts after her brain had been firing off like the fifth of November for nearly two days straight.

She missed Rory too. A painful, tearing sensation in her chest, as though they would not see each other for months. She had a mind to go downstairs to her mother, to ask if she'd felt a similar thing when her father had proposed, but she decided against it.

The feelings would be gone in the morning. She'd cuddle up with a movie in bed until she fell asleep. Maybe Rory would wake up and text her. She remembered the vanilla Häagen-Dazs in the freezer, and for a moment this made her so happy, she nearly cried.

Her emotions were not as much like a rollercoaster as one of those pendulum rides that spin as they swing. Exhilarating but nauseating at once.

She threw aside her duvet, jumped up, and headed for the door. She doubled back, checked out the rain-blurred window for her dad's car, then headed out again.

Mrs Fletcher. Soon she would be Mrs Saffron Fletcher.

It was her birthday soon too. She was going to be a proper adult.

She inspected her ring in the hallway light before heading downstairs. She was still perplexed at how it looked in different lighting. The elegant twist of white gold around a single, sizeable diamond. Rory had refused to reveal its cost, but she knew it hadn't been cheap from the Holts box.

Warm lamp light spilled from the living room. The TV was playing loud enough to mask her footsteps. She fished her ice cream out of the freezer, grabbed a teaspoon, reconsidered, and swapped it for a dessert spoon.

She'd avoid her mother until the morning, in case she sensed something was wrong, and tried to pry. Saff didn't know if she'd be able to keep her thoughts to herself if her mother did ask.

As she headed for the door, light swept the kitchen from the front garden. She peered out of the window to see her father's black Jaguar skulking into the garage.

Soon she'd be able to buy a car of her own. Something with lots of seats. She should save some money, of course; they'd need money for a deposit on a house, and she didn't want to rely on her father's money. He'd want her to invest it aggressively, to create a niche portfolio in markets she knew well. She supposed it was okay to accept her parents' support in the meantime. And Rory had a better handle on all the technicalities.

A car door slammed in the garage. Saff hurried upstairs before her father saw her. She heard him talking to her mother - or perhaps just himself - as she slipped into her room.

She scanned the videos and DVDs on her bookshelf, before settling on *Beauty and the Beast*. She felt a little childish loading the VHS into her TV, but it had always been her favourite movie. Even if she told people it was *Pulp Fiction*.

As the shooting star arced over the castle of the Disney logo, she climbed into bed and opened the Häagen-Dazs in her lap. She checked her Nokia, but Rory still hadn't replied.

She doubted she'd make it to the end of the movie. She'd probably fall asleep and wake in the morning to find the melted ice cream all over her sheets - if she didn't eat it all before then.

She sank her spoon into the ice cream, closed her mouth around it. The sweetness melted on her tongue. Birdsong and a floating piano melody introduced the film's prologue, and for a second, she drifted back into bliss.

ANDREW

Karen jumped in her seat, sloshing wine into her lap. 'Oh, Jesus.' She set her glass down and dabbed ineffectually at her blouse with a tissue. The stain was there for good.

'Sorry,' he said.

She regarded him with a tender smile. 'How are you doing? How was the board meeting?'

'Fine. It was fine. Listen, I'm going to take a shower and head out. I'm meeting Darren in Soho.'

'Oh, okay.' She sounded crestfallen, but he didn't have energy to pursue his own emotions right now, let alone other people's. 'But you'll be around tomorrow?'

'Yes. I said I would. I'll have to make some calls in the morning, but I'll be there for your parents. You hear about the Queen Mother's death?'

'Yeah, it's awful, isn't it?'

'Mmm. Good for the business though. Draws the spotlight away a bit.'

'Right. I hadn't thought about it like that.'

Andrew nodded slowly. 'Anyway, I'm gonna hit the shower. I'll j-'

'Is that blood on your shirt?' she asked, pointing.

Shit.

'What? Oh, yeah, I had a nosebleed in the office. Just a

little one. Must have been the stress.'

'The stress?' she asked, in a tone that said, *I know exactly what caused it and you're not fooling me for a second.*

'What do you want from me, Karen?' he said, and that silenced her. Before she could reel in a retort, he slipped away to the kitchen. He took a bottle of Dalmore and a whisky tumbler and went upstairs. He poured himself a glass of the honey-coloured single malt, knocked back a smooth-burning mouthful, and stripped out of his suit. He carried the whisky and his work phone into the en suite and set the shower running.

He stared down at his phone, took another swallow, and then opened his contacts. He scrolled through the corporate names - company directors, board members, financial consultants - and stopped at 'Simon'.

So, he hadn't deleted her number after all. He'd deleted the incriminating text messages but not the number itself. He didn't think he'd ever loved and hated himself so deeply at once.

Steam was coming off the shower now, and he didn't have time to waste.

He clicked on Selina's alias and typed, **Hey, beautiful. Sorry about the other week. My head was a mess. What are you up to tonight?**

He stared at the message for a second, added a winky face to the end, and sent it. God, who the fuck was he? He grimaced, knocked back the Dalmore, and grimaced again, this time with pleasure.

He stepped into the shower and let the water scold the aches from his shoulders and back. He closed his eyes, thought of Selina's tender arms around his neck, her warm breath whispering secrets in his ear.

He glanced at his mobile through the haze, then turned away to wash himself. Maybe, if he waited long enough for her reply, he would talk himself out of it. An unlikely but interesting possibility.

He inhaled deeply through his nose. It stung up by the

bridge, as though he'd just been punched in the face.

Please don't bleed again. If it did, he'd just let it run until it clotted itself.

But he was in the clear.

When he shut off the water and checked his mobile, a reply was waiting from Simon AKA Selina.

I knew you couldn't stay away... Tonight I'm up to whatever you want ;)

He drained the whisky and fastened a towel around his waist, his erection pinned painfully against one leg.

SIMBA

Simba's body was weeping for a fix. Sweat had already stuck his t-shirt to his back when the train stopped at Liverpool Street and a dozen more bodies forced their way onto the carriage.

Only two more stops, he told himself, looking out the window as the train took off again and darkness raced by.

The aches had firmly taken hold of his limbs like setting concrete under his skin. Soon he would get his fix and his discomfort would dissipate - much sooner than if they'd walked the distance.

Not soon enough.

When they stopped at Aldgate East, he and Daisy moved closer to the doors.

One more stop.

He closed his eyes, followed his breath as the air soughed between the train and tunnel.

Fingers interlaced his, squeezed.

The train slowed and the doors hissed open. Still holding his sweaty hand, Daisy led him onto the platform and from there, the current washed them out of the station, like foreign bodies from a venous system.

His own veins were swelling hungrily now that they were in the dusk. He had a mind to tell Daisy to forget Terry and just shoot up in a toilet or something.

'It's just a few minutes from here,' she said as though reading his mind.

She lit a cigarette as they walked and handed him one.

'You sure?'

'Of course, man.'

They headed south and turned off the main street into the estates. They passed garages and takeaways in the shadow of towering council blocks. On the wall of one, simply the word 'cunt' was spray-painted in black.

Simba felt new eyes on him as the concrete jungle slowly swallowed them. He imagined faces peeping out from curtains, watching him from parked cars. Middle-aged Bangladeshi and other South-Asian men eyed them cautiously as they passed.

Stranger danger.

But they weren't the ones Simba was worried about.

'You sure we're in the right place?' he asked Daisy.

'Yeah, man. It should be down here.'

They passed a courtyard playground, surrounded on three sides by council blocks. A group of youths lingered by the swings, smoking weed and playing music from a tinny speaker. Their gazes peeled after Simba and Daisy.

'Oi,' a male called. 'Do I know you two?'

'Just keep walking,' Daisy said, digging one hand into her jeans pocket. Clutching her knife, probably.

Voices overlapped; footsteps followed them.

'Hey, I'm fucking talking to you.'

Two of the youths were right on their tail, one with a hand under his hoody. He was either strapped or he wanted them to think he was.

'It's cool,' Daisy said. 'We're just visiting a mate, innit.'

'Who's your mate?' the first youth shot back.

'Terry.'

The youth frowned, looked to his mate. 'Nah, fam. I

don't know no Terry around here.'

'He just moved in. Round that corner.'

'Is it?' the youth asked. His tone suggested he didn't believe Daisy for a second.

Daisy kissed her teeth and walked on. 'Allow this, man,' she told Simba.

He did not look back again, but he heard them following. Were there more footsteps now? More voices?

'They're fucking junkies, man.'

'Yeah, you should dash them, fam.'

'Show them the ting.'

Simba's breath was coming thick and fast. Sweat was still dripping off him, and the aches weighed him down like bricks. All he'd wanted was his fucking fix, and now he was about to get jumped in the ends.

'It's that one,' Daisy said, pointing to a terraced house as they rounded the corner. She walked briskly to the door and hammered on it.

Simba stole a glance behind him. The youths lingered on the corner, watching them like wolves.

No sign of movement came from behind the door. The seconds dragged by like a razor.

'Fuck.' Daisy knocked again.

If Terry wasn't home or Daisy had the wrong number, they'd be trapped between a locked door and a group of nervy youths. With or without arms.

A shadow behind the frosted glass. A bolt slid away, a lock clicked, and the door swung back to reveal a big white bloke in a West Ham shirt. He frowned down at them, at the youths on the corner.

'Daisy?'

'You said to swing by sometime.'

'I did. I did,' he said, as though only just remembering. He had the air of a man suddenly woken. 'Well, you better come in then, I suppose.' He stepped back to let them in.

With the sound of the closing door, relief fell out of Simba in a breath.

'Those kids giving you bother?' Terry asked.

'Nothing we can't handle,' Daisy said. 'This is Simba, by the way.'

'You alright, mate?' Terry shook Simba's hand, and waved them into the small living room. 'I'm still unpacking shit as you can tell, needs a lot of work, but make yourselves at home. I was about to put the kettle on actually. Tea, anyone?'

'Yeah, man, safe,' Daisy said. 'Simba?'

'Yeah, please, mate.'

Terry nodded to himself and went into the kitchen, but was still visible behind the pass-through window. Simba had the impression of watching an actor in a monotone stage play.

He sat beside Daisy on the sunken, faded sofa. The half-decorated living room looked as though it had been robbed in the night. It had the musty smell of a pub. Cigarettes and damp.

'Where you living now?' Terry asked over the chink of mugs and murmur of the kettle. 'Still in that Camden squat?'

'Nah. We got kicked out last week. Someone swiped some cash from these refugees with a baby, so obviously we took the rap for it. Just sleeping rough and sofa-surfing for now.'

'Sorry to hear that,' Terry said. 'Well, you're welcome to crash here for the night, but I've gotta be up early. Scored myself a job interview.'

'Oh, nice one, mate,' Daisy said. 'Where at?'

'Just B&Q - they have this scheme for people like me - but it'll be a good start. I'm off the junk, you know? And if I stay clean, I might be able to see my kids in a few months.'

'That's great, man. I'm proud of you.'

Yes, that's all well and good, but when are we going to get our fix? We're starving, Simba. You need to feed us.

If Terry was clean, he probably wouldn't approve if Simba cooked up a shot and injected himself there on the sofa. This was not that kind of house, despite its aesthetic.

Maybe he could shoot up in the bathroom.

Before he could follow that thought down its rabbit hole - *You're late, Simba. You're late. For a very important date* - Terry came jangling in with their tea.

A prickling itch went up Simba's back and he clawed at it, forcing a smile.

'Thanks, mate.'

'Thanks, Terry,' Daisy echoed.

'So, what's new?' Terry asked.

Daisy glanced at Simba and he read her thoughts easily: what the fuck could be new with a couple of junkies who spent every day in a constant back-and-forth of withdrawal and placation, like an endless game of Pong? Did Terry want to hear about the new pairs of socks and clean needles they'd got from the soup kitchen a few days ago?

'Not a lot, mate. Just doing our thing, you know.'

'Right, yeah,' Terry said, and looked away. 'So, you wanna stick the telly on?'

KAREN

Karen heard the front door shut and went to the window to see Andrew walking down the drive. An idling car waited in the street.

She returned to the sofa, re-filled her wine glass. The wine had already gone to her head, but this was a time for celebration, wasn't it? She just wished Saff had stayed a little longer. She'd imagined they would stay up all night, gossiping and getting more than a little tipsy, but Saff had been yawning away like Sleepy of the Seven Dwarfs, and the wine hadn't invigorated her either. Good news wasn't as sweet when you had no one to share it with. But there would be plenty of time for that, once things had settled down with Andrew. In truth, the secrecy was a little exciting. It made her feel youthful again.

Who would she tell first? Her own mother probably, or her entire reading group at once. And then there would be so many preparations to make: dress-shopping with Saff, venue scouting, choosing flowers and food for the wedding. Assuming she wanted to do all of that with Karen, that was. They would catch up on some well-needed mother-daughter time.

Before she left the nest forever.

Of course, Saff would want to move in with Rory soon, and after her birthday, she would have the financial freedom to do so.

Panic struck like an airbag in her stomach.

The sudden need to act gripped her. Saff was slipping through her fingers, and Karen couldn't let her go.

As if she had a choice.

She was just being emotional, of course. Saff could not remain a child forever, to be fussed over, cooked for, and cleaned up after. Karen could not sit her on her lap and brush her hair like her favourite doll. Saff had not been a child for a long time.

A tear streamed down Karen's cheek. She wiped it away and drank her wine.

Nothing much would change, she reassured herself. Saff spent most of her time in her bedroom anyway, and they rarely ate together these days. Yes, she would see Saff less frequently, but the time they did spend together would be better quality. And it wasn't like Saff would move far away. She would be confined to the Greater London area, just as Karen was now. They would go on dinner dates together, Karen would visit often at her and Rory's house, and when they had a child of their own, Karen would be there to support them every step of the way.

The idea of Saff having a child filled her with inordinate hope and dread. Karen was not old enough to be a grandmother. Saff was certainly not old enough to be a mother. But at the same time, it would give Karen a deeper purpose in life. She could help decorate a nursery for the child and babysit so Saff could catch up on sleep.

Karen imagined herself sitting in a rocking chair, cradling the baby in the crook of her arm and watching it drink drowsily from a bottle of formula.

There she went again, skipping ahead to thoughts she had no business thinking.

Saff had to finish sixth form first, and she might not

want to move out for another few years.

Karen's bladder was full of wine. She rose, but her feet carried her past the bathroom and up the stairs. She was Princess Aurora following an ethereal emerald light up the spiral staircase.

She stopped outside Saff's bedroom, reached to knock, but only laid her hand flat on the door. There was no sound from within, no light under the door.

Karen turned away, followed her feet not to her bedroom but upstairs to Andrew's office.

She leaned back against the door, scanning the room's red leather chesterfield and matching armchairs, the numerous bookshelves, and the giant walnut desk.

Why was she in here? Something had drawn her there. It hung in the air like a smell she couldn't quite place.

Her gaze settled on the triple filing cabinets behind Andrew's desk and the secrets they hid. Inside the drawers, their entire lives were locked away, compartmentalised into neat files.

They were nothing compared to the morgue she'd seen in Andrew's Canary Wharf office, but it overwhelmed her just the same. She didn't like to think about the endless paperwork that underpinned her complicated life, and she was lucky Andrew savoured control of such things.

She fell into the leather desk chair and turned to face the filing cabinets. Her bladder clenched like a fist, but she ignored it. Two of the three cabinets were dedicated to Andrew's work, the other to familial affairs. The three drawers were labelled *Andrew*, *Karen*, and *Saff*. She tried the second drawer - her own - not expecting it to give, but it was unlocked. Perhaps the same force that had guided her up here had opened the cabinet for her. The heavy drawer slid out slowly, as though it contained a corpse instead of mere paperwork. She wouldn't have been particularly surprised to see her own dead eyes staring up at her.

She scanned the colour-coded dividers: *Medical*, *Automative*, *Banking*, *Assets*, and so on.

Where was it?

She pulled the drawer further out. There, right at the back, was an unmarked maroon file divider.

She lifted it out and spread it across the desk. Inside was the contract she'd signed on her eighteenth birthday. Twenty-three years and a few months ago.

She'd seen Andrew poring over countless contracts during the evenings or in bed at night, identical in layout save for the royal crest embossed in the top left corner: a crowned lion and unicorn either side of the royal arms' shield. That and Karen's maiden initials, KJ, which were scrawled in her eighteen-year-old hand in the bottom corner of each page.

Her contract - soon to be Saff's contract - was with the sovereign state of the United Kingdom, pre-signed on its behalf by the Queen herself.

How many contracts were there like hers? How many others lived with the same secret in London? Probably not many, but surely there were others, if her understanding of their purpose was correct.

She scanned down the clauses and subclauses, though she knew their content by heart.

Don't ever leave the confines of Greater London.

Don't leave the house without taking your mobile with you.

Don't tell anyone about this little secret, except for blood relations and your spouse no sooner than your wedding day.

Also, you need to have a child before your fortieth birthday, who will inherit the contract on their own eighteenth.

In return, you'll receive top-tier private healthcare, private education for your children, and a handsome salary paid monthly.

None of this was of particular benefit anymore, now that Andrew brought in a seven-figure salary. But the greatest benefit - also the one Karen had lost the most sleep over - was unparalleled.

In the event of a threat to national security, your life, and the lives of your immediate family, will be saved.

It was an insurance policy, when it came down to it, and

the geographical limitations and surveillance - they were definitely watching her - were a small price to pay. Her father had lived out his contract, as would Karen in a few months, and they had escaped nuclear holocaust so far. On the other hand, the very existence of her contract told her that the authorities believed it to be a very real possibility, and her father was convinced that the initiative had been organised in the wake of the second world war. Presumably, the contract covered them for natural disasters too.

A new consideration rode in on the back of a sharp bladder pang. When Saff married Rory, Karen would lose her place in this mystical covenant. Only their lives would be spared, and any children they had at the time. But that wasn't so bad. Saffron's safety would always be Karen's first priority.

She regarded the contract sadly, not entirely sure which part of it depressed her, before returning it to the filing cabinet.

Whichever spell had brought her here had released her. She was notably sober, considering the half-bottle of wine she'd drunk.

Silence rang in her ears and waves went through her bladder again.

She got up and went to piss.

MAC

'Are you okay?' he asked Charlotte, closing the kitchen door behind him. 'Really?'

'For God's sake, Mac, I'm fine.' She set a pan down heavily on the hob. 'Can we just drop it, please?'

He weighed his words carefully, or as carefully as he could through his fatigued haze. 'I'm just concerned that you're taking on a little too much.'

Charlotte upended a bag of pasta into the pan, drowning out his voice.

'I was going to put those pizzas in,' he said. 'Why don't you put your feet up with Luke?'

'We can't just eat junk every day. I'm making a proper meal.' Charlotte turned away to fill the pan with water, and Mac closed his eyes in exasperation. She set the pan down and turned on the gas. The ignition switch clicked ineffectually over the hiss.

Tick-tick-tick-tick.

'Honey, listen, I know you're strong as hell, but you still have limitations. You're still human.'

The spark clicked on like a clock at double speed.

Time's ticking. Time's ticking. Time's ticking. Time-

31

'Charlotte.'

'What?' She turned on him as the spark caught the gas build-up and the flame illuminated her face. She glared at him through bloodshot eyes, daring him to go on, but behind her mask of rage, he saw fear and panic.

'I love you,' he said.

'I love you too.'

He held out his arms and Charlotte let him hug her, rested her head on his shoulder.

'I'm sorry,' he said. 'I'll let it go, but we do need to talk about this sometime.'

'I know. Maybe next week, when Luke's at school.'

'Okay,' he said, and kissed her forehead.

Byron whined from the hallway.

Charlotte sighed. 'He needs to go out.'

'I'll take him.' The monkey on his back - or the inner child he'd never truly shaken off - cried out for a cigarette.

'Alright.'

'See you in a bit then.'

He took his leather jacket and Byron's lead from the hallway, patted his jeans down - phone, wallet, keys, other phone - and headed out.

Maybe he had overreacted. Was he being overbearing? He'd been so locked in his own head lately, it was hard to tell. In truth, he was so exhausted, he felt like he might fall down at any minute himself.

He lit a Benson as he walked, Byron obediently tailing him.

Should he steal a couple of hours' sleep after they'd eaten? He knew he should, but somehow, he'd already decided against it. A flask of coffee would see him through the night, and he could recoup tomorrow and Monday. That way, he'd have a little more time to appease Charlotte and Luke. Fuck it, he'd let Luke have his chocolate bar too. It was cruel to hold Luke to such high standards when he leaned so heavily on his own crutches. Although wasn't the whole point of parenting to teach your kids to be better than you? To not pass on your own failures?

A group of youths rounded the corner - the same ones from the petrol garage? - and Mac started, pulling Byron to one side. One of the kids smirked at his jumpiness.

A heavy breath escaped him, and he pressed a hand to his stomach. Three secret mouths gaped with laughter. For a second, he was back in that room, and the kid was staring right into his eyes as he plunged the knife into Mac's abdomen, withdrew it, and then stabbed him twice more.

He took a deep pull on his cigarette and followed the path towards Holloway Road. The corner shop he passed had a rack of flowers outside, and he doubled back to buy a bunch.

Byron fouled on the pavement on the way home. He walked back up their road, carrying flowers in one hand and a bag of shit in the other, thinking there was something depressingly poetic about it.

He dropped the bag into their green bin and let himself in.

Charlotte was frying bacon in a saucepan when he peered around the doorway. The scent lulled him, like a siren song, to something approximating comfort.

'Hey,' he said.

When Charlotte turned, he revealed the flowers.

She smiled tiredly. 'Carnations. Thank you, honey.' She touched his arm and kissed his cheek as she took the flowers. 'They're lovely.'

She filled a vase with water and put the flowers in.

'I'm going to check on Luke,' he said.

'Okay.'

Luke was in the living room, watching *The Phantom Menace*. A young Anakin Skywalker was throwing his podracer around an impossible desert track. The podracer on his tail took a shot from the valley and went up in a cloud of flame and smoke.

The sofas were both clear, but Luke sat on the floor in front of the TV.

Mac lowered himself to the ground with a grunt. 'How you doing?'

Luke shrugged. 'Alright.'

'You not bored of this yet?'

Luke frowned, as though Mac had said something childishly stupid. 'It's my favourite film.'

'I know. I know. I prefer the originals myself but I'm old.'

'You're not that old,' Luke said.

He was right. If Charlotte died – *when* she died - he'd still have another thirty, maybe forty years left. Another lifetime lurked beyond the event horizon. He would watch his son grow to be a man. Alone.

'No. I guess not,' he said. 'Hey, you know the second film's coming out this year? *Attack of the Clones*. We can go see it in the cinema. Leicester Square if you want.'

'Will Mum come?'

'I don't think it's her kind of film, but if you want her to be there, I'm sure she'll join us.'

'Okay.'

Anakin shot past the finish line to tumultuous applause.

Luke smiled. 'Can I have my chocolate bar now?'

Mac sighed. 'You can have it after dinner. How's that?'

Luke considered, shrugged. 'Okay.'

'Mum's making carbonara.'

Luke smiled. 'I like carbonara.'

'We know,' he said and ruffled Luke's hair.

Luke swatted Mac's hand away indignantly and glued his eyes to the TV.

'I'll be back in a minute then. Just going to make a coffee.'

Tonight was going to be a long night.

ANDREW

Rain fell in sheets over Soho, pattering on the glass canopy above their heads. Aside from the odd flourish of neon in the distance, the skyline glowed orange, like a sea of candles.

Like a wake.

Andrew parted his lips and let the cigar smoke drift out of his mouth and into the night.

Darren surveyed him over his tumbler. 'I don't envy you, mate. I really don't. But I've got your back every step of the way. You know that.'

Andrew nodded, forced a smile. 'It's not you I'm worried about, Darren. What are the other principals saying?'

'I won't lie to you, it's not good. Most are sympathetic to your cause, but you need to keep an eye on Neil. He'll sing your praises to the board, and then spit another story to the shareholders.'

'Oh, I'm well aware of his priorities.'

'But in the event of a vote, you're safe. As long as you have the internal directors on board, of course.'

'I run a tight ship.'

'I know you do,' Darren said and raised his glass. 'They'll have to try a lot harder if they want to topple you, my friend.'

Andrew nodded, rang Darren's glass, and drank, wishing he were half as confident himself.

'So,' Darren said, leaning in, 'who's taking the fall for it?'

Andrew's mobile pulsed against his left thigh. His work phone.

Selina. He imagined her caressing his inner thigh, smiling deviously.

'Andrew?'

'Mostly the regulatory directors. Some of media. We acquired a new quality manager from Orion, offered her twice what they were paying her.'

He felt for his phone and glanced at it under the table.

Simon: **Just got out the shower. Going out in Brixton later but can't be bothered to get changed just yet ;)**

'That should appease any uncertain shareholders,' Darren said. 'There are plenty of sharp investors who see this as the flesh wound it'll be in the long run. We've just got to pray that the deaths are over and let the storm pass… They are over, aren't they?'

Images flashed of Selina writhing beneath him, as though she were making a show of trying to get away but not truly wanting to.

He stirred.

'I don't fucking know, Darren. The recall stats look positive, but they're never entirely accurate. I'm praying just like you.'

Darren nodded slowly, staring out at the rain.

Andrew looked down at his mobile, tried to formulate a plan.

He knocked back his whisky and typed, **Fuck Brixton. Come to Soho for cocktails.**

He sent the text, took another swallow of whisky, and filled his mouth with cigar smoke.

His head throbbed like a plasma globe with someone

36

pressing their thumbs into his temples. The electric spectres of his afternoon coke binge surged through his neurons. His body ached, but his mind pulled back with nauseating strength. He had things to do tonight.

The alcohol had dissolved his impotence like a hot bath. He needed to stop the snow for the night, but he could drink.

He drained his whisky. 'Same again?'

'Sure,' Darren said. He looked around for the waitress, but Andrew got to his feet.

'I'll go to the bar. I need to stretch my legs.'

'Alright. I'll make a quick call then.'

Andrew ashed his cigar and left it smoking in the porcelain dish. He checked his phone on his way to the men's, but Selina hadn't replied.

He pissed, splashed water into his face, and stared himself down in the pristine mirror.

He didn't need to do this. He could just delete her number, head home, and slip into bed with Karen.

But he couldn't. He'd go crazy and end up fighting with her. This way, he could have a peaceful day tomorrow with her parents.

His mobile vibrated. He fished it out so fast that he lost his grip, and it slipped down the bowl like a bar of soap. He snatched it out, wiped it on his shirt, and checked the screen.

Simon: **I'm going to the Fridge with some friends, but after midnight I'm all yours ;)**

What the fuck kind of student piss-up could rival drinking in London's most expensive bars? The kind where you could cut a line and snort it right there on the table and no one batted an eyelid.

Midnight.

That was over three hours away. He could drink with Darren for another hour, maybe two, but he didn't fancy waiting around for her, not least because it gave him time to change his mind. He needed her, and she needed him, so why was she fucking about?

The bathroom walls were unyielding barriers, closing him in. The room was too silent, but the ventilator humming in the corner was too loud. Why didn't they have some fucking music on? Some cafe jazz bullshit?

He typed, **You know I can't wait that long. I'll come to Brixton?**

God, you're pathetic. This is low, even for you.

His temples throbbed. His back ached. His ears rang with the highest note of the ventilator fan.

He tore away from his reflection and headed for the bar.

SAFF

Saff nodded awake. She'd only drifted off for a few minutes, judging by the scene on TV: Belle and the Beast dancing in the grand hall, bathed in golden light.

Rory had better dance with her on her wedding night. But which song? They didn't really have 'a song', but there was time enough for that.

She scooped a spoonful of ice cream soup into her mouth and smiled. She checked her mobile, sat up straight at Rory's text: **Hey, honey x**

She set the ice cream aside, jumped to her feet, and dialled his number.

'Hey, baby. Or should I say fiancée?'

'Mmm, I like the sound of that,' she said, watching the silver curtain of rain falling outside. 'How are you?'

'I'm good,' he said in a laboured breath. 'I just told Mum.'

'How did she take it?'

'Pretty well,' he said. 'She really likes you, you know. Says you're the best thing that ever happened to me.'

Butterflies skittered around her stomach and fell still again. 'She doesn't think it's too soon?'

'Well, she does a bit, but she's happy for us. She wants to take us out to dinner next week if you're free.'

'Of course.' Dinner with the mother-in-law. No

pressure. God, what would she wear?

'You still with your mum?' he asked.

'No. She was trying to get me drunk, so I went to bed. Just watching… a movie.'

'Sounds nice. Oh, speaking of your parents, I just saw your dad on the news.'

'Jesus,' Saff said. 'He has a way of drawing attention to himself.'

'You haven't told him yet, right?'

'No. No. I'll wait a week or so.'

'Alright.'

'Rory?'

'Yeah?'

'I miss you.'

'I miss you too.'

'Yeah?'

'Of course.'

'Sorry,' she laughed. 'I don't know. I just feel a little fragile right now. It's still so overwhelming.'

'I know. I had a little cry before, I won't lie.'

She laughed, and a sob escaped beneath it. She wanted nothing more than to bury her face in Rory's shoulder, feel his warmth envelop her as they melted together.

That was the pain she felt: incompleteness. Her and Rory's souls were becoming one, and being away from him was like being away from half of herself.

'But hey,' Rory said, 'I'll see you in a few days.'

'Yeah.'

Silence fell but still she found the sound of his breathing comforting.

She needed to tell him about the contract. She needed his opinion, and most of all, she needed to not be alone in it. But what if they were listening to her phone calls? Or had microphones hidden in the walls? She couldn't jeopardise everything a few months before she was due to inherit the contract.

She hated having secrets from him - her parents kept

things from each other, and she told herself she'd never be like that - but her hands were tied on this. For now.

Rory yawned on the line, and she found herself yawning.

She laughed. 'I think we're both in need of a good night's sleep.'

'Yeah. I'll call you tomorrow though, my love.'

The emptiness within her widened. She hadn't meant to suggest they end the call, but she didn't want to be pathetic either.

'Alright. Goodnight, Rory.'

'Goodnight, babe. I love you.'

'I love you too.'

Just like that, he had dissolved into the endless dead line, into that dream-like quality where he was and wasn't.

She shut off *Beauty and the Beast* a few scenes before the end and climbed into bed. She pulled the covers up to her chin and settled down to face the tub of melting ice cream on her bedside table.

SIMBA

Simba closed the bathroom door behind him, the handle shaking in his grasp. He looked for the lock but there was none.

The sound of the television - an *Only Fools and Horses* repeat - and Terry's laughter, which more often than not had given way to a racking cough, had been too loud for him. The oppressive silence of the bathroom was louder. Not even the hum of a fan.

Feed us, Simba. Feed us, feed us, feed us.

His withdrawal symptoms had started to bleed into each other. His forearm burned. He drew back his hoody sleeve and scratched at his skin: a constellation of needle holes in a bruised sky. He needed to get that checked out.

But with the appeasement of his itch, a tremor rolled over him, and he imagined his very bones were shaking.

He looked up at his reflection in the dirty mirror over the sink. Had his skin always been so dark?

A vacuous ache washed through his gut, as the self-loathing chattered on and on.

Look at the fucking state of you. If your mother could see you now. But it's okay. Just cook us up a shot and it'll all fade away.

He held his gaze, feeling like a silhouette on a stage himself. But who was watching?

Maybe, if he stared long enough, the cosmic song and dance would cease. The house lights would come on, applause would ripple, and he'd give a bow - the man behind the feeble act.

He set the tap running and clutched the lip of the sink with both hands.

He could shoot up in here, if he could only get his wrap from Daisy and the syringe and spoon from his bag. It would be an obvious move, especially to an ex-junky like Terry, but Simba was growing desperate. What little control he had left was melting away.

How long would Terry stay awake? If Simba knew that, he might be able to keep his shit together. Terry had said he needed to be up early for an interview. Surely it couldn't be too much longer. Although, Simba sensed the loneliness in Terry, the desperation for human connection, albeit from a couple of junkies.

Why had they come here anyway? A roof over his head and a relatively comfortable sleeping spot were not worth this torture.

He grimaced, turned away from the mirror, and pissed. The toilet, like the sink, was filthy, ringed with black mould and yellow grime.

He returned to the living room with some semblance of composure and sank into the sofa. The cushions swallowed him, as though they'd never forgotten his form.

Daisy laid a hand on his leg. 'You alright?'

'Yeah,' he lied.

She nodded knowingly. She looked exhausted herself, like she'd just outrun the devil himself. 'Soon,' she breathed.

Terry was smoking another cigarette. Grey tendrils of smoke rose seductively. He grunted with laughter at the final *Only Fools* gag and broke into a coughing fit over the end credits.

When it subsided, Daisy stretched, yawned deliberately.

Simba looked at Terry expectantly.

Come on, take the bait, you stupid fuck. Take the bait.

Simba held his breath as Terry checked his watch. What time even was it? What if it was too early, and Simba had to sit there watching TV for another half an hour? An hour?

'I suppose I better hit the hay. It's getting late.'

'Alright, mate,' Daisy said.

'You guys have your sleeping bags, right?'

'Yeah, man. We're good. Don't worry about us.'

'Alright then.' Terry got to his feet, scanned the room with a slow sweep, and then nodded to himself. 'Night then.'

'Night,' Simba and Daisy echoed.

Terry closed the door behind him, and the musty living room transformed into a sanctuary, as though one backdrop had been switched for another.

Simba rummaged through his rucksack, loaded the table with his spoon, syringe, lighter, cotton wool, and the shoelace he'd been using since he'd lost his last tourniquet.

'Let's wait a few minutes,' Daisy said, 'just to be safe.'

A hot flush passed through him and his whole body tensed. 'Alright,' he breathed. His legs were shaking in anticipation, sweat beading on his brow.

On TV, an animated advert for mouthwash was playing.

'Alright, fuck it,' Daisy said, reaching into her jeans pocket. She dropped the cling film balloons onto the coffee table and jumped to her feet. She lifted her top, exposing her pale, emaciated mid-drift, and drew the thin pink belt out of her jeans, the one she'd lifted from Claire's Accessories. She fell back to the sofa, tied her bicep off with the belt, and unwrapped a balloon.

Heart racing, Simba opened his own shot and cooked it up in the spoon, as though he and Daisy were competing in a junky *Master Chef* final. He siphoned the murky liquid into a syringe, tied his arm off with the lace, and tapped for a vein with two fingers. When the vein surfaced, he pushed the needle in, careful to avoid the bruised skin, and pulled

44

back on the plunger. Blood seeped into the barrel.

He glanced at Daisy, who shot him a drowsy smile from the sofa, then pushed the plunger.

Warmth washed through him, starting in the back of his legs and sweeping over his entire body like a heavy blanket. He withdrew the needle from his vein and unfastened his tourniquet with the last of his energy. A ribbon of blood ran down his forearm as he lay back and closed his eyes.

He floated, weightless.

The sound of the TV was growing distant, insignificant, but he could hear Daisy's heavy, almost sensual breathing beside him.

He followed it down.

ANDREW

'Well, it's been a pleasure, even under the circumstances,' Darren said as they stepped out into the Soho street. The rain drummed on the canopy.

'Always,' Andrew said, offering his hand.

Darren shook it, reconsidered, then opened his arms for a hug.

'Call me if you need anything, yeah?' Darren said into his ear. 'Work or not.'

'Thank you. I will.'

A line of black cabs idled in the street.

'After you,' Andrew said, gesturing.

Darren nodded solemnly, climbed into the first cab. Andrew took the second.

'Alright, mate,' he said. 'Good business tonight, it seems.'

'Oh yeah. The rain is great for us,' the driver said. 'Where to?'

'The Fridge,' he said. 'Brixton.'

The cabby lifted his eyes to the rear-view. 'This is more a student club, you know?'

'I know,' Andrew said firmly.

'Okay.' He shifted into gear and pulled away.

Andrew sat back and watched Soho roll by, obscured by a layer of rain and another of intoxication. He'd lost count of his drinks.

He checked his phone. No new texts from Selina since she'd headed to the Fridge, which meant she was either already inside or she was close. He had half a dozen work texts and a couple of calls he'd ignored, but they could wait.

Traffic was all but gridlocked between Piccadilly Circus and Trafalgar Square, and it wasn't much better heading south along the Thames. The streets were a haze, and he was becoming steadily more aware of the cab's confines, of its humid atmosphere, the note of the driver's aftershave floating above the generic air-freshener.

The radio played chart music, but Andrew could barely hear it over the drumming rain. At any moment, he imagined the music would break off and a news reporter would lecture Andrew about his occupational failures.

There was no way out. Not for the next twenty minutes at least.

So just turn the cab around. Go home to your wife and daughter.

It was too late. He'd made his bed and now he had to lie in it. With Selina's hands running down his body. Her sharp, intoxicating smell.

His spine ached, his temples throbbed, and his fingers clawed restlessly in his lap. He gripped the door and focused his attention outside the cab. As long as they were moving forwards, everything would be okay.

His ego was bloated, like a weather balloon pressing against the roof, the windows, the Perspex screen separating him from the driver.

Each breath was laboured, as though something were physically restricting his lung capacity.

The cab stopped dead in traffic, its idling engine grating in his ears. Andrew reached into his jacket and took out a Marlboro. He wound down the window and lit the cigarette.

'Hey,' the cabby called. 'You can't smoke in here.'

Andrew took two twenty-pound notes from his wallet and pressed them against the Perspex partition. The cabby grunted, opened the window, and took the bribe.

Andrew laid his head back and exhaled out of the window.

Traffic moved on, and he closed his eyes, tried to listen to the sound of the rain, the revving engines and car horns in the street. But in the swimming darkness, there was no telling where the confines of the cab ended. He knew rationally, but a voice told him they were much closer. Perhaps he wasn't in a cab after all, but a cupboard.

Don't you love me, Andy? If you love me, why would you make me sad?

His eyes snapped open. He took a deep drag of his cigarette and ashed it out the window.

A distant siren rose above the hubbub.

They were over the bridge now, and traffic moved a little more freely.

When he'd smoked his cigarette down to the butt, he tossed it out the window and lit another. The cabby eyed him in the rear-view but said nothing.

Andrew followed each laboured breath until the cab turned into Brixton and pulled up outside the Fridge. Its facade was brightly lit in neon spotlights, and a crowd was gathered in the rain.

The cabby told him his fare, and Andrew handed over the cash. 'Keep the change,' he said, climbing out.

He joined the queue and checked his mobile. Nothing.

She's forgotten about you, Andrew. She's probably gyrating on some young guy right now.

I'm outside, he wrote. **Where should I meet you?**

The Fridge's facade provided little shelter from the rain. His hair and jacket were growing damp. He checked his wallet, considered paying his way past the crowd, but the queue moved ahead to admit him.

He entered the lobby. Bass pounded from the auditorium. He paid his entry, checked his jacket into the cloakroom, and walked inside.

He checked his mobile. Still no reply. There was no signal inside the venue, which explained Selina's silence, but didn't get him any closer to locating her.

He scanned the room. Where would Selina congregate? Was she the kind of girl to hang around by the bar, or up by the stage, in the heat of it?

You don't know, because you don't know anything about her, do you? You only know the mask she wears.

He went to the bar, ordered a whisky, and checked his phone again.

So now he was supposed to find a girl he barely knew amongst hundreds in a dark auditorium? Needle in a haystack didn't do the situation justice.

Should've just gone home, Andy. You only have yourself to blame.

He knocked back the whisky and made for the stage. He took off his wedding ring as he walked and put it in his wallet. He'd wander around a bit and then go for a fag. She would go out for a cigarette eventually. Then he'd find her.

He waded through the bodies, scanning faces in the roaming RGB spotlights. The crowd swallowed him and for a moment, the tension drained out of him. The combined heat was making him sweat already.

He was just another face in the crowd. No journalists forcing cameras and microphones into his face. No boy-faced executives asking his advice or predictions. To the clubbers - students and young professionals - he was just a lost old man. A nobody.

His claustrophobia was mostly deceived by the high ceilings and large auditorium. Bodies surrounded him as far as he could see, but as long as he kept moving, he would be okay.

He stopped a few feet from the stage, looked around, and checked his work phone.

'Fuck,' he breathed, and headed back.

He was nearly at the bar again when a hand snatched his arm from the crowd. He turned as Selina pressed her mouth against his. Her sharp, sweet fragrance flowed through him, an intoxicating wave of synaesthesia, illuminating his darkest, numbest depths.

'Hello, stranger.'

She was even more beautiful than he remembered. There was an ethereal brightness to her eyes that threatened to shatter the greatest of illusions. A tight black dress hugged her figure, glistening like a starry sky. Her straightened, blonde hair hung about her shoulders.

'You look… amazing,' he said, and kissed her.

It was only then that he noticed the couple dancing behind Selina.

'This is Dan and Izzy,' Selina called, gesturing to her friends. 'This is Andy.'

He shook Dan's hand, but Izzy went for a hug.

'Oh my God, it's so nice to meet you.'

'And you.'

Christ, he needed to get Selina away from these morons.

The change of music stunted any further conversation. He faced Selina, who moved her hips fluidly in time, like a fondue fountain. He grasped her hips.

'Aren't you drinking?' he said into her ear.

She shook her head with a sly smile, reached into her bra, and withdrew a small baggy.

The animal in him roared.

Was it coke? He was already drunker than he'd intended, and he couldn't risk another nosebleed.

'What is it?' he asked.

'Molly. You want some?' She regarded him with that same sly smile, that sparkle in her eyes. She was too perfect.

He took the baggy, scooped his house key into the powder, and shot it up his good nostril.

He hesitated, then did a second hit. He needed to be on her level.

Selina smiled, kissed him. He was soaring down a tunnel and she was the light at the end.

Soon he could not tell where Selina ended and the drug

began. His senses glowed like city lights, and beneath it all was something evanescent. Something he was forever chasing but never found.

Selina turned her back to him and placed his hands on her hips. Her dress was softer than silk, guiding his touch down.

The music pounded on distantly, and the ocean of bodies rippled around them, but it was all peripheral, fading away until it was just him and Selina. A bubble of absolute bliss.

She's lying to you. This isn't who she is. And let me tell you a secret, Andy, this isn't who you are either.

Even the voice was outside of him now. She was gyrating against him, and every thought went out of his head like a broken vacuum.

He lifted her hair away from her neck with the back of his hand, like a diaphanous veil, and ran his lips along her neck, drank her fragrance.

She ran a hand up between their legs and squeezed him.

He stirred in her hand. The animal roared.

'You want to get out of here?' he asked.

'We just got here,' she sang, 'but I could go for a smoke.'

'Alright. Whatever you want.'

She turned to Dan and Izzy and made a smoking gesture. Dan flicked her a thumbs-up.

Selina took Andrew's hand and guided him through the bodies. As they broke out of the thick of the crowd, he realised Dan and Izzy had followed them.

He groaned internally. Fuck smoking. He just wanted Selina, alone.

But as they stepped out of the lobby, the cool air diffused through him in a wave of euphoria. The coloured searchlights of the Fridge's facade were like UFO beams shooting into the cosmos. The rain had slowed to a drizzle now, but each drop melted blissfully on his skin.

God, he was high. His coke and spirits tolerance clearly did not translate to other drugs.

'Good vibe, huh?' Izzy asked.

'See, I told you,' Dan said. He regarded Andrew anew in the light, then lay his head back against the wall and closed his eyes.

Andrew took out his Marlboros and handed Selina one.

'Thanks.' She smiled her sly smile.

'So, what do you do, Andy?' Izzy asked, exhaling slowly.

'I'm a manager. I work in management.'

Selina laughed, a girly giggle that didn't suit her. 'He's being modest. He's a CEO.'

'Oh, wow. That's so cool,' Izzy said. 'Is that a Rolex?' She took Andrew's wrist and held it up to the light.

'Patek Phillipe,' he said.

'Nice,' Izzy said. 'You know I've always wanted to start my own fashion label.'

'Oh yeah?'

'Yeah. I'm thinking like Prada mixed with Dior, but like an affordable price point.'

'That sounds good,' Andrew said. Selina was leaning against him, her hand roaming up his leg. He slapped it away.

'Sorry,' Izzy laughed. 'I can't stop talking when I'm high. Just tell me to shut up.'

'Izzy,' Selina said. 'Shut up.'

Izzy looked crestfallen as she put her cigarette between her lips.

'I'm joking, babe.'

'Oh,' Izzy said and broke into hysterical laughter.

He was losing his high out here with them. He wanted to be back inside with the music and Selina moving on him. Maybe he should ask her for another hit of the Molly; if he felt this good now, how good would he feel from twice the dose? But didn't too much make you impotent? He couldn't risk that. Not tonight.

Selina turned to face him. 'You okay?' she asked.

He smiled. 'Yeah. Just… impatient.'

'Oh yeah?' she said, leaned in, and kissed him.

Her lips were ecstasy, but a coldness manifested in his stomach: the sinking realisation that this moment would not last forever. Soon he would return to his job, his life, his home, and any recollection of this pleasure would be through the lens of regret and self-loathing.

He kissed her back, raising one hand to cup her neck and pulling her waist closer with the other. She was his lifeline, and if he let go now, he would be lost forever.

Don't you love me, Andy? I thought you loved me.

She made soft moans of pleasure. He stroked her earlobe and trailed his thumb over her thigh.

She jerked back, and his heart raced after her. Wasn't this what she wanted? What was the fucking problem?

She swiped ash from her leg. Her cigarette lay smouldering on the pavement.

Cool waves met him. Maybe it was just the wind, but it soothed him like a mother's lullaby.

'You okay?' he laughed.

'Yeah, but I blame you for that one.'

'You blame me?' He stabbed a finger theatrically at his chest.

'You… distracted me.'

'Oh, I see. Well, I won't do it again then.'

'No, that's okay,' she sang, leaning in close.

'Okay,' Izzy said, slapping her thighs. 'We're going to get a drink. We'll see you in there, yeah?'

'Alright, babe,' Selina said.

The thought of a drink made him suddenly aware of his throat. He wanted nothing more than to knock back a cold beer or, better still, water.

'Have a good night, guys,' Dan added, following Izzy inside. Did Andrew detect a note of admiration in his glance back?

'So,' Selina said, pursing her lips as though suppressing a laugh. 'What do you want to do?'

'You want to go to the bar?'

'We could do that,' she said, glancing away, as though

she were hiding something. Goddamn, she played her part well. 'Or, we could go somewhere quiet.'

Shit. He had not expected her to cave this quickly. And now that the option was in front of him, he kind of wanted more of a tease. But on the other hand, this wasn't some great Austen romance; this was a dirty betrayal.

His cock was pressing through his pants now. There was no way she couldn't feel it against her.

'No time like the present,' he said. 'I'll get us a taxi.'

'No need. I only live around the corner,' she said, waving back lazily.

'Oh. Okay.'

She took his hand and led him up the road.

Her place? Where did she live, in student digs? Would he have to pass her flatmates in the corridor?

He squeezed her hand, suppressing the urge to dig his heels in and pull her back. He glanced around the street. Would journalists have followed him here? What if he saw his face on the front page of tomorrow's paper?

Apollo CEO Affair with Student.

Selina squeezed him back, and a wave of calm followed it.

She was a mature student; she would not be living in digs with eighteen-year-olds. And they'd be in her room anyway.

They crossed the street and walked for a couple of minutes, before he pulled back on her hand.

'What?' she asked.

He kissed her there for a while before asking, 'How far is it?'

'It's that building there,' she laughed, pointing up the road.

'Okay, let's go.'

She let them into the building and called the lift. He opened his mouth to request they take the stairs, but the lift was already on the ground floor. Selina pulled him inside.

His heart raced as the doors closed. Selina had barely pressed the floor button when he pulled her close and kissed her.

The same panic he'd felt outside now echoed around the lift, growing louder with every heartbeat. He was too drunk, too high to be compressed into such a tight space. He was back in the taxi with car horns and sirens all around him. He had his knees pressed into his chin in the shoe cupboard of his mother's house.

You can come out when you've decided if you love me or not.

Selina was his exit from all the noise. Her body and her mouth on his were bliss. When she filled every one of his senses, everything felt just fine. The feel of the floor shaking beneath him and the whir of the motor paralysed him, but when he was with Selina, he was not himself. He was something above or outside of himself, in the same way that he was not himself when he was high on coke, drunk, or in a flow state at work.

The doors opened with another chime, and it was over. Selina pulled him into a corridor, inside her flat.

He kissed her against the wall before she could fumble for the light switch.

Inside her room, she pushed Andrew away, and went into the en suite.

'Give me two seconds,' she called.

He was alone in her room, his ears ringing from the Fridge's sound system.

Shit. He'd left his jacket at the venue. He'd pick it up on the way home. He didn't expect to be here long. Although maybe he could stick around for a second round. It wasn't too late yet.

No, but you do have to be up early to work on... oh, you know, the hardest difficulty you've ever faced with that little business you run. You need to get back to your wife and daughter, and then you'll show your teeth and smile in front of your wife's parents.

This time, the calming waves stopped short of him. A physical yearning drew him to face the en suite door.

Selina would be out soon.

He looked around the bedroom apathetically. It looked

just as he'd expected, perhaps a little more sophisticated. It was just a set to him, like the sterile hotels he'd rented when they'd fucked before. They came in, they acted their parts, and they went home.

But it wasn't as impersonal as the others, not if he really looked. The shelves beside him were filled with her things: books, makeup products, a half-empty bottle of Smirnoff. Her pyjamas hung off the back of the chair. There were photographs tacked on the side of her wardrobe.

This was the room of a girl he did not know.

The girl in the photographs - the holiday pictures, club printouts, and photo booth reels - was not the Selina he knew. In fact, he wasn't one hundred percent sure that was even her real name.

All he knew was the masquerade mask she wore, which was only ever a big shining mirror. He was a scared little boy staring back at himself and seeing nothing.

At least she was nice to look at, though.

She wasn't always.

He scanned the photos, frowned. There was something about the photos, some secret they hid.

The woman in the bathroom was an imposter, a skin-snatcher from a TV horror movie.

The door opened behind him. She'd left the en suite light on, and through his drunken haze, she was bathed in a cinematic golden vignette.

She wore only a bra and G-string. Matching. Scarlet.

Her father.

The photos' secret.

He turned back to the collage and scanned the photos.

Her father was in none of them. Was he dead or had he left? What did it matter? Andrew had known all along, hadn't he? It was obvious when he really thought about it.

He turned back and stared at her.

'I can't do this.'

Selina laughed, then stared back at him for a long time.

'I'm sorry.'

She went back into the bathroom and returned in a pink dressing gown, an actress between scenes. She fumbled in her bag for a cigarette, popped it into her mouth, and lit it. Then she handed him one.

'Thanks,' he said. He started to pace up and down in front of her bed, slowly at first, then faster.

'You want to talk about it?' she asked.

'No.'

'Okay. I think I'll change my number, make it easier for both of us. For what it's worth, I think you're a really nice guy. I hope you figure out whatever you're struggling with.'

'Thank you. Oh, and Selina, this all stays between us, yeah?'

'Yeah, don't worry. I won't talk to the press.'

'Right.' His cigarette needed ashing but he could see no ash tray, and he couldn't work out how to open her window.

The ash fell to the carpet and they both watched it.

'I'm sorry. I'll-' He looked around.

'It's fine,' she said, producing an ash tray from her desk and setting it on the windowsill.

'You know what, I'll just leave you to it.' He stubbed the cigarette out and looked for the door.

Selina opened her arms in question.

Andrew hugged her.

'Goodnight, Selina.'

'Goodbye, Andy.'

He let himself out, clutching at the sharp pain in his stomach. Out on the periphery, the euphoric glow of the Molly lingered, like dusk before a long night.

He took the stairs down.

MAC

Mac shifted his seat behind the wheel, but his backache did not ease.

His job sounded easy on paper - sit around most of the night, waiting to drive clients between meeting rooms, hotels, and watering holes - but in reality, it was a kind of insomnia. He spent most nights in a daze, never truly awake but never truly dormant either. He could rarely concentrate enough to read, and sleeping in the car was all but impossible. When he wasn't driving, he spent most of his time staring blankly out of the window, listening to the monotonous drone of the radio. He went through the motions, but he was never entirely present.

He climbed out of the Range Rover, stretched, and lit a Benson. It was raining lightly, and a gentle breeze came across the car park, ran its fingers through his hair. He paced slowly beside the car, then stopped, leaned against it, and looked up at the Renaissance Hotel. Light glowed behind nearly all of its windows. For a second, he was frozen by its sublimity; some great magic lingered in its shadow, but the sensation passed as quickly as it had come.

At least he was not cruising the streets for weekend

offenders and reckless drivers in a squad car. This job was safer, but God, it could drag by, and sometimes he missed having a partner. His clients were rarely great conversationalists, although he'd take poor conversation over chasing delinquents any night.

The wind and rain had the hairs standing up on the back of his arms and neck. He stubbed his cigarette out and climbed back into the Range. He was more awake, for now, but his tiredness had not faded so much as metamorphosed into a crippling headache. He could fill his flask with water in the hotel toilet, but he'd have to empty out the rest of his coffee.

Fleetwood Mac played on Smooth FM. Huge surprise. He found himself drumming on the steering wheel nonetheless. He liked the song actually; it reminded him of the years before Luke had been born, when it was just him and Charlotte. Back then, it had seemed they could conquer the world together. The Mac and Charlotte who had gone out for city dates and fucked on the sofa were gone. Now they were hanging on by their fingertips and praying the storm did not sweep them away. What he'd give for just one more day in the sunshine.

A blur of suited figures came down the hotel steps - Mac sat up straighter - but they were not his clients.

He checked the time on the dash. It was exactly midnight; four red zeroes shone back at him like the end of a countdown.

Luke would be in bed now, Charlotte too, probably.

He yawned at the thought, settled back into the seat.

Fleetwood Mac gave way to Spandau Ballet. He killed the radio.

Rain tapped on the windscreen and roof. Traffic rolled endlessly up Euston Road.

He opened the glovebox, took out the paperback he'd been reading, then returned it. He did not have the focus to read now. He knew what would happen; he'd scan the words and his fingers would turn the pages, and after a few minutes chasing thoughts like a dog chasing its tail, he'd realise he hadn't been paying attention and have to start again.

He needed a holiday. They all needed a holiday. Even a weekend of R&R without thinking about hospital bills and life insurance would be a blessing. But he couldn't leave London. He'd traded that freedom for the money when the man in the dark suit had come to the house with his contract. But the money would count for nothing when Charlotte was gone.

More figures emerged from the Renaissance Hotel but there were too many to be Mac's clients.

He only wished he knew how long they would be inside. If he had ten minutes, he could run to a shop and grab a sandwich.

The figures drew closer, headed directly for him. He squinted through the rain. The two men were his clients; they had simply acquired a female companion each.

Mac climbed out and opened the back door for them.

'How'd it go?'

'Not bad,' the older man said, climbing into the back. 'But we're done with business tonight. It's time to have some fun.'

The girl giggled as she climbed in after him.

'Sounds good,' Mac said.

The second man and girl got in, and Mac returned to the driver's seat.

'So where to?'

'We were thinking somewhere expensive but not too in-your-face,' the older man said. His younger associate was too preoccupied with the girl beside him.

'I know just the place in Soho,' Mac said, starting the engine.

'So-ho be it,' the man quipped, and his girl giggled again.

Mac pulled out of the car park and joined the southbound traffic.

The older man in the back started making out with the

girl, and the next time Mac glanced in the rear-view, the girl had disappeared from view.

Just what he fucking needed.

Mac used only his side mirrors from then on. It wasn't worth the risk of making eye contact. They were only five minutes from Soho now, maybe ten with traffic. What was he supposed to do if they were still at it when they arrived? Pull up and wait for them to finish or drive around in circles?

Mac was passing the corner of Regent's park when his phone rang. He fished it out of his pocket and glanced at the caller ID, but the screen was blank. Because it was not the phone in his hand ringing. It was his other phone.

Everything slowed.

He fumbled for the other phone and stared down at it. He was still driving the car somehow. He'd split into two equal parts like a cell dividing under a microscope. One part navigated the traffic, the other focused entirely on the ringing phone in his hand.

He was wide awake.

He answered it, and raised the phone slowly to his ear. 'Hello?'

'Hello, Mac. My name's Warren Clarke. We met two years ago when you signed the contract. Do you remember me?'

'Yes.' He couldn't picture the man's face, but his voice was like something out of a dream.

'Good. I need you to pull over for me, Mac.'

So they *were* watching him. There must be trackers in the car, in his phone.

The windscreen wipers cleared the rain from his view. He looked down at the hand gripping the steering wheel, white-knuckled. It was his hand. He was driving.

What had happened? Why had this dream man surfaced now? Were Charlotte and Luke in danger? Was the city?

'Okay,' was all he could manage. He pinned the mobile with his shoulder and pulled up on the pavement.

'Good. I need you to listen very carefully to me, Mac. There is an unprecedented threat to the country. I need you to drive home immediately and as fast as possible. Ignore the highway code when it's safe to do so. You'll collect your family and then drive to an address in Hampstead, collect another family of three, and drive to St Mary Axe. I'm texting you both addresses now. Say that back to me, Mac.'

'I collect my family, pick up a family from Hampstead, and then drive to St Mary Axe.'

'Good. As fast as you can, Mac, and don't stop for any other reason. Time is of the essence, as they say.'

'What's the threat?' Mac asked.

A pause. 'Everything will be explained when you arrive at your destination. For now, I need you to focus on the task at hand.'

'Okay.'

'What's happening?' one of his clients asked from the back. He ignored them.

'Good. Oh, and the code to the safe in the boot is 2374. There's a handgun and ammo inside, if you need it. I'll text you that too, in case you forget.'

'Okay,' Mac said again.

'Good luck, Mac.' And he was gone.

Mac stared out of the windscreen at the gathering rain, before the wiper swiped it away.

He needed to be sick. No, that was just the adrenaline.

His mobile buzzed in his hand: the addresses and safe code.

'You all need to get out,' Mac said. His voice was cold, alien.

'Excuse me?' the man behind said, leaning between the seats.

Mac climbed out, hooked around the bonnet, and pulled open the back seat.

'Out. Now,' he barked.

Judging by his facial expression, the man couldn't seem to work out if he were angry, amused, or both.

'We weren't even doing anything,' the man in the back said. The girl's head and shoulders were visible again beside him.

As he stood there arguing, the seconds were bleeding away.

Time's ticking, Mac. That's what it does. Tick, tick, tick.

He stepped back and pulled open the Range's boot. He lifted the floor and keyed the code into the safe.

He slid the Glock out of its holster, pocketed the spare magazines, and aimed the gun into the car.

'I said get the fuck out.'

He hadn't held a gun in a couple of years now, let alone discharged one, but the weight of it brought him right back to his Met days. The Glock was only an extension of his arm now, an extension of his brain. The ability to subdue, to kill, was automatic.

'Alright, alright,' one of the men said. They filed out onto the pavement. One of the girls hid behind her male counterpart.

'I'm sorry,' Mac said. He slammed the door behind them and returned to the driver's seat.

'I'll have your job for this, you cunt,' one yelled after him.

Mac set the Glock and mobile down on the passenger's seat and pulled away. The engine growled from the excess gas, before he shifted into second gear.

He felt around for his main mobile and dialled Charlotte.

'Come on, pick up, pick up,' he muttered.

The traffic lights ahead turned red. He floored the accelerator and cut through it.

'Mac, honey, what's up?'

Relief flooded him, but it was dissolved by panic just as quickly.

'Charlotte.' He sighed. 'I need you to listen very carefully.'

KAREN

Karen woke to a phone ringing.

Who would be calling at this time?

A light blinked on, half-blinding her for a moment. Andrew sat up in bed. She hadn't sensed him getting in; the wine had sent her to a deep, dreamless sleep.

'Are you going to get that?' she asked, scanning the room for the source of the ringing.

'It's not mine,' he said.

'Well it's not-'

But it was hers. Her other phone.

She was paralysed. She was dreaming, of course. Only in her dreams could the phone be ringing.

Andrew climbed out of bed, located the mobile, and handed it to her.

She answered the phone - that's what she was supposed to do, wasn't it? - and raised it to her ear.

'Hello?'

Who was on the other end? Had her dream architect thought that far? But surely that was her. Would she hear her own voice through the phone?

Wake up, Karen.

But the voice was male. 'Hello, Karen. My name's Warren Clarke. I came to your father's house on your eighteenth birthday. Do you remember me?'

She looked to Andrew for support, but his stare only demanded more answers. What if she wasn't dreaming after all?

Her tongue unlocked itself. She rolled it around her mouth for a second as though feeling the shape of her jaw and teeth for the first time.

'Yes. I remember you.'

'Put it on speakerphone,' Andrew said. She did.

'…unprecedented threat to the country. To the world in fact. There's a car en route to your house as we speak. It'll take you and your family somewhere safe. You have around ten minutes to pack any personal effects. Do you understand, Karen?'

'Yes,' she said after some deliberation. She didn't understand at all. What kind of threat? Was there a nuclear attack or some freak natural disaster?

She glanced at the windows, as though she might see a flash of white light and a slowly rising mushroom cloud in the distance, but the curtains were closed anyway.

'Good. I'm sure you have many questions, and I promise they will be answered shortly, but we need to move quickly. Pack a bag and wait outside. I'll see you soon.'

'Okay.' There was nothing else she could think to say.

Warren ended the call, and if it weren't for the dead tone ringing, she would have convinced herself she really had dreamed it all.

Andrew was already in motion. He switched on the wall-mounted TV, tuned it to BBC News, and scrambled around for his clothes.

'Wake Saff. Get her to pack a bag.'

'Okay,' she said.

The news broadcast showed a packed train station which could only be Waterloo. People ran, pushed each other to get away from something. The ticker along the bottom of

65

the screen read: Hundreds dead in London massacres. Suspected terrorist attacks in -

'Karen.' She hadn't moved.

'Right, sorry.' She jumped to her feet, panic pulling her like a puppet master.

She took one last look at the TV and bolted out.

'Saffron,' she called, hammering on the door, and opened it. She didn't have time to waste.

Saff sat up in bed, grimacing, as Karen flicked on the light. She mumbled something from behind both hands.

'Saff, honey, you need to get up. You need to pack a bag. We're leaving in a few minutes.'

'What? Where?'

Karen pulled open Saff's closet and snatched a rucksack from the floor. 'The phone rang. My other phone. There's some national threat. A car's coming for us. We need to go.' Into the rucksack, she stuffed a few tops, underwear, and a pair of jeans.

'I'm not going anywhere. Not without Rory.'

Karen froze, a lacy bra she'd never seen before in-hand.

She should have seen this coming, but everything was happening so fast. Of course, Saffron would not leave without Rory, especially now that they were engaged.

They all needed to be in that car when it arrived. How long did they have now? Six minutes? Five?

'Saff, honey. I know this is hard for you,' she started, but Saff wasn't listening. She fumbled for her mobile and dialled Rory's number.

Karen set the rucksack down on Saff's bed. 'Okay, call him, but pack in the meantime. We don't have long.'

Saff acquiesced, opening her bedside drawer and packing things into the bag. The phone rang out, but she re-dialled.

Perhaps their escort would let them pick up Rory on the way - on the way to where? - but surely he wouldn't leave his mother alone.

'Oh, fuck,' Saff cried, throwing her head back. Tears

filmed her eyes.

'Just keep trying,' Karen said. 'And keep packing.'

Time was melting away, and Karen had so many other things to do. A tornado had blown through their lives, and she had only minutes to loot the wreckage. What should she pack? Food? Toiletries? Cash? Did they need their passports, or was that a stupid idea?

She tore out of Saff's room and hurried back to the bedroom.

Andrew was zipping up a bloated suitcase. A bulging rucksack and holdall lay on the bed beside it.

'I've packed everything we need from here. Is Saff up?'

'Yes, but she's refusing to leave without Rory.'

'Like fuck she is.' He snatched up the TV remote and turned it off, but not before Karen heard the news reader mention Apollo Pharmaceuticals.

Andrew shouldered the two bags and dragged the suitcase across the floor.

'Why were they talking about you?' she asked.

'Don't worry,' Andrew called back.

Karen looked stupidly around the room, then followed.

She had so much ground to cover and so little time. She checked her other phone as she followed Andrew down the stairs. It was twenty-seven minutes past midnight. Her call log showed the call had come through at nineteen-past and lasted two minutes.

They had four minutes.

'Saff, are you ready yet?' she called, but no reply came.

'I'll sort her,' Andrew said, dropping the bags by the door, and mounted the stairs again.

'Alright.'

What did she need again? Food. Money. Pills. She needed her pills.

'Did you get my meds?'

'Of course,' Andrew said.

She hit the kitchen first, snatching a canvas bag from the back of the door and filling it with food from the cupboards.

Biscuits. Cereal bars. Tinned veg and soup. Things that would last. She didn't know where they were going or how long they'd be away, but it seemed like the right thing to do. That's what people packed in movies.

She added the rest of the Bordeaux and another bottle of wine for good measure, then dropped the bags in the hallway, and moved onto the living room.

She scanned the room, and the past couple of decades of her life stared back at her: artwork they'd acquired - some of which were originals - shelves of books she might never read again, a cabinet of records, tapes, and CDs of her favourite music.

She opened the cabinet first, took her iPod out of the dock and pocketed it. She hadn't got around to transferring all of the CDs, but it was something.

She took the Eiffel Tower ornament from the mantelpiece, the one Saff had brought back from her trip to Paris.

She scanned the bookshelves next. Her heart jumped, like an emotional radar, as her gaze fell upon the photo album. She pulled it out and added it to her bag, feeling the weight not just of the leather-bound book but the memories it contained. The other books stared back at her desperately. The hundreds of lives she had lived for the duration of their pages. Novels in which she had lost and found herself again.

She dropped *Alice in Wonderland* into the bag, and looked between *Jane Eyre* and *Wuthering Heights*. She could not leave without a Bronte, but which one?

She looked between the spines, heart racing. She was wasting time.

She added both and was scanning the room one final time when Saff cried out from the hallway.

'Get off me. You can't make me leave.'

'I can and I am,' came Andrew's voice.

Saff yelled out again, and Karen rushed to the hallway to see Andrew pulling her down the stairs by an arm. He had her rucksack over his other shoulder.

'He's my fiancé,' Saff yelled. 'I'm not leaving without him.' Mascara-tears streamed down her face. Her messy bun had collapsed onto one shoulder.

Andrew released her. 'What?'

'He proposed to me,' she sobbed. 'On Thursday.'

'Jesus Christ,' Andrew said, slapping a hand to his forehead. 'I don't have time for this shit - watch her,' he told Karen. 'I need to finish packing.'

He went into the kitchen, leaving Karen as... what, Saff's jailor? What was she supposed to do if Saff made a break for the door, subdue her? Karen didn't think she could restrain Saff if she wanted to. But what if Saff did escape? Stole one of their cars and drove away? She would put them all in danger, not least of all herself.

'You couldn't get through?' she asked.

'Obviously not,' Saff said.

'Well, we'll keep trying him in the car. Maybe he'll be able to join us.'

'You don't know that. You're just trying to shut me up. You're just as bad as Dad.' She sat down heavily on the stairs and buried her face in her hands.

'We just care about you. Like Rory cares about you. And I'm sure he'd want you to be safe too. I know you want to make sure he's okay, but you need to think about yourself, too. The way you feel about Rory, that's how we feel about you. We need to protect you, honey. So, let us keep you safe, and we'll do everything we can to help you with Rory.'

Saff lowered her hands and stared at Karen through a curtain of fringe. 'Fine.'

'Yeah?'

Saff nodded, covered her face as another wave of tears came over her.

'Oh, honey.' Karen sat on the step beside her and pulled her into her shoulder. Saff resisted, but not for long.

'Have you texted Rory? Or left him a voicemail? So he knows what's happening as soon as he sees his phone?'

'I texted him already,' Saff said. 'He must have it on

silent.'

'Have you tried his home phone?'

'They don't have one.'

'They don't have a home phone?'

'No,' Saff whimpered. 'His mum… his mum… No, they don't.'

Andrew emerged from the kitchen, carrying a new canvas bag in one hand and an axe in the other: the one he cut firewood with when they fancied a fire in the lounge on those cosy winter nights.

He regarded them both carefully as he set the bag down, looked inquisitively to Karen: was everything under control?

She shrugged, nodded.

Andrew opened the front door, stepped out.

Saff pulled away from Karen and dialled Rory's number again.

Andrew returned as Rory's voicemail message spilled from Saff's phone.

'No sign yet.' His form filled the doorway, sweat blotting his shirt armpits, the axe at his side. He looked like a man ready to kill. This brought Karen equal measures of fear and comfort. Was he on coke now or just adrenaline? Had he done a line while she'd been waking Saff or was this just what raw instinct looked like?

'No luck?' he asked.

Karen shook her head, laid a hand at Saff's back.

'We'll ask the driver. He should have answers for us.'

Should. But how much rested on the should?

Saff redialled the number. It was pointless at this point, of course, but perhaps it gave Saff some semblance of agency, which was good. They needed Saff as calm - sedated - as possible for the foreseeable future.

Andrew turned as Karen caught the vaguest sound of an engine. Behind him, headlights grew out of the shadows.

A Range Rover pulled into the driveway.

'About time,' Andrew said.

SIMBA

You shouldn't be here.

A voice from the shadows.

Simba struggled to sit up, but he saw nothing in the darkness.

He was back in solitary confinement, his hands sticky with his cellmate's blood. No, the room was too spacious for that. He was in the Camden squat. Daisy was murmuring in her sleep nearby. There were other voices in the room.

You don't belong here.

He sat up, shuddering as though every cell in his body were repelling each other.

He was in Terry's living room, of course. The other voices were only from the TV. He was safe.

He took deep breaths to calm himself, though his racing heart lagged behind in panicked dreams.

He stood up, rubbed his neck, and stretched to alleviate the worst of his aches. Somehow, Terry's sofa had beaten him up worse than the cardboard-on-concrete bed on which he'd slept more times than he wanted to think about.

His hand was sticky. He rolled his arm over in the weak light of the television screen. A crimson ribbon traced down his wrist, drying in his palm lines.

It was only then that he noticed what was actually playing on the TV - a breaking news report - and the screen drew him in like a window to a Lovecraftian landscape, so terrible he couldn't bring himself to look away.

A mousey reporter stood in front of Waterloo station. Behind her was an army of police vehicles, armed response officers, and other journalists. A suspected terrorist attack had occurred inside, killing hundreds of people.

Worse still, King's Cross was also locked down in what was believed to be a second coordinated attack. Together, they made the highest death count since 9/11, and the figures were still coming in.

Then there was the third story: a pile-up on the M3, killing dozens. Both Surrey and Met police were on the scene, but it was unclear as of yet whether this third event was isolated or coordinated.

A shout came from the window. Multiple voices in the street. Was this normal Saturday night ruckus, or had something bad happened? Surely no terrorist would attack Whitechapel.

Daisy jerked awake from the sofa, where she'd been slumped over the armrest. 'What the fuck?' she groaned.

'I don't know,' Simba said. 'Something's happening.' He pointed to the TV and Daisy silently read the ticker.

A moped engine echoed around the street. More voices.

'Jesus Christ,' Daisy breathed, sitting forwards.

Movement from the corridor. Light appeared under the door. Daisy had just long enough to sweep their shooting paraphernalia into her bag, before Terry opened the door.

He held a cricket bat at his side.

'What the fuck's going on?'

He watched the news for a moment, but glanced towards the window when the noise from the street drowned out the broadcast.

He went to the window and peered through the curtains.

'It's just kids out there. Fuck, what about my kids? I need to call them.' He hurried out of the room.

'Why does this have to happen now?' Daisy groaned. She pulled on her hoody and shoes, packed the rest of her things into her bag, as though she were getting ready for school rather than preparing to flee for her life.

Simba moved slowly himself, as though he were wading through liquid tar, but soon adrenaline would cut through the junk haze.

And then the real fun started.

He was too old for this shit. He should have died with his last OD.

Oh, you think you've suffered enough? You haven't seen nothing yet, boy.

Terry wandered back in, holding a phone to his face.

'Fuck,' he cried in a voice Simba didn't expect from a man like Terry. It was the voice Simba had used himself only in his lowest moments. So desperate, so infantile, it was almost funny.

'I've gotta go,' Terry said, patting his pockets. 'I need to find my kids. You can stay here if you want. Watch the house. I don't know.'

And then he was gone again.

On the news, the chaos was unfolding. Accounts of numerous smaller killing sprees came in, mostly on roadsides or near train stations. No explosives had been confirmed, and it was unclear exactly what had killed so many people, aside from those in traffic collisions.

Outbound flights from all London airports had been grounded, inbound flights turned around or redirected. Just minutes ago, the Prime Minister and his family were seen leaving the back entrance of Downing Street in their armoured Jaguar, accompanied by a procession of unmarked Land Rovers.

The Queen's whereabouts were unknown.

'Fuck,' Daisy said. 'What are we doing? You wanna stay

here or you wanna kick?'

'Where would we go?' he asked. Taking to the streets seemed counterintuitive, especially with the commotion outside, although he had a sinking paranoia about staying at Terry's, too.

'I don't know.'

There were quiet places in London if you knew where to look, places where no one went - abandoned office blocks and disused warehouses - but to get to them, they'd have to brace the open streets.

Terry reappeared in the doorway in a black puffer jacket with a bag slung over one shoulder. He still held the cricket bat. What if Simba needed to defend himself? Daisy had her knife, which wouldn't be much good against a gun or explosive, but it was something.

There was something else he'd need too, not in the next few hours, but certainly today.

I might be quiet now, but I'm coming back, Simba, and you better be ready for me.

He pushed the thought from his head for the time being.

'So, what are you guys doing?' Terry asked. 'I can leave you my spare key if you want, or I can drop you off somewhere on the way to Ilford, but I have to go now.'

Simba looked to Daisy, but her expression only reflected his own desperation back at him.

'I guess we'll stay here,' Daisy said. 'If that's cool.'

Terry nodded, handed Daisy a key. 'I don't know when I'll be back. Bell me if anything happens down here, yeah?'

'Of course, man. Don't worry about it.'

'Alright. And if you do leave, just post the key through the letterbox.' He scanned the room one final time and headed out.

'Good luck,' Daisy called after him.

The front door opened and closed, and then they were alone. There were still voices coming from the window and from the news broadcast, but Simba became acutely aware of the silence between the sounds.

'The fuck do we do now?' Daisy asked, slumping back into the sofa.

Simba had no answer. He fished a half-smoked cigarette out of the ash tray, blew it off, and lit it.

They watched the chaos unfold on-screen, until he eventually reached for the remote and killed the TV. The crowd outside seemed to have drifted on, leaving a cosmic tinnitus in its wake.

MAC

Mac climbed down from the Range Rover and went to meet the man emerging from the house. Two more figures stepped out of the porch behind him.

'You must be the Cummings,' Mac said.

'Andrew,' the man said. He transferred the wood axe to his other hand to shake with Mac.

'Mac. I'm here to escort you to a safe place. I assume you've been briefed?'

'Barely,' Andrew said. 'We were hoping you could fill us in.' His gaze found the Glock on Mac's hip and lingered there.

'I probably don't know much more than you. I'll tell you everything I know in the car, but we have to go now. Let me help with your bags.' He gestured to the doorway.

'Alright,' Andrew said, lifting a suitcase from the hallway, 'but we have a problem. My daughter can't get in contact with her boyf - fiancé. We need to pick him up en route.'

Mac gathered two bags from the hallway and led them to the car. 'Sorry, mate, but I can't do that. I'm on strict instructions to drive you directly to St Mary Axe. They have trackers in the car.'

'St Mary Axe?' Andrew asked. 'The Gherkin site?'

'That's the one,' Mac said, opening the Range's boot and putting the bags in beside their own.

'Okay.' Andrew frowned. 'What if he made his own way there? He is family.'

'I don't know. I'm just the driver here. You'd have to take it up with them. I'm sorry.'

Andrew grunted as he hoisted the suitcase into the boot. 'Alright.'

Charlotte and Luke faced out from the back seats. Byron tried to look between the headrests. Mac didn't even know if they'd be allowed to take Byron in, let alone another person.

They walked back to the house and the wife handed over more bags.

'That's it,' she said.

'What about Rory?' the girl asked as they headed back to the car. Black tears ran down her face.

'We can't pick him up now, but he might be able to join us there,' Andrew said.

'Might?' the girl asked. 'What about his mum?'

'I don't know, Saff,' Andrew snapped behind him. 'I'm doing my best here.'

They hauled the last bags into the boot and Andrew zipped his axe inside the top bag.

'You know how to use that thing?' he asked, nodding to Mac's Glock.

'Yeah. I was in the Met for twelve years.'

'Alright. Let's go.' Andrew shepherded his wife and daughter into the car with minimal protest and climbed in the passenger side.

Mac reversed out of the drive and gunned the engine.

He navigated the winding one-way roads, doing as much as forty-five on some corners.

By the time he joined Heath Street, it was apparent that the residents of Hampstead - those who'd still been awake or woken by friends and family - were as eager to leave as they were. The already busy Saturday night traffic had coagulated to a near stand-still. The box junction outside the tube station had descended to anarchy as everyone tried to force their way through at once.

If only the Range had been fitted with a siren, they might have cleared a little space. Still, there was a reason they'd chosen Mac; he'd spent over fifteen years navigating the streets of London, and he'd lead his fair share of police chases.

'Fuck this,' Mac grunted, driving up onto the pavement. Horns screamed as he cut past the line of traffic, and swung around the box junction.

The main roads flowed a little faster and the pavement was wider here. He managed to keep ahead of the traffic mostly by manoeuvring onto the pavement and the oncoming lane.

His sat-nav gave him an ETA of just over half an hour with traffic, but this wasn't ordinary weekend traffic.

The girl behind him, Saff, was dialling her fiancé, but otherwise the car was silent. The street outside was chaos, but somehow everything felt slower inside the car. That was probably just the adrenaline.

Traffic slowed ahead, and Mac mounted the kerb to get past - pedestrians scattered - but when he tried to re-join, the cars ahead blocked him.

'Fuck,' Mac growled. He inched forwards, praying the next car would let him in. If not, well he had the Glock. He could always aim it out of the window if things got desperate.

The car blocked him too, but Mac pushed into the road, grinding against the bumper of the Mini behind. The woman behind the wheel leaned on her horn.

They moved ahead as the traffic light turned green. The boot of the car in front was packed with suitcases and bags.

Mac cruised on, constantly scanning for an opportunity to overtake. At least the south-bound traffic was moving faster than north - he imagined most people evacuating the city were heading north - but even then, it was the usual stop-start.

When they reached Chalk Farm, the lane split into two and he managed to mostly maintain the speed limit between lights. But as Chalk Farm gave way to Camden Road, traffic dissolved into further anarchy. The extra lane had been usurped by the volume of extra traffic coming north and he was forced back into the left-hand lane. The driver of a navy BMW behind him held his position, leaning on his horn, but Mac didn't wait around to find out what happened. The Golf ahead mounted the wide pavement and Mac followed. He clipped his right wing mirror on a lamp post but cut back into traffic in time for the next box junction free-for-all.

Now the road was one-way, and with multiple lanes and wide pavements, traffic was like a white-water river.

They were making good progress when they bottlenecked into a single lane again approaching St Pancras.

The pavement was strictly off-limits now: pedestrians flocked up and down the streets, many running. Sirens echoed, but Mac couldn't locate their sources.

'Fuck,' he breathed, sitting back in his seat. He should have given King's Cross a wide berth. He'd be lucky if none of the roads were closed. On the other hand, most of the congestion was caused by people flooding in and out of residential areas. No one wanted to be in the city in the wake of the attacks. With a little luck, traffic would ease up once they passed St Pancras.

He considered switching on the radio to follow the news but decided he didn't want to know. His entire focus was on getting them to St Mary Axe before the streets clotted completely. All it took was one person to crash or abandon their car in the road and everything ground to a halt.

Byron barked in the back. He glanced in the rear-view as Charlotte hugged him to her chest, muttering soothing words.

A motorbike came up on his right side just as a group of

pedestrians filtered between the cars ahead. The motorcycle struck a woman head-on, and she hit her head hard as she went down.

The chaos was unfolding exponentially. He needed to get out of there, but there was nowhere to go.

He drummed his fingers on the steering wheel, holding the revs behind the clutch.

People crowded around the fallen woman. A barrage of horns sounded from behind.

'Take the pavement,' Andrew said.

'I can't. There are too many people.'

'They'll move,' Andrew said.

Mac hesitated, then edged forwards and mounted the kerb. The pedestrians parted, and he manoeuvred slowly around the people, trees, and lamp posts on the pavement. He rounded a corner, avoiding the crossroads, and joined Euston Road.

It was hard to believe that he'd been right here in the car park of the Renaissance Hotel less than an hour ago.

People ran towards him on the pavement, traffic blocking the bus lane immediately beside him.

A car changed lanes ahead, and Mac seized the opportunity. He flattened the accelerator, raced towards the pedestrians, and turned at the last minute into the bus lane.

Relief escaped him in a breath as he closed the gap between the car in front.

Only then did he realise that the pedestrians were running from something. Outside the St Pancras Underground entrance, a woman was pinned to the wall by a man who seemed to be kissing her neck, but as he released her, the woman fell limply to the ground. The man jerked around to face Mac, wearing a surgical mask of blood around his mouth. There was no way the man could see Mac through the tinted windows, but somehow he saw him.

'What the fuck?' Andrew called.

Mac fingered the grip of his Glock, inching the Range forward. Traffic was moving, but not quick enough.

The man's attention was soon diverted by the crowd of pedestrians and he sprinted after them.

Traffic pulled ahead, and Mac flattened the accelerator.

It was too much to process. Beyond the edges of his adrenaline-fuelled focus, everything had a dream-like quality. Even the violence he'd just witnessed didn't feel real. Terrorists attacked with bombs and guns - *And knives*, the mouths in his stomach jeered - they did not bite people's throats out.

It was like the news report he'd heard that afternoon about the drugs trial. Some schizophrenic man had killed his wife by biting out her jugular. It was too great a coincidence.

But he didn't have time to ponder it all now. His attention was drawn ahead as the lanes opened up. He gunned the engine, doing forty-five half in the cycle lane, half on the kerb.

There was another siren behind him. Lights flashed in his rear-view. An ambulance was parting the traffic, and as soon as it passed Mac, he joined its tail.

Traffic was relatively easy now. If he hadn't just seen what he'd seen, he might have assumed it was just a normal Saturday night.

They were on the A1, heading south. His sat-nav, which was pretty much useless at this point, estimated arrival in ten minutes.

And then what?

As they approached Holborn, traffic slowed to a crawl, bottlenecked into one lane. A black cab lay upside down in the bus lane, its back windscreen scattered across the road. A man sat on the kerb, nursing a broken arm.

He drove east for a stretch at forty. The city of London was emptier as he'd expected.

'Okay, we're nearly here,' he told the rear-view mirror as they passed Liverpool Street. He scanned the skyline for the half-constructed Gherkin, but it was hidden by surrounding buildings.

Only when he pulled onto St Mary Axe did the Gherkin

come into view. It towered over the street, its emerald and black glass spiralling up to the halfway point where only its metal carcass foundation was visible.

The building was blocked off by a construction fence, but Mac couldn't even get to that for the half dozen cars parked before it.

He stopped behind an identical Range.

This was the place, but where was everybody?

'Wait here,' he told the car. He climbed down, drew the Glock, and walked between the cars towards the half-finished Gherkin.

Were they too late? Had they left without them? But left where? Wasn't this their destination?

He walked up to the construction gate and rang his Glock on the corrugated steel.

'Hey! Is someone there?'

Nothing.

He reached into his pocket and took out his phone to call Warren when he heard voices behind the gate. The doors opened inwards, and two soldiers in gas masks stepped out, aiming automatic rifles at his chest.

'Hey, I'm Mac. The driver,' he said, raising his hands in surrender, the Glock pointing to the sky. 'My family and the others are in the car.' He jerked his head back to the street.

'Bring them in,' the first soldier said with a Glaswegian twang, and stepped forward. 'Let's go.'

Mac led the way back through the cars. He pulled the back door open and leaned in. 'Okay, come on.'

The soldier walked out to cover the entrance to the street.

Mac pulled the back seat forward, and Byron jumped down. He helped Charlotte and Luke out.

'You okay?' he asked them.

'Yeah,' Charlotte breathed.

Andrew lifted their bags down from the boot. Mac shouldered a rucksack and took Charlotte's suitcase in one hand.

'We'll need two trips,' he told the soldier.

'Alright. Quickly.' He gestured for them to go, and Mac didn't need telling twice.

'Come on,' he said, gesturing Charlotte and Luke forward. He'd done his job, albeit by the skin of his teeth. His family were his priority now.

They filtered through the parked cars, carrying bags on their backs, and passed the soldier at the gates.

'Wait here. I'm-' *Going back for the other bags*, he was about to say, but Byron cut him off with a series of sharp barks from behind.

Mac dropped the suitcase and the bag, and hurried past Andrew and his family on his way back to the car.

'Stop right there,' the soldier yelled. A figure was approaching them from the end of the street. Byron barked again, growled deep from his throat like Mac had never heard before.

Another figure rounded the corner. The first started to run towards them.

Mac racked the Glock's slide and aimed it at the man. Byron raced forwards to meet him.

Gunfire rang against the buildings on both sides: the spray of the soldier's rifle.

The first man went down like a puppet with its strings cut. Byron jumped at the gunfire and again as the soldier neutralised the second target.

Byron took a sweeping look of the street, and then bolted away, whether to look for other targets or to flee from the gunfire, Mac couldn't tell.

'Byron,' he yelled, running forwards.

'Leave it,' the soldier called, waving his arm back. 'Get inside.'

Mac hesitated, then snatched up the last bags and hurried back to the others.

The soldier followed him and closed the gates behind him.

'Where's Byron?' Charlotte cried. 'What happened?'

'He ran off,' Mac said.

'We'll keep an eye out,' the Scottish soldier said. 'Just get inside.' He gestured to the Gherkin's entrance.

They carried their bags into the unfinished shell of a lobby.

'Leave your things here,' the Scottish soldier said. 'We'll bring them down for you.'

He led them down a short corridor to a series of lifts. He turned a key in a panel on the wall, and the doors of the nearest lift slid open.

Mac holstered his Glock and stepped inside. The others filed in, all except Andrew.

He stared into the lift, let out a deep breath, then followed.

The doors closed and they were sardines in a box, their heavy breathing echoing.

A whirring sounded, and they sank down the shaft.

Mac held his breath until the car stopped and the doors opened.

They spilled into a cool tunnel, dark, save for small LEDs embedded in the walls leading to a huge steel door.

Andrew led the way, but before he could reach the door, a deep mechanical click echoed around the tunnel, and it swung slowly back. Light flooded the tunnel from another corridor, and a third soldier was revealed. He, too, wore a gas mask. Was there a chance they were breathing in some noxious chemical, or was it merely a precaution?

'Have any of you come into contact with an infected person tonight?' the soldier asked.

Infected?

Like a Super 8 projection, an image flashed in his head of the man pinning his victim to the wall of the St Pancras Underground. The blood around his mouth. Was that what that had been? An infection?

They all looked around each other and shook their heads.

'Alright. Come in,' the soldier said, stepping back.

They walked into a teal-coloured corridor, which made Mac think they were underwater as opposed to just underground.

You're gonna drown, Mac. You're gonna drown down here.

The soldier closed the door behind them with a groan of hinges and a heavy thud.

He regarded them all in the better light, his gaze falling upon the Glock at Mac's hip. 'I'll take that for you,' he said.

Mac handed it over, feeling suddenly naked without it. They were safe here, whatever *here* was, but the vacuum in his stomach didn't relax.

The soldier emptied the round Mac had chambered and stowed the Glock in his belt.

'Alright. Follow me.' The soldier led them down a corridor of numbered doors. Further down, a sign on the wall pointed to various rooms: dining hall, common room, library, gym, chapel, garden. How was there a garden this far beneath the street?

They turned a corner and headed down another identical teal corridor. They stopped outside the chapel door and the soldier gestured them inside.

'Wait in here. Someone will come for you.'

Mac followed the others into the chapel, small like a hospital's. There were only a dozen or so pews, a few potted plants, and a small altar beneath a stained glass window.

The walls, thankfully, were painted cream.

They stood silently in the aisle, before Andrew fell into a pew, and the others followed suit.

'You okay?' Mac asked Charlotte, and she nodded slowly.

'I'm just glad we're all safe.'

'Yeah,' Mac said. The weight of his body pressed down against the hard pew. His temples throbbed. Adrenaline had pulled him through the whole ordeal, but now the exhaustion was creeping in.

He rested his arms on the pew in front and buried his face in his hands.

'You did amazing,' Charlotte said, touching his bicep. 'It's over now.' But he heard the lie in her voice. This was far from over.

'Yes, thank you,' Andrew said from across the aisle. 'We owe you our lives.'

Mac nodded, forced a smile.

'This is my wife Karen, by the way, and our daughter Saffron.'

Karen reached across the aisle and shook his hand, but Saffron only stared blankly ahead. How old was she? Seventeen? Eighteen? Too young to be engaged, that was for sure.

'This is Charlotte and Luke,' he said. They exchanged awkward pleasantries.

'So you had a contract too?' Karen asked.

'Yeah. A few years ago he came to the house. Warren. He gave me the Range Rover and a phone, told me in the event of a threat to national security, he would need me as a driver. You had one too?'

His question was directed at them both. He'd expected Andrew to answer but it was Karen who spoke.

'He came on my eighteenth birthday. My father had the contract before me, and his before him. I guess I never thought anything would come of it.'

'Jesus. What did the contract say you're supposed to do?'

Karen shrugged. 'Just survive, I suppose. I was forbidden from leaving London or going anywhere without the phone, and I had to have a child before forty.'

She'd been a prisoner all this time too, but he figured they were all prisoners now in a different way.

'I wonder how many others there are,' Charlotte said.

'A lot,' Andrew said. 'Dozens, judging by the size of this place.'

Surely there must be other drivers like him to bring everyone here, other Met officers perhaps. That brought him some comfort, but it was short lived.

Karen turned away and rubbed at Saff's mascara tears

with a thumb. Saff stared on.

The chapel was too calm after the night's chaos - the chaos that was still unfolding out there - even with the trauma lingering in each of their minds. The coolness of the room caressed his arms and face. Would it always be this cool? Was it just one of a thousand changes he'd have to get used to?

He shivered.

He'd always found something slightly unsettling about churches - or perhaps it was just the people within them, the collective delusion that brought them all together - but there was something different about this chapel. He'd assumed it was just its location and the circumstances surrounding them, not to mention his encroaching exhaustion, but as he followed Saff's empty gaze, it hit him. The stained-glass window above the altar shone subtly, but there could be no natural light down here. It could only be artificially lit.

His eyes might never see natural light again. He might never feel the warmth of sunlight on his skin or the cool rain.

The door opened behind them, and Mac started. A man in sky-blue scrubs and a surgical mask stood in the doorway.

'Malcolm?'

Mac stood. 'Yeah.'

'Come with me, please.'

He touched Charlotte's shoulder and kissed her head. 'I'll see you soon.'

'Okay.'

All eyes were on him - even Saff - as he squeezed out of the pew and walked to the door.

The nurse, Mac could only assume, gave him a perfunctory smile and led him back into the corridor.

Go here, do this, wait here. He was beginning to feel more and more like cattle than a survivor. It was surely a blessing and a curse, but he had the sinking feeling that the scales would tilt towards the curse.

He followed the nurse through the aquatic labyrinth.

Mac had lost all sense of direction when the nurse led him into a door marked 'Hospital'.

He found himself in a uniform doctor's waiting room. The room, like the chapel, seemed to have been lifted directly from the real world, as though each door on the corridor were a portal back to the real world. If it were not for the lack of windows, he might have entirely forgotten he was in an underground government facility. Where did the other doors lead? Would he find the observation deck of a spaceship straight out of *2001: A Space Odyssey* behind one? Or a Victorian billiard room? A smoky opium den? Would a haggard old man hand him a pipe to sedate him?

The nurse crossed the waiting room and knocked on the door marked 'Office'.

'Come in,' a voice said, and the nurse gestured Mac inside.

The office, too, was like any consulting room Mac had seen. A South Asian man in scrubs only a shade darker than the corridors looked up from his desk.

'Malcolm. My name's Kamal. Take a seat, please. I'd shake your hand, but it wouldn't be appropriate yet under the circumstances.'

He, too, wore a surgical mask, which bobbed as he spoke.

'Of course,' Mac said, sitting down.

The door closed behind him, and he was alone with the doctor.

'Now, I'm sure you have many questions, and they will be answered soon, but for the time being, I need to run some routine tests.'

'To make sure I'm not infected?' Mac asked.

Kamal hesitated, then said, 'Yes. I'd like to start with some bloods.'

'Okay.' Mac didn't get the impression he had a choice in the matter. Would he or Charlotte be there when Luke was tested? He couldn't bear the thought of Luke being alone for a moment in this place, especially as a stranger stuck needles in him.

Kamal prepared a syringe and examined Mac's arm.

'Sharp scratch coming,' Kamal said. As the needle sunk into his vein, his stomach turned over. The mouths in his belly opened to scream and then gritted their teeth. A ghost of the pain flashed and for a moment he was back in the dark room, the knife plunging into his stomach, tearing open one, two, three gaping holes that would never quite heal.

He clenched both fists. Each breath was heavy, strained, stretching his lungs.

And then the needle was gone, and Kamal was pressing a cotton pad to his forearm.

'Put pressure on it here.'

Just keep pressure on it, Mac. The ambulance is coming. You're going to be okay.

'Not so good with needles?'

For a moment, Mac was overcome by the urge to tell Kamal everything: the pain; the shock; the thought of slipping from the world like a needle from the edge of a record and leaving Charlotte and Luke alone in the world; the months of hell following the incident; the days where he couldn't get out of bed.

'No,' he said. 'I guess not.' He lifted up the corner of the cotton pad. A little blood had stained the inside but no more oozed from the hole.

'Would you like some water?'

His head was heavy, a bowling ball that might drop at any moment. 'That would be good. I can get it,' Mac said, looking around. 'Where's the-'

'It's no problem,' Kamal said, getting up. He went out to the waiting room. Through the open door, Mac saw the nurse leading out a man and young girl.

Kamal returned, handed him a plastic cup of cool water.

'Thank you,' he said. 'Are you the only doctor here?'

'No,' Kamal said, taking a tube from a basket and withdrawing the swab from it.

'How many are there?'

'Your questions will be answered,' Kamal said, handing him the swab. 'In the meantime, I just need a cheek swab.'

Mac complied, thinking there was no reason Kamal couldn't answer his questions and conduct the tests simultaneously.

He handed the swab back, and Kamal gave him a plastic container in exchange.

'I just need a urine sample from you to finish up,' Kamal said, getting to his feet. 'If you'd like to follow me.'

He led Mac through the waiting room and to a door labelled 'WC'.

At first, he couldn't piss, despite the night's coffee bloating his bladder. He leaned over and turned on the tap. He closed his eyes, focused on the sound of the running water, and eventually managed.

He washed his hands and returned the warm container to Kamal.

'Thank you. If you'd like to take a seat out here, I'll be back soon with your results.'

'Okay,' Mac said. He sank into a chair as Kamal headed out, and looked around the waiting room again: the pale blue paint job, the potted plant - surely fake - the fan of magazines on the coffee table that would never be replaced; the impressionist painting on the wall where a window should have been: a European village against an orange twilight.

He gripped the chair's armrests with shaking hands.

You're going to die down here. You're going to watch Charlotte die and then you're going to die yourself in this cold, dark hell.

There were multiple doctors down here, Kamal had said. Surely the masterminds behind this place had anticipated that some of them would get sick if they were expected to be down here for years. There had to be facilities for treating cancer.

But still he couldn't shift the black hole of dread in his gut.

He buried his burning face in his hands, but he didn't let himself cry. Even here alone. If he let the impulse consume him, he didn't know if he could ever stop it.

The clock on the adjacent wall ticked away, the only sound in the silent room. Time was inconsequential down here. Day and night were abstract concepts when their only light was artificial.

It was fifteen minutes before Kamal returned. Another man followed him in, and it took Mac a moment to register who it was.

The man who had knocked on his door three years ago and changed everything.

Mac got to his feet, looked between Warren and Kamal. 'You're clean,' Kamal said.

A breath of relief escaped him. 'Thank you.'

Kamal nodded, smiled. 'I'll be in my office. Just let me know when you're finished.'

'I'll keep it brief,' Warren said.

Kamal returned to his office and closed the door.

'Please, have a seat,' Warren said, pulling a chair around to face him. 'It's a pleasure to meet you again, despite everything.'

He offered his hand, and Mac shook it with trembling fingers. Warren noticed, regarded him with a wan smile. How the fuck was he so calm?

'Likewise.'

'I suppose I should introduce myself properly. My name's Warren Clarke. I'm the director of this place. The Ark. I didn't choose the name, by the way.' He paused. Did he expect Mac to laugh? 'If I'm being honest, I never thought this place would be needed, but I suppose that's besides the point. I asked for you to be screened first of your group because I wanted to ask your help. People are scared and they need direction. They need order.'

Mac had the impression that Warren was choosing his words carefully. Perhaps he'd had this speech prepared for years.

'The coming hours and days will set a precedent for the foreseeable future. I chose you largely because of your background. You must have met Callum, David, and John outside. They have decades of military experience, but your own expertise will prove invaluable. Can I count on you to keep things under control if things get heated?'

What exactly was Warren asking of him? To police the Ark? He'd only been a foot soldier, following the orders of those who understood the true DNA of law and order. Did he really have a choice?

'Of course.'

'Great,' Warren said, clapping his hands. 'I'll show you to the common room, where your family will join you shortly.'

Mac followed him through the teal corridors to his new life.

PART TWO

HARRIS

The killer walked slowly up the porch steps and into the house, a silenced pistol in his gloved hand. The screen door flapped back behind him and the shot faded to black.

The credits rolled over a cold piano melody.

'Well, shit,' Laura said, turning to Harris. 'Price'll get there in time though, right?'

'I don't know,' he said.

She turned to face him. 'Something on your mind?'

'No.' He smiled. 'Just tired is all.'

'You wanna turn in?'

'Sure. I'll take Murph out.'

'Thanks, hon.'

He killed the TV, stretched his back so it clicked, then walked to the kitchen.

Their German Shepherd raised her head expectantly from the floor.

'Come on then, girl,' Harris said, unlocking the patio door and sliding it open.

The automatic yard lights flashed on as Murphy trotted out. Rain fell in silver sheets against the black sky.

Harris looked back into the house. Laura was gone; he

heard her footsteps going up the stairs. He stepped out under the lean-to and lit a Camel.

Murphy circled the yard before catching the scent of something and slinking into the shadows.

He checked his watch: just past eleven. His days away from the medical school went by so slowly, but he was never quite content when they were over. Something in him itched to be around the books and the students and the heated debates. Well, he'd be back at the school in a week and he had reading to busy himself with in the meantime. Maybe he should take Laura out someplace tomorrow, get out of the goddamned house.

He smoked his cigarette down to the butt and dropped it in the ash tray.

'Come on, Murph,' he called to the shadows.

Still darkness behind the curtain of rain.

'Murph?' He stepped out onto the lawn, rain tapping on his head. He took another step and Murphy emerged from the shadows, dragging something across the lawn with her teeth. At first he thought it was a cat, but then he saw the ringed tail trailing behind.

A raccoon.

As Murphy dropped it under the patio lights, Harris saw that it had been dead for some time. It looked like a hand puppet whose insides had been emptied by weeks of decay. The smell hit the back of his throat like smoke.

'Jesus, Murph,' he coughed, waving her away from the corpse. If only he could wave the raccoon back to the shadows with the same motion.

He went back into the kitchen, searched under the sink for a pair of rubber gloves, but could find none. What would he do with it anyway? Toss the rotting thing back in the bushes for the worms to have their way or throw it in the trash like a spoiled meal? Neither option seemed particularly appealing. Probably he should bury the thing in the morning, but that wasn't exactly what he'd had in mind by getting out of the house.

His cell rang in the living room and he jumped.

Who the fuck was calling at this hour?

He closed the patio door after Murphy and grabbed the phone.

'Hello?' he said, hearing the frustration seep into his voice.

Silence, then, 'Professor Harris?' A female voice. Middle-aged. Unfamiliar.

'Yes?'

'My name's Julia West. I'm the Director-General of the World Health Organization. Are you sitting down, Professor?'

Rain swept against the front window, illuminated by the warm glow of the street light.

'Yes,' he lied. 'I'm sorry, it's late. What is this-'

'I'm guessing you haven't seen the news.'

'No, I haven't. Has something happened?'

'I think you'd better see for yourself, Professor.' Her voice was cold, almost militant.

He snatched up the clicker and tuned to CNN.

Breaking news from England: a virus was spreading across the South East at an unprecedented rate. London was in gridlock as the population raced to evacuate. Thousands were dead within hours.

'Shit,' was all he could manage.

'Are you home?' Julia asked.

'Yes.'

'Good. The UN is mobilising, and I've been tasked with recruiting a team of world-renowned specialists in response to the outbreak. Can we count on your assistance, Professor?'

A grainy video feed showed a man tearing a fleeing victim to the ground and burying his face in their throat. In horror movies, there was always a certain theatrical artifice to it, no matter how good the special effects were, but this... this shit looked more real than real and it sent long, cold shivers snaking down his arms that didn't go away.

'Professor?'

'Of course. Anything I can do to help.'

A sigh of relief came down the line. 'Thank you. What's your address?'

He told her.

'We'll have a car there in about... a half hour. It'll take you to Logan International, where you'll board a flight for Geneva. That's where the team will converge. I'll meet you there.'

'Okay.' What else was there to say? What seemed to be the deadliest virus in recorded history was spreading across England and he was one of the superhero team assembled to fight it? Surely he had fallen asleep watching HBO and his dream self had woven its very own hero's journey in which he, Richard Harris, would save the world from the brink of destruction. Laura would shake him awake any second and he'd laugh like he'd never laughed before. But he knew this was real, just as he knew the host in the grainy news report was real.

'Do you have any questions, Professor?'

'A thousand,' he said, 'but I guess they can wait.'

A half hour. He had a half hour to pack for a flight to Geneva and assimilate some kind of foundational understanding of this outbreak. And there was Laura. How could he explain this to her? How could he leave her?

'Alright,' Julia said. 'Well, I've texted you my cell number, if you need anything in the meantime. I'll try to call you before you board, but if not, I'll see you in Geneva.'

'Okay.'

'Oh, and Harris?'

'Yes?'

'Thank you. Your help is invaluable to... well, to humanity.'

Harris let out a breath. 'I hope so.'

The line went dead and he stood there for a moment, frozen with the cell to his ear, before adrenaline got him moving.

The stairs groaned in all the usual places as he hurried up to the bedroom. Laura was in the en suite, humming a tune over the ventilator.

He pulled the closet open and took down a carryall, stuffed it with clothes. How long would he be away? Days? Weeks?

Months?

He all but emptied his bedside drawer into the carryall, tore his cell phone and laptop chargers out of the wall, and packed them too. Where was his laptop? In his office probably. That was his next mission.

He should change into a suit for the United Nations - his Ralph Lauren - but before he could walk back to the closet, the en suite door opened and Laura stepped out.

She stopped in place, looked between the carryall and his face.

'Honey?'

'I have to go.' It was all he could manage; how could he explain the situation to Laura when he was still grappling with its impossibility himself?

He moved past her into the en suite, pulled the light cord, and gathered his toothbrush and meds.

'Honey, you're scaring me.'

'I'm sorry. A virus broke out in England. The UN need me in Berlin. A car's coming for me.' The words sounded crazier out loud than they had in his head.

Laura only frowned from the doorway. 'You're going to Europe? Now?'

'Yes.' He slipped past her, searched the closet for a book bag. 'In fact, you should leave too. If the reports are accurate, I've never seen anything like this before. It's only a matter of time before it spreads across the pond. Go to your mom's. You'll be safer out of the city.'

He crossed the hallway to his office. Laura followed.

'What kind of virus? Like rabies?'

'Yes and no. You'll have to see for yourself.' He packed his laptop into its carry case and scanned his bookshelves.

'Jesus,' she said.

He added Sherrington, Virchow, Plato, and Pythagoras to his book bag, alongside a couple of pathological encyclopaedias and both of his own books. He packed a few Science journals and his external hard drive filled with catalogues of digitised papers, and carried it all downstairs.

He and Laura watched the news from the doorway for a minute before Harris stole away to the bedroom. He raided the closet safe, tucking the Smith & Wesson into his waistband and pocketing the three thousand dollars' cash, passports, and 9mm ammo.

He hauled his carryall downstairs and dropped it by the door, trying to think what else he needed.

Laura was still fixated on the CNN report. She reached blindly back for his hand, pulled him into her. 'This is bad. This is really bad, isn't it?'

He kissed her head, held her for a moment before turning her round. 'Here,' he said, handing her half of the cash and her passport. 'I want you to take this as well.' He offered her the Smith & Wesson and ammo.

She looked up, fear in her glassy eyes. 'Won't you need it?'

'I'm flying international, honey, and we'll have military protection, I'm sure.'

She stared at the handgun a second longer, then took it.

'You'll have to take Murphy too. Your mom won't mind, will she?'

'No. It's fine.' Her face contorted, as though she were in great pain. 'I don't want you to go.' She flung her arms around him and he hugged her tightly. 'And just like that, with no warning.'

'I know. I'm sorry. With a little luck, I'll be back in a few weeks.'

She took a deep breath, holding back tears. 'I'm scared, honey.'

'I'm scared too, but we'll get through this. I promise.'

'Will you pray for us?' she asked, holding his gaze as they

withdrew.

'Oh, come on. You know I don't belie-'

'Will you? For me?'

He sighed, forced a smile. 'Okay. For you.'

She reached behind her neck and unfastened her crucifix. 'If I'm taking the gun, you're taking this. It'll keep you safe, like it's always kept me safe.'

'Okay.' If it came to life or death, he'd rather have a gun in his hand, but he let her fasten the chain around his neck, and tucked it under his shirt. The pendant was cold on his collarbone. It was calming for a second, maybe.

Laura smiled to suppress further tears. 'You'll need some food for the journey. I'll pack you lunch.'

She turned away and busied herself making sandwiches. Harris filled the coffee pot and hunted for a flask as it brewed.

He checked his watch. He had sixteen or seventeen minutes until the car was due.

He regarded Laura, bent over the counter in her night things, and a great yearning shot through his stomach like a dozen ball bearings. He stepped up behind her and pressed his body against her. He kissed her neck, folded his arms around her middle.

She laid her head on his and stroked his arm. 'I'm gonna miss you.'

'Well, what if I leave you something to remember me by?' he said, trailing his lips underneath her earlobe, raising a hand to cup her breast.

He fucked her there on the counter, like he hadn't fucked her in years, tears filming his eyes as he climaxed.

'Well, that was something,' she laughed through tears of her own, and laid her head on his shoulder. 'You'd better do that again when you come home.'

'Oh, I will.'

When he'd filled the flask with coffee and packed the food into his bag, he checked his watch again.

Time was melting away, but they had a few minutes left

at least. Now that he'd packed and made his peace with Laura, he had only to absorb what few details he could from the CNN report.

Everything was suddenly real. Until this point, he might have convinced himself he was embarking on a regular business trip - another book tour perhaps - but it was too close not to look in the face now. He was flying across the Atlantic towards what was already the fastest spreading disease in recorded history. His entire academic and personal life had been preparation for this moment; every rung of the ladder had got him closer to the top but now it was time to jump and he had no time to check his parachute.

They watched the news in silence, holding hands, before sweeping headlights drew their heads. Harris went to the window and looked out. A station wagon cruised to a stop outside the house.

'It's here.'

Laura swallowed, nodded. 'Call me as soon as you can, yeah?'

'I will. You going to your mom's then?'

'Yeah. I'll get some coffee, drive through the night.'

'Well drive carefully. If you get tired, pull over and take a pit stop, won't you?'

'I'll be fine,' she said.

They kissed, and for a second he was back in Detroit, kissing her in the park for the first time. He tried to commit the shape of her lips to memory as he opened the front door and carried his bags out onto the porch. Rain flickered in the car's headlights: silver ahead and red behind.

A man in a dark overcoat climbed out of the station wagon and walked across the yard.

'Professor Harris?' he called. Thick Boston accent.

'Yes, sir.'

'Are you ready?'

'Just about,' he said, looking back at Laura.

'I'll take your bags while you say goodbye.'

'Thank you.'

He turned to Laura. 'I love you.'

'I love you too.'

They hugged, and Murphy padded out and sat beside them.

He could think of nothing else he could say to somehow express the tornado tearing him apart from the inside, so he turned away and walked down to the idling car. He looked back from the sidewalk, forced his best smile, and climbed in.

Laura's rain-blurred shape drifted out of view as the car pulled away.

'So what have you got for me?' Harris asked.

'What's that?'

'You got news for me? Some kind of background?'

'They didn't tell me nothing, sir. I just drive. All I know is it's bad.'

'Right.' He leaned his head back against the leather headrest and closed his eyes.

Only then did he remember the racoon.

SAFF

'Just follow the signs for the common room. You can't miss it,' the nurse told her, and doubled back to the hospital.

She watched him go, his plimsolls echoing faintly around the corridor.

She was clean, which meant that everyone else was too. But she could not settle into the fact, not when Rory was still out there. It was a cruel joke that he had proposed to her, and her dreams had been true for two days before it was all torn away from her. And now she might never see him again.

She pinched her arm as she walked, closed her eyes. If she were dreaming, she'd wake up. But she didn't. The corridor still ran on before her.

She glanced at her phone, but of course there was no news from Rory. She swallowed to stop herself from crying again, took deep breaths. She tried to tell herself that it meant nothing. It had been less than two hours since her mother had woken her, and if she'd not been able to get through to Rory already, it was because his phone was on silent. Trying him again and again was futile. She just had to wait until his alarm went off, or pray that he woke to use the bathroom.

Unless he's dead.

It was true, hundreds were dead across the city, maybe even thousands by now, but the violence had erupted in central London, not in the residential boroughs. He was safest in his Harringay home. No terrorists attacked people in their houses.

Was that what she still believed this was? Some kind of political statement? She'd seen that man biting the woman's throat out, although *man* was not the right word. There had been something seriously wrong with him - something inhuman - and that wasn't the first time a man had killed by biting in the last few days, was it?

Perhaps it was a coincidence. Perhaps not. What if the pockets of violence had been caused by other subjects of the drug trial? Crazy people with defective medication for whom suicide or a single murder was not enough? Or perhaps she really was dreaming, her unconscious drawing a tenuous connection with her father's scandal.

But Rory was safe in his bed. She had to believe that. In a few hours, he would wake, and she had to be ready for it. She had to clear the way for him, find who was in charge and guarantee that Rory and his mum would be allowed in. But that was just the first step of the process. Then they'd have to cross London to get there.

As she approached the double doors of the common room, the din grew out of the silence. Through the glass panels, she saw people inside. Dozens of people.

She pushed through the doors, and the din became a roar so loud, she had the urge to press her hands over her ears. The nearest faces turned to her, regarded her like some lost child in the woods.

The room was about the size of her school hall, furnished with elegant burgundy sofas and armchairs. Half of the crowd was talking animatedly in clusters - more than a few were weeping and embracing each other - and the other half was transfixed with the BBC News report playing on the projector screen on the far wall. A helicopter view of a gridlocked motorway filled the screen. She tried to read the ticker but there were too many heads in the way.

She slunk over to the wall, and watched the news report with horror. A car crash she could not tear her eyes from.

Thousands were dead, as many injured. London was in a state of chaos as more violence rippled across the city, and most of the population hadn't woken up yet. Previous speculation of bombings in Waterloo and King's Cross had been incorrect. Reports of murders on trains from Woking and Slough predated the train station attacks and countless eyewitness reports pointed to ordinary citizens as the perpetrators. In the past hour, indiscriminate violence had erupted across West and North London, especially in and around train stations, major roads, and hospitals. The Met police were operating on the hypothesis that a viral infectious agent was responsible for the deaths and the commissioner urged civilians to stay in their homes.

Maybe it was best that Rory stayed in Harringay. The streets were not safe and there was no driver to escort him. She should never have come here. She should have run when she had the chance.

'We've got Daniel Harper, Professor of Sociology at King's College on the line,' the reporter said. 'Thanks so much for getting in touch, Daniel. Reports of terrorist attacks have now been discredited and countless murders are cropping up across Greater London and the South East. So, to what do you attribute the mass violence?'

A graphic visualizer appeared beside the reporter, soundwaves rising and falling as he spoke. 'Everything's happening so fast, and it's too soon to truly gauge the source of the outbreak, but if I were a betting man, I'd put my money on the defective antipsychotics pedalled by Apollo Pharmaceuticals. The parallel in the mode of violence, namely biting of the throat, is undeniable. I think Apollo have a lot to answer for.'

A sharp chill washed down Saff's back. She hugged her

arms around her stomach and pinched with both hands.

'Well, I'm sure you're not alone in that speculation,' the reporter said, 'but how then would you explain the spread from those predisposed to psychosis to ordinary people? Surely psychotics don't make up enough of the population to account for the volume of violence we're seeing?'

'Well I'm neither a psychiatrist nor a biologist but the greatest recorded incidents of mass hysteria don't hold a candle to what we're seeing here, especially not on such a short timescale. There's little doubt in my mind that a biochemical agent plays a big role in the catalysis of the outbreak, and it seems only logical that the defective drug trial is to blame.'

'Thank you for your insight there, Daniel. Stay safe.'

'My pleasure,' he said.

The reporter filled the screen again. She looked off camera for a moment and then stared back. 'Erm, we're getting reports of a commotion in the street outside - Do we have a feed?' she asked off camera, failing to keep a note of panic from her tone.

The screen was taken over by a view looking down onto the street. Half a dozen figures were running by. Another straddled a body on the pavement.

'Saff.'

She turned to face her mother. She pulled her into an embrace and held her there. 'Are you okay?'

'Yeah, I guess.'

'Any word from Rory?' she asked, reading the answer in her face before Saff shook her head.

'No.' She glanced back to the projector screen. 'They think it's to do with Dad,' she said, leaning in so no one else would hear.

Panic washed over her mother's countenance, quickly replaced by a fixed, calculating stare. 'Did they show his face?'

'No,' Saff said.

'Okay.' She closed her eyes, let out a deep breath. 'Don't

tell anyone. If anyone asks, he's an accountant.'

Saff nodded.

Her mother was transfixed with the news report for a moment before turning away. 'God, do we have to watch this?'

Saff scanned the common room. There was space across the room where they could avoid the view, perhaps the sound too, and an archway led to another section of the room, but if they moved too far from the entrance, it would be difficult for her father to find them.

'Where are Mac and Charlotte?' her mother asked.

'I don't know.' She looked around but could not spot them.

Her mother sighed, pulled her over to an empty sofa.

On-screen, the camera zoomed in to the street. The figure jumped up from the body it had been feasting on. It was a woman, blood dripping from her face, matting her hair. She stared up at the camera and Saff shivered. Her face was pale, the veins behind her cheeks and forehead a dark, inky purple.

The double doors flew open and her father walked in. He spotted them and strode over. Her mother got to her feet and they hugged, kissed.

'Thank God we're all okay,' her mother said.

'What's happening in here?' he said, looking around. His gaze was needle-sharp, but at the same time he looked like he might collapse at any moment.

'Nothing,' her mother said. 'Everyone's just watching the news.' She leaned into his ear then and Saff watched the fear paint itself onto his countenance as her mother relayed what Saff had told her.

He looked around the room, as though sizing up potential assailants, and nodded.

The doors flew open again and a soldier walked in. He had removed his gas mask, exposing his thick ginger beard and bald head. She noticed he was not holding the rifle anymore, although a pistol was holstered at his hip. Behind the soldier walked a man in a dark suit, older than her father, judging by his wrinkles and the grey creeping into his dark hair.

They cut through the crowds to the front of the common room. The projector screen blinked off as the suited man stepped onto a chair and raised his hands to silence the room.

The murmur died down to a whisper of anticipation.

'If I could have your attention for a moment, I'd like to fill you all in. For those of you who don't know, my name's Warren Clarke. I'm director here at the Ark. Not everyone has arrived yet, but we're hopeful that a few more will join us in the coming hours. I know emotions are running high at the moment and it's all a lot to take in, but I can guarantee that you're safe down here and that you're in good hands. The Ark was built in preparation for a major threat to the population, to foster the greatest chance of survival as a nation and as a species. You were chosen as individuals and families of the most value to our future, occupationally, characteristically, and genetically. We have technicians, doctors, and psychiatrists who will look after our needs. It will take time to adjust to the environment and routine, but I assure you in time you will be comfortable. As for how long we will be down here, I cannot comment. We can only observe the outside world and act accordingly.

'I'm sure you all have many more questions about the Ark and I'll be happy to answer any individual questions you have shortly, but for the time being I'd like to get everyone settled in. I'll be coming around to assign flats. In your rooms, you'll find booklets that explain the ins and outs of the facility. Meals, technology, health and safety. There's a map on the back of each booklet too, but I'm sure you'll get used to the layout in no time. Your bags will be brought down in the morning and brought to your rooms. Our head cook Alison will be serving refreshments in the dining hall next door or if anyone fancies a drink or a snack, and there are toilets across the corridor. For any smokers among us, there's a smoking room to your right.' He pointed to the different rooms like a flight attendant: your exits are here, here... and here. Except, there was no leaving this place, was there?

'Cigarettes will be rationed out to smokers in time, but for now there are packs in the room.' Someone gave a weak cheer from the far wall. 'But I must stress that smoking is strictly restricted to the designated smoking room. Everything is explained in your handbook. I'll come around now to allocate accommodation. Please be patient and we'll get everyone settled in as smoothly as possible. Thank you.'

He stepped down from the chair and the hum of conversation started up immediately. Those nearest to Warren moved in, eager to be accommodated first.

Saff turned to face her parents but they met her with blank expressions.

What were they supposed to make of it all? There was too much to take in, but at the same time, so many unanswered questions.

'What about Rory?' Saff asked.

'We'll talk to him when he comes around,' her mother said.

'He said they're still expecting people,' her father said. 'If we tell him Rory's on his way, they might let him in.'

'And what if they don't?' Saff said.

'Tell him you're pregnant,' her mother said. 'Surely they couldn't deny the father of her child entry. Her fiancé.' She took Saff's hand and lifted it up to show her ring.

Her father vaguely winced. 'Maybe. But he'd still have to get here, and he'd have to leave his mother.'

'At least we'd have the option. It'd buy us some time until Saff can get through to him.'

Her father nodded slowly. 'Yeah, it's a good plan, for the short term. What do you think, Saff?'

It offered little progress in the possibility of Rory joining her, but it was the best option she could see.

'Yeah.' She glanced at her phone, but of course there was

no news.

'Okay, shall we go?' her mother asked, moving towards the crowd.

'Not yet,' her father said. 'If we ask about Rory with everyone else around, he's more inclined to say no. I mean, how many people do you think have family and friends they want to join the Ark? If we wait for him to come to us, we'll have a better chance.'

There was some strong logic to that, Saff thought. Despite her father's brutish ego, he was always on the ball.

'One at a time, please,' the Scottish soldier shouted to the crowd closing in. 'We'll get through everyone quicker if you're all patient.'

'I'm going to have a cigarette,' her father said, paused as if to leave a narrow window for objection, and then headed for the door.

Saff perched herself on the sofa and laced her hands on her legs. Her thumb automatically ran across the fingernails of her left hand, searching for a flake to pick off. Usually, she tried to stop the impulse when she noticed it, but tonight, she didn't give a fuck.

Her mother sat beside her and laid a hand on her back. Saff leaned into her and found herself crying within seconds.

'Hey, it's gonna be okay. One way or another, we'll figure it out.'

She supposed the lie was intended to make her feel better - an empty reassurance - but it only made her cry harder. Two days ago, she'd felt like she could walk on clouds and the world was waiting for her and Rory to seize it. Now her naiveté had come crashing down on her, and she could only watch it all fall.

The crowd peeled away bit by bit as they made for their new homes. Just after her father returned, Saff saw Mac, Charlotte, and Luke leaving. Charlotte shot them a smile and Saff tried to return it but found her facial muscles had been anaesthetised.

Cement set in her stomach as Warren walked over, holding a clipboard.

'Is it just the three of you?' he asked.

'Well, actually,' her father said, 'we're one short. Saffron's fiancé is still en route. I'm assuming the soldiers will let him in when he arrives.'

Warren looked at Saff with an unreadable expression. 'Your fiancé?'

'Yes.'

'No one is supposed to know about the Ark, not except for spouses and blood relatives.'

'I'm pregnant,' Saff said, looking directly into Warren's eyes.

His eyebrows raised and the corners of his mouth curled for a fraction of a second.

'Okay,' he said. 'So, two double rooms?'

She drew a breath to ask about Rory's mother, but hesitated. In truth, she hadn't expected Warren to agree to it. Would she be pushing her luck with his mother too? But if she didn't ask, Rory might never come.

'That'll be perfect,' her father said.

'Alright, you're in flat number eight,' Warren said, and turned to Saff. 'If your fiancé makes it here today, and he's clean, we'll take him in.'

Warren moved on to others waiting, and the relief came out of her in a sob. It was a small victory in the grand scheme of things, but it was the first good news she'd heard all night.

ANDREW

Andrew closed the bathroom door and leaned against it. He ran his hands over his aching face, his closed eyes.

The ventilator hummed in the wall, an endless 'om' of a chanting monk.

When he opened his eyes, his vision did not clear immediately. A fog of glaucoma closed in on him.

He set the cold tap running, splashed a double handful of water into his face, and straightened up.

He was so tired, it was a wonder he had not collapsed already, yet sleep was hidden from him behind a dark veil.

The weathered face staring back at him from the vanity cabinet mirror had ten years on him, maybe more. His skin was like old leather, his sunken eyes sharp with knowledge of the impending rapture.

Coke. He still had the coke.

His panic locked onto it like a seeking missile. He emptied his pockets onto the counter surrounding the sink: both phones, his wallet, keys, and a crumpled wad of tissue.

Shit. Shit. Shit.

He snatched up his wallet and searched the coin pocket and note compartment; he took out every card and drew the business cards out from the space behind the coin pocket.

His heart leaped as a baggy fell onto the counter. Warm, liquid relief flooded his stomach, but a vacuous chill followed right after.

He had a gram, maybe a gram and a half. That would last him a day at the rate he'd been going recently. If he rationed it out - one hit now to get him through the night and then only a thin line a day, for instance - he might be able to stretch it out for a few days. His jumping heart and flu-like exhaustion roared in protest, but he had to think rationally. The baggy was some small mercy, but he would not have access to any more for a long time, quite possibly for the rest of his life. And he was addicted. He could not hide from the fact. Withdrawal would catch up to him sooner or later, but if he paced himself, he might soften the brunt of his cravings.

Or was that just the addiction changing its voice to seduce him, like a cognitive chameleon? Perhaps he should empty the whole lot down the sink right now and be done with it.

He picked up the baggy, opened it, and paused. The running water streamed down the white porcelain, disappeared into the dark eye of the drain.

He imagined standing on the precipice of a great canyon, looking down into the shadowy gorge.

Jump.

Behind the trickle of the tap, the ventilator hummed on, echoing around the small bathroom.

He shut off the tap, took up his keys, and snorted a dusting of snow up his nostril. He licked the bitter key, returned the baggy to his wallet, and filled his pockets again.

His sinus burned as though the key had been coated with burning petrol instead of snow. Something dripped from his nostril, and he instinctively swiped at it - fuck, he'd forgotten about the nosebleeds and used his right nostril again - but it was only mucus.

He'd got lucky this time.

He rolled off some toilet paper and stuffed it in his pocket.

His vision blurred again. Jesus, he needed to sit down. No, he needed to lie down. If not sleep, at least rest. But there was no time for that. Saff was panicking. Karen was panicking. The whole situation was fucked, and he was hanging by a thread behind an accelerating freight train.

He tensed every muscle, clenched his fists, and waited for the haze to dissipate once more.

'Andrew?' A knock on the door. Karen.

He unlocked the door, opened it.

She stood in the doorway, the Ark 'Handbook' open in one palm, a concerned frown on her face. How long had he been in the bathroom? No more than a minute, surely.

'What's up?'

'Are you okay?'

He shrugged. 'I'm keeping it together.'

'Hey, we're in this together, okay?' She smiled, and a pang went through his stomach.

You don't deserve her. You never did.

'Yeah.'

Karen stepped back and he walked through the short hallway to the open-plan kitchenette and living room. The place was like a four-star holiday apartment, just without the view out of the windows. Always with that caveat. The lights embedded in the ceiling had a barely perceptible blue tinge. They seemed more realistic than normal LEDs, but there was something not quite right, something artificial about the quality. Two paintings - Hockney prints, he was sure - were framed on the far wall where windows should have been: one of a mildly psychedelic mountain range, the other of a winding country road. The art scheme within the Ark seemed to be impressionistic exteriors. No reason to remind them of their imprisonment.

Saff lay on the sofa, scowling as though she were in physical pain. 'My phone's nearly out of battery. Can I use yours?' she asked Karen.

Karen handed Andrew the booklet and dug out her phone for Saff. 'Of course. I don't need this one anymore.'

Andrew leaned against the kitchen stool and scanned the booklet. Meal times were on there, with a request that the kitchen staff be made aware of any dietary requirements. The food would offer a balanced diet and include any supplements they needed, such as vitamin D and melatonin. They could keep snacks and refreshments in their private kitchens, retrieved from the kitchen each Monday on a rationed basis. The TVs in the common room, gaming room, and kitchen were free to use on a first come, first served basis, save for collectively organised events. Movies, TV box sets, music, and books could be borrowed from the library at any time, given the borrower noted their items in the book. Art could be traded at will. There was a keypad on each flat door, currently inactive, but which could be programmed to a four-digit code. And so on, and so on with the tiny details and arrangements of their new lives.

The walls were closing in on him again. His own sweat was rancid in his numb nostrils. His arms prickled as though insects were crawling across his skin. He set the handbook down on the breakfast bar and got to his feet.

Only when Karen glanced back at him with a frown did he realise he'd started pacing. He stopped in place, breathing heavily. He needed to get out of here. A cigarette would calm him down, maybe a short walk around this supposed garden. But he could not keep slipping away from Saff and Karen. He was supposed to be their strength, their fire, and he had no business to bury his head in. All of that was gone. All he had now was the two of them and these four walls.

His nose dripped. He wiped at it with the toilet roll, reluctant to blow it, in case he had a nosebleed.

But what use could he be? He could hold them while they cried, but what would that really achieve? He needed to carve out the best possible life for them down here, and he could not shoulder that burden on his knees.

'I'm gonna go for a cigarette,' he said.

'Okay,' Karen said. 'You sure you're okay?'

She knew something was wrong. They'd been married for sixteen years; of course, she knew.

'Yeah, just a little claustrophobic. I'll be back soon.'

Guilt stabbed at him as he strode down the teal corridor. He imagined himself from a bird's-eye view: a rat in a maze with no end and no cheese.

He pushed into the smoking room and drew a deep breath, as though surfacing from underwater. He snatched up the cigarettes on the table, only vaguely aware of the other men in the room, and lit up.

He fell into one of the leather armchairs. He'd first imagined the smoking room to be some cold, sinful place like a brick courtyard in a prison, but the place was already becoming a haven. Like his office had been until tonight. It was an elegant reading room as much as it was a smoking room, the kind of room in which he'd have a cigar and a long discussion about future business plans.

The other men smoking were Mac, the bald, Scottish soldier, and two other men he did not recognise.

'Alright?' Mac said as Andrew leaned in to ash his cigarette. 'Did your daughter manage to contact her fiancé?'

Andrew shook his head, sniffed. 'Not yet. To be honest with you, I only found out that they were engaged tonight.' The other men looked at him.

'Jesus, that must be quite a blow.'

Andrew raised his eyebrows. Why had he told Mac this? Probably just the coke running his mouth. Christ, he needed a drink of water. 'Did they find your dog?'

'He hasn't come back yet,' Mac said without hope. 'But if they see him, they'll let me know.'

'And they'd let him in?'

'I'm assuming so,' he said, looking to the soldier.

'That'd be up to Warren.'

'I see,' Mac said. 'This is Andrew by the way,' he told the others. 'Andrew, this is Callum-' he gestured to the soldier '-Ian, and Grant.'

'Pleasure,' Andrew said, shaking Callum's hand, then Ian's, but Grant only stared at him.

'Don't I know you?' he asked.

'No. I don't think so. I might have bumped into you before.'

'No. I remember now,' Grant said. 'You're the Apollo CEO, aren't you? I saw you on the news.'

MAC

The boy in the oil painting was about Luke's age, leaning over a village pond to launch a wooden ship with canvas sails. It was a bright summer day and the breeze cut ripples across the pond surface.

It was the only painting he'd seen in the Ark with a human subject. There was something uncannily realistic about it which went beyond its mere placement as a proxy window. Mac was staring through a portal into a dream; he imagined he could see the light dancing on the pond, the wind buffeting the boat's sails.

He heard Luke's voice narrating the boy's thoughts: the careless wonder and adventure of a life he would never live.

He looked down at Luke, sleeping in Charlotte's arms, watched the gentle rise and fall of his chest. He liked to think that Luke would be free from the gravity of it all in his sleep, that his dream state would prove a sanctuary from the horrors of waking life. But he'd told himself the same thing about Charlotte, and he couldn't have been more wrong.

Her eyes were closed too, but he didn't think she was asleep. Perhaps she drifted somewhere in between.

Mac rubbed her back tenderly, wishing some semblance

of comfort would filter through to her unconscious.

Where was his own sleep? Where was the dark veil descending over his senses? The adrenaline and physical exertion had left him feeling like he had the flu. His body was a sandbag sinking under the surface, but his mind was still acutely aware. Perhaps it was only the coffee. Perhaps it was the paranoia feasting on him like eels.

Thousands had died, and the man whose company had likely caused it all was down here with them. Mac had risked his own life as well as Charlotte's and Luke's to escort Andrew and his family here. Well, word would spread quickly down here and a consensus would soon be reached. But what if the decision fell upon Mac as newly appointed head of security? Could he throw Andrew out to fend for himself? It would only bring greater distress to his family, who could not be held accountable for his actions. And there was Andrew's reasonable defence - that he was only the CEO and was not responsible for the pharmaceutical side of things - and protestations that the outbreak had nothing to do with the recent recall.

Grant had not believed it, and Mac struggled to believe that many others would either. People were scared and charged up, and Mac had seen how easily mob mentality could turn pointed fingers into calls for violence. Perhaps they'd have to throw Andrew out for his own protection.

That was a question for the morning. He would need his strength for then.

He rolled over, closed his eyes, but sleep still eluded him.

There was something about the room. It did not feel natural. It did not feel safe, like a hotel room at the end of the world. Just because he could not hear the screams or see the buildings burning did not mean the chaos had stopped.

It was too quiet. That was it. He was used to the white noise of their Holloway street, but in here, there were only the faint hum of a ventilator and Luke and Charlotte's breathing.

He sighed and rolled over again.

He lay there in the darkness, sleep grinning an inch from his face. To some sinister part of his mind, his inability to sleep was the funniest thing in the world. The scars in his stomach opened wide and roared with laughter.

Charlotte moaned under her breath, and then again.

Mac turned over, stroked her shoulder.

'Hey, hey, it's okay,' he whispered, praying she did not wake Luke.

Her breaths came in restrained sobs. He found her hand between the sheets; she gripped him tight like a vice, her nails digging into the back of his hand.

'It's okay,' he said, squeezing back and kissing her forehead. 'You're safe here with me.'

And then, just as soon as her distress had come on, it melted away, and her breath returned to normal.

He lay back against the pillows and sighed.

He needed a cigarette, and then a nice, strong sedative to plunge him deep down where nothing could reach him. If he couldn't sleep tomorrow, he'd ask Kamal for some sleeping pills.

They were already in the early hours of Easter Sunday. On Tuesday, Charlotte had been scheduled for chemo. Would Kamal and his medical team be able to treat her? And how the hell would they hide it from Luke in here?

Christ, and he was worrying about sleeping pills.

KAREN

'You sure you're okay? she asked Andrew as he started pacing again.

'I'm fine. I just need to think.' He walked to the kitchen sink, poured himself a glass of water, finished it in one drink, and sat back down in the armchair. He sighed. 'Some of the guys know. Who I am.'

Saff looked up from the TV, which played a repeat of some panel show.

'Jesus Christ.' Things kept going from bad to worse and Karen didn't know how much more she could take. 'What happened?'

'A man in the smoking room recognised me from the news. Grant, I think his name was. Mac and one of the soldiers were there too. A guy called Ian. I think it's best you keep to yourselves for the time being.'

'Why would they blame us?' Saff said.

'Because they're scared, Saff,' he said, 'and they want somewhere to point the blame. You don't know what people are capable of in their darkest moments. Just... let me deal with this, okay?'

'I'm not sure that's the best idea,' Karen said.

'What?' Andrew snapped around to face her, thinly veiled fear in his eyes. He was hanging by a thread, she could tell, but then which of them wasn't?

'I just think, if we avoid everyone and don't have a chance to show who we really are, it's too easy for people to project shit onto us and scapegoat us.'

'Scapegoat? So, you think this is my fault too?'

'I'm not saying that, Andrew, for fuck's sake. We're on your side here. But we have to tackle this as a team.'

'Shit,' he muttered, ran a hand through his hair. 'Okay. I'm sorry. Just-'

The phone rang in Saff's hand. She jumped to her feet.

'It's Rory,' she almost squealed with equal parts panic and excitement.

She held the phone to her ear and started pacing the same line Andrew had. 'Rory. Are you okay? Where are you? … Okay, just stay in the house. Turn on the news…' She reached for the remote and switched their own TV to BBC News. The report was currently focused on the Dover crossing, where a flock of fleeing civilians was trapped between the Army barricades and the murderous infected. From the bird's eye view, burning cars and floodlights lit up the darkness.

How long before the virus crossed the channel into Calais? From there, it would no doubt spread across mainland Europe like wildfire. And that was assuming some unsuspecting victim hadn't already carried the virus onto a plane or ferry before transport had been shut down. All it took was one person.

Beneath the horror of it all, Karen felt some vague glow of relief. They were safe down here. If they shut off the televisions and phones, they could remain completely oblivious to the unfolding hell outside.

'We're okay. We're safe,' Saff told Rory. 'We're in a government facility under the Gherkin. Mum had a secret contract I couldn't tell you about. I'm sorry. I'll explain later. You just make sure you're safe.' She got up from the sofa and went into the hallway.

Andrew stared vacantly after her, his fingers drumming on the armrest. Karen reached across and laid a hand on his.

She needed him now more than ever. They needed each other.

It would bring Saff some relief to know that Rory was okay, but with the roads blocked off and the increasing danger in the streets, there was no way he would be able to join them in the next twenty-four hours, which meant, in turn, that he would never be able to join them.

What was Karen supposed to tell her? She was all out of reassurances and tenuous promises. All she had left was the notion that Rory was safe in his home. For now. And she wasn't convinced for a second that it would suffice.

At least the three of them were safely inside the Ark. For all the distress and the heartbreak it would bring Saff, at least she was physically safe. It was horrible to think, but relationships collapsed in the real world. People died in the real world. It was a nasty business, but she would get over it.

Or was this all just a defence mechanism, a justification for her own inaction to stifle the guilt that she ought to feel?

Christ, it was a fucking minefield. Whichever step she took - forwards, backwards, sideways - she was doomed.

She itched for the feel of a blister packet in her fingers, of popping a tablet through the foil membrane and swallowing it down. The action alone always brought her some infantile comfort: a child engrossed in a sheet of bubble wrap. But her Prozac was in one of their bags in the lobby. She would have to wait until morning.

The minutes passed in silence. The news report ran on, but Karen largely filtered it out. The details didn't seem to matter anymore. She could conceive of individual events, like the train station slaughters, and she could picture the death counts in a football stadium, but as the chaos spread beyond the city, the deaths blurred into empty statistics. What did a hundred thousand deaths look like compared to ten thousand?

Soon, millions would be dead, or simply infected. She didn't know where the line was.

The news reader's voice became white noise. The disturbing footage blurred into the background. It may as well have been a poorly dramatised apocalyptic movie, something on the Horror channel. Was this how quickly the brain became desensitised to death and destruction, or had the safety of the Ark rendered her emotional responses vague and abstract?

She found herself looking around the room instead, taking in the surroundings that would become their new normality. The neutral decor was appeasing but not homely. The whole flat had the impersonal atmosphere of a hotel room or a holiday flat. It gave Karen the impression that dozens of people had stayed here before her, that she was the last string of faceless strangers who had come and gone with no trace. She yearned for some totem, some anchor to their previous lives, without which she might lose herself entirely. If only she had the photo album or her iPod to conjure some suggestion that her life was real and not some vague dream of a dream.

The Bordeaux wouldn't hurt either.

Saff had been gone for some time now. She focused her hearing, listening for the sound of Saff's voice, but there was only the television.

'I'm going to check on Saff,' she said, getting to her feet.

'Okay,' Andrew said, staring fixedly at the wall as though trying to discern some grand illusion which had baffled mankind since the dawn of time.

The small hallway was empty. Light spilled from beneath one of the bedroom doors.

'Saff, honey?' she said, knocking.

Silence.

She opened the door to find Saff lying in a foetal position on the bed.

'Just leave me alone,' she sniffed.

Karen hesitated, then stepped inside and closed the door gently behind her.

'Hey, it's okay,' Karen said, sitting down beside Saff and rubbing her back. 'Tell me everything.'

'Tell you what? That he's trapped out there? That I might never see him again?'

'At least he's safe. That's the important thing.'

'Yeah,' Saff snorted derisively. 'About as safe as the rest of London.'

'He's a clever guy. If he stays inside, blocks the doors and windows, and waits it out, he'll be okay. Maybe, once things have calmed down, he'll be able to join us here after all.'

Saff shot her a look of daggers. 'Don't tell me what I want to hear. It's all fucked, and nothing you or anyone can say is going to change that.'

This burned Karen from the inside. Saff had been so happy only last night. The girl before her seemed a different person entirely, one beaten and broken by the world.

And after all, why was she trying to bend reality? Because she could not bear to see her daughter suffer, that was why. Because the truth was hard enough to swallow herself; it was harder to spoon-feed it to someone she loved, someone with whose happiness and well-being she was forever charged.

She was not prepared for this. There was no manual on how to coax your daughter through terrors you can barely conceive of yourself. She doubted there was a relevant section in the Ark's handbook.

'I'm sorry,' she said. 'I don't know what to do.'

'I know,' Saff sniffed. She sat up and leaned into Karen's shoulder.

Time melted away as they cried together, and by the time Saff pulled away, the tears had dried on Karen's cheeks.

'You should get some sleep. We all should.'

'I can't,' Saff said. 'Rory said he'll call me back soon. But you sleep. I'll be okay.'

Karen frowned. 'That's okay. I'll stay with you, if that's what you want.'

Saff considered, then nodded.

'We're in this together,' Karen said, but Saff didn't seem to hear. She was staring down at her engagement ring, as though it had turned her finger black.

ANDREW

Andrew was simultaneously not there and painfully present in his own head. Pressure mounted in both of his temples like 10mm drill bits twisting in behind his eyes.

The coke bump had only lifted him so high before it had dropped him on his head again. The worst part was that he couldn't tell if he'd hit the bottom yet or if he was still falling.

All of the whisky, the coke, the Molly, and the adrenaline of the night were catching up with him.

He was crashing hard.

His skin was stretched taut over his bones, his jaw ached like it had been recently broken, and nausea curdled deep in his stomach. The recessed LEDs were like artificial suns burning his retinas, even dimmed as they were.

His every thought was coated in black, viscous dread. The shadows crawled towards him with clawed fingers.

The news report was still playing on the TV. He reached for the remote and switched it off.

How long had Saff and Karen been gone? He checked his Patek Philippe: twenty-to-four in the morning. The second hand scratched by, dissecting time into individual frames from which he had no escape.

You can come out when you've proven your love.

A shadow passed over the greyed-out television screen as Karen walked into the room, and leaned against the breakfast bar.

He closed his eyes and called on any flicker of courage to guide him. If he could just make it through the next couple of hours, until his body and mind would let him sleep, maybe, just maybe, everything would be okay.

'How is she?' he asked Karen's reflection.

'Oh, everything's fucked. Don't you know that, Andy?'

He wheeled around to see Selina sitting on a breakfast stool. She wore the same black dress and stilettos as last night, one leg crossed over the other. She held a cigarette lazily in one hand, dark grey tendrils of smoke rising to the ceiling.

He blinked, but she was still there.

He knew he was hallucinating, but still the apparition would not abate. The scent of her perfume and cigarette smoke filled his nostrils. If he touched her, would he feel her or would his hand go straight through her, like a ghost?

'So, this is the family you betrayed for me?'

'Fuck off,' he said, making for the bathroom. His legs ached under him, threatened to spill him to the floor with each step. If he fell down, he didn't know if he'd be able to get back up again.

He locked the bathroom door behind him, set the cold tap running, and splashed water into his face. *She wasn't real*, he told himself, staring into his black-hole pupils.

A scratch came down the door, and he shivered, imagining acrylic nails on the varnished wood.

'You can't shut me out, Andy. Not forever.'

Watch me, he thought.

She wasn't real. It was just the gritty comedown and the trauma fucking with his mind. The real Selina was somewhere in the city above, probably still in bed in her Brixton flat. He needed to forget her, to erase the whole affair with the great cognitive shredder of repression.

It was over now. He had more immediate problems to attend to.

But she was still there. He could hear the thespian sigh of her breathing on the other side of the door, even over the running tap.

A finger tapped gently on the wood.

'I know you want me, Andy,' she moaned. 'I know you need me.'

He stepped back from the door, flattened his back against the towel rail, and slid down to the floor.

'Andy,' she called, pounding the door with a fist. The graceful seductress gave way to the vengeful matriarch behind the act. 'Don't fucking ignore me, you pathetic worm. I know what you are. I see right through you.'

He buried his face in his hands, latched onto the nearest suggestion of motion: his own strained breathing. He hugged his knees to his chest, drowning out her knocking and shouting with the mantra: she's not real, she's not real, she's not real.

And then, stillness.

He opened his eyes and exhaled slowly. His whole body was shaking, as though he'd been outside all night in sub-zero temperatures. The only sound now was the trickle of water down the sink drain.

She was gone. His mind had lapsed momentarily, like twisted tape in a cassette, but it was over now.

His head throbbed, as though his brain were swollen and pressing against his skull.

The walls were closing in again. He was out of time to collect himself. He shut off the tap, unlocked the door, and stepped out.

The entranceway was deserted, as was the living room beyond.

He drew a breath and knocked on the second bedroom door.

'Yeah.' Karen's voice.

He opened the door and leaned in.

Karen lay on the bed, Saff's face buried in her shoulder.

'Everything okay?' he asked.

Karen nodded slowly. 'Rory's okay. He's at home. The streets are too dangerous.'

'Right. At least he's safe.'

Saff let out a noise which might have been a laugh or a sob. He did not have the energy to discern which.

'I need to lie down for an hour or so, if there's nothing I can help with.'

'You get some sleep. We'll be okay.'

'Alright. Wake me if anything happens.'

'Sure.'

He lingered in the doorway a second, then closed the door and staggered to the other bedroom.

Part of him yearned for comfort, for Karen's arms around him, but it was crushed by the relief of being alone. Alone with his guilt and insanity.

He collapsed on the bed, crawled under the covers with his shoes hanging off the side, and turned off the light.

His heart was still thumping away like a fist knocking on a door.

Sleep flickered on the cusp of consciousness like radio interference.

The pillow was soft against his cheek, a maternal caress. Two reactions - tranquillity and panic - rose simultaneously, entwined in some cosmic conflict.

Ethereal fingers reached inside him, pulled in opposite directions. He felt the fabric of his being tearing, breaking apart, but the feeling was not entirely uncomfortable.

In the void between sleep and waking, a voice whispered his name.

HARRIS

Harris dreamed he was a warrior leaving for battle, some great hero from a Homeric epic. He donned his armour, loaded his horse, and kissed his family goodbye. Laura and the children they'd never had waved from the hill as he departed on his great journey.

He awoke with a start.

He could only have slept for a few minutes, but the dream still drifted around him like smoke. There was a residual burning in his chest: something like parental ferocity, not for the ghosts of his own children but for the entire human race. The lives of billions rested upon his shoulders.

He stared out of the plane window at the Atlantic Ocean hypnotically drifting by. The deep blue threatened to draw him down into its depths, but it was not lethargy that distracted him from the colossal task at hand. It was fear - that was his Achilles' heel - fear that his life's studies, the rational and intellectual faculties he'd shaped over the years, would not be enough. What if he froze in the blinding headlights? What if all of his knowledge and reasoning abandoned him like jetsam from a sinking ship?

He touched Laura's crucifix at his throat. She was right; he needed faith, in himself if nothing else. His own cognition would tie him into knots under the pressure. He needed to relinquish some of the weight, or it would pull him to his knees.

He took deep, measured breaths and returned his attention to his laptop and books on the table. He opened his flask and drained the dregs of his coffee, for all the good it would do him.

His open Word document stared back at him: bullet points and rambling notes, going round and round in circles like the proverbial serpent biting its tail. His data was incomplete to begin with, and he'd been in the air for over nine hours with no radio or phone signal. How much had happened during this limbo? What little information he had was like a drop in the ocean, but wasn't that always the case? You had to work with what you had.

He re-read his notes a half dozen times, searched his external hard drive for a journal he remembered reading for a class, but before he could locate it, the flight attendant came through the curtains.

'Just to let you know, Professor, we'll be landing in ten to fifteen minutes. Someone will be waiting to escort you when we land.'

Already?

He glanced out of the window to find the endless Atlantic had been supplanted by swathes of green and grey. Geneva swept by like a changing backdrop in a Broadway show.

No burning buildings yet. That was something. And they hadn't been turned away en route, which meant probably the virus had not spread much further.

'Shit,' he said. The flight attendant frowned. 'I mean, thank you.'

She nodded and turned away.

What had he been thinking about? He stared at his laptop screen for a moment, before closing it. It didn't matter; he had no time to follow rabbit holes in the vague hope of finding divine inspiration. The best of his theories and enquiries would surely be lost in the deluge of new developments.

He packed his laptop, books, and papers away with a sense of defeat. His shoulders and back ached. His body had suffered the arduous journey, but his mind had skipped through without the time to process anything.

He stretched in the aisle and went to the restroom. He emptied his bladder of the coffee and water, but not the anxious stone lodged there.

His reflection in the scratched mirror was rugged, years ahead of him. He splashed water in his face and returned to his seat.

As the plane began to descend, his heart rose to his throat, fast and hard. He gripped the armrests and watched the city crystallise. The toy roads, cars, and buildings popped into reality like high-definition models in a computer simulation.

Geneva was no longer a distant, external world; it enveloped him with no sign of escape.

And then, just like that, the runway was beneath them. The front wheels made contact, then the rear wheels, and the plane slowed.

When they came to a full stop, Harris got to his feet, and shrugged his book bag onto his back.

This was it.

With no preparation, no self-actualisation along his hero's journey, the battle lay before him. His armour was scant, his shield lost en route.

The flight attendant emerged from the curtain, shot him a sympathetic smile - *better you than me*, it said - and opened the door.

'Good luck.'

A golf cart was heading towards them: a man in a high-vis vest driving and a soldier beside him.

'Thank you,' Harris said and carried his bags down the

steps.

The air cut through his clothes, sending shivers up his arms and back. A fine haze of rain kissed his face. Geneva's weather made Boston feel like LA. He should have packed a coat.

The soldier climbed down from the golf cart and walked out to meet him.

'Professor Harris?' he asked in a thick French accent.

'Yes, sir.'

Harris's gaze was drawn to the automatic rifle hanging from his chest as they shook hands. The sight of the soldier's gun and camouflage relaxed an iota of tension from his stomach, although he would have felt a lot more comfortable with a weapon of his own, if only a 9mm sidearm.

The soldier loaded Harris's bags into the backseat of the golf cart.

'Please.' He gestured for Harris to get in.

The airport rushed towards them, and then Harris was led inside the terminal, deserted save for stationed soldiers and police officers. Harris's escort nodded to them all, exchanged brief words with a few, but never stopped.

Behind the glass entrance doors, a mob was gathered, held at bay by crowd control barricades and armed police.

'This way,' the soldier said, guiding Harris away from the main entrance to a side door.

A police officer held the door for them, bowing his head low to Harris.

The soldier led him to a black car with tinted windows idling in the road. He opened the door for Harris and handed his bags through.

'Thank you,' Harris said.

The soldier gave him a curt nod and slammed the door.

The driver pulled away immediately.

'Excuse me,' Harris said, leaning forwards, 'can you tell me what's happened in the last eight or nine hours?'

The driver met his eye in the rear-view, frowned. 'My

English not so good, sorry.'

'Do you have any English radio?' he asked, pointing to the central console.

The driver reached over and tuned through stations of music, French and German voices, and static.

'Sorry. No.'

'Shit,' Harris breathed. So, he was supposed to arrive at the UN meeting with no idea what had happened since he left Boston. He felt like one of his students turning up ill-prepared to a seminar, save for the fact that it was a lot more than a grade at stake.

They slowed to a stop, joining a queue to turn left. How many of the cars around him were headed for the WHO HQ like him?

Harris squinted at the driver's sat nav. Its ETA stated ten minutes, but Harris wasn't sure whether this accounted for the heavy traffic. At least it was moving, unlike the gridlocked aerial views he'd glimpsed of London.

Had the panic hit State-side yet? It must have; people flocked to stock up on groceries and gasoline after minor hurricanes, and this was beyond anything the world had seen before.

How was Laura?

He reached for his cell, but there was no signal. He'd never thought to check if his SIM worked overseas.

'Can you make international calls from your telephone?' Harris asked, gesturing to his own cell. When the driver looked blankly at him, he added, 'Can I call America from your phone?'

The driver shrugged, passed back his cell.

Harris dialled Laura's number, but his only response was a pre-recorded German message.

'Fuck. Thank you, anyway,' he said, handing the cell back. He'd have to call her from a landline.

He took out his laptop and re-read his notes as they navigated traffic. The rain picked up, tapping on the window as though trying to gain his attention, and obscuring his view of the streets.

The drive was strangely sobering. The streets were packed but relatively calm. They turned off the main street onto a private road that could have led to any business park or university campus. He hadn't been to Geneva in over ten years and the whole ride had the quality of a dream: that lingering déjà vu that threatened to snap him out of his senses to some new reality.

Traffic slowed, and Harris looked out of the windshield to see the military blockade.

He closed his laptop. He could not concentrate anyway.

The line of cars moved slowly forwards as each car was checked. Harris's driver rolled down the window and spoke to the soldier in French. The soldier walked over to Harris's window and tapped on it with a knuckle.

'You have identification?' he asked when Harris lowered the window.

'Yes,' he said, fumbling in his wallet for his driver's licence.

The soldier studied it for a long pause, looked between Harris and the licence, and then nodded curtly and handed it back. He shouted in French and the barrier lifted.

His driver navigated through the parking lot and stopped outside the main entrance.

'Thank you,' Harris said, pushing open the door and trying to get hold of all his bags at once.

'Good luck,' the driver said.

He walked through the automatic doors into the lobby of the WHO building. People walked briskly past him, going in and out, dressed in suits and oriental garments. Some dragged suitcases along the polished floor; others carried tote bags and briefcases.

A woman rose from a seat along the wall and cut a line through the crowds to him.

'Professor Harris?' She offered her hand. 'I'm Julia West. We spoke on the phone.'

'Nice to meet you.' He shook her hand.

'You arrived just in time. The Assembly has been pushing to make a start, but I managed to hold them off for your arrival. Leave your bags here,' she said, gesturing to a suited man to his left. Harris handed them over. 'Okay. Follow me.'

Their footsteps echoed around the lobby and then, with no pause, she walked past the armed peacekeepers and pushed through the double doors into the chamber. The room was even bigger than he remembered, especially now that it was packed with people. Its size put even Harvard's Sanders Theatre to shame. A wall of noise washed over him - the incoherent din of a hundred voices talking at once - but the sound gradually faded as he followed Julia down the aisle, as though someone were gently fading a stereo.

She stopped at the front aisle and gestured to an empty seat three places down.

'Take a seat, please, Professor. We'll begin shortly.'

He sat down as she walked up to the stage and spoke to a board member.

'Richard?' The man to his right was staring at him. Thomas Campbell, the British neuroscientist whose ground-breaking research into HIV had resulted in an unprecedented drop in AIDS-related deaths. They'd met in London a few years ago and corresponded by email a few times since.

'Tom. You don't know how good it is to see a familiar face.'

'Oh, I do,' he said. 'I've been here all day.'

'I just got here,' Harris said. 'I've been on a plane for ten hours from Boston. I haven't heard anything since.'

'You haven't heard about the light?'

'The light?'

'The photophobia, yeah.' Campbell caught him up with the bullet points just before Julia stepped up to the podium and called for quiet. As if things hadn't been crazy enough before, the light had driven the hosts indoors. And the virus had spilled into France in the early hours of the morning. If the military didn't manage to establish a secure perimeter before night fell again, the infection would spread across the country. And then to Geneva.

'We are now faced with the greatest threat in living memory,' Julia said. Her voice was amplified from speakers around the auditorium. 'And it will take the very best of humanity to overcome this challenge, but I look around me and the very best is what I see. The greatest academics, strategists, and scientists of our time from all corners of the earth. Hear me loud and clear when I say this virus will not be the end of us. This is our purpose, and we will respond with the united force of the world's nations.'

A roar filled the chamber, sending a shiver through Harris's body. It was not quite a war cry, but an invigorating rally nonetheless. If only their optimism and passion were enough.

'We have assembled a world-class team to combat this vicious disease. We have the greatest pathologists and doctors the world can offer under this roof. We have Nobel prize winners and professors of Oxford, Harvard, John Hopkins, and Karolinska universities. As we speak, Swiss police and peacekeepers are securing the University of Geneva's medical school, where the campus and any willing faculty members will be dedicated to our cause. We are working closely with forces in France to have samples of the virus transported to Geneva for testing this afternoon.

'In the meantime, I'll hand over to President Garcia of the Security Council, who will explain the consensus of their recent meetings.'

Julia sat back down and, in her place, a burly Latin American man with a thick black beard took to the lectern.

'Thank you, Julia. We talked for many hours how to combat this problem, and the United Nations have passed several resolutions to slow the transmission of the virus. All nations have agreed to close their borders and suspend all air travel immediately, except for authorised government and UN personnel. Any other flights will be given one warning and then shot down. Each nation is responsible for control of the virus within their own borders, but we will allocate peacekeepers to countries in most need. As the Director-General already mentioned, we have also allocated twenty percent of the force to the World Health Organization to aid its mission and protect the Geneva university.' He paused, staring down at the lectern between his hands. 'We also passed a motion to tactically strike London in defence of mainland Europe.'

The chamber erupted with cries and boos.

'That's genocide,' Campbell yelled beside Harris.

Garcia raised his splayed hands with a furrowed brow. 'I said we have passed the motion. I did not say the strike will be launched yet. It was the will of the Security Council that we give the World Health Organisation at least twenty-four hours to assess the situation first.'

'Twenty-four hours,' Campbell repeated. 'What a fucking joke.'

Not a good one, Harris thought. But they needed to find a way to slow the disease down some way or another before it spread throughout Europe. He couldn't imagine the borders were guarded sufficiently to stop the influx of fleeing Britons from transmitting the virus, but he didn't think it should come to bombing innocent people. There were other ways to stop it.

'The Security Council will also discuss alternative measures but it's my job to inform you of the resolutions that were reached.'

Julia returned to the lectern and the rest of the conference went by in a blur. He could barely pay attention to the rest of the agenda with his jet-lagged mind racing with panicked thoughts about what the fuck he was going to do now.

And then the time for listening was over, and it was time to act. He followed the others out of the chamber, down the steps, and into an idling SUV.

He opened his laptop on his knees as the car pulled away

in procession.

Campbell borrowed Julia's cell to make a call, but the line did not connect.

'Fuck,' he growled, winding the window down, and lighting a cigarette.

There was a thick fog of dread in the car. None of them spoke as they followed the line of cars out of the WHO park. Harris tried to focus on his laptop screen, but his mind kept flashing with images of London skyscrapers falling like trees in a storm.

There seemed little hope, even with a small army and the medical faculty behind them, but he had to somehow ignore that fact, hide it away in a safe in his mind.

He had work to do.

SIMBA

Simba jerked awake, and reached for the kitchen knife on Terry's bedside table. The danger was only in his dream; he was safe. For now, at least.

'What's happening?' Daisy asked, sitting up.

'Nothing,' he muttered, setting the knife back down, and rubbed the sleep from his eyes. 'Just a bad dream.'

Sweat covered his back, and his legs hummed with ache. He felt like death. He'd been robbed of his score by the panic and adrenaline of last night, and with the city in a state of terror, how would they secure another?

Daylight bled through the lavender curtain.

'What time is it?' he asked.

Daisy checked her Hello Kitty watch. 'Eight-fifteen.'

He lay back against the musty, mildew-smelling pillows and let out a groan. His body needed to sleep, to sink back into sweet oblivion, but his heart was racing.

'You got any more junk?' he asked.

'Nah, man. We shot it all.'

'Fuck,' he breathed.

'I'll bell K,' she said, climbing out of bed.

Simba got out too and went to the window. The street outside was deserted. No sign of last night's chaos. He didn't dare think about what had happened since they'd barricaded Terry's bedroom in the early hours. How many more were dead?

'Help me with this, man,' Daisy said, pushing at the chest of drawers blocking the bedroom door.

Together they moved it aside and uncovered the door. Simba followed her out, doubled back, and grabbed the kitchen knife.

In the living room, Daisy snatched Terry's home phone from its cradle and punched in K's number. They stood in place, waiting. The call dropped instantly.

Daisy kissed her teeth and slammed the phone back down.

It was no surprise. Who the fuck would be dealing in the middle of an apocalyptic outbreak? And even if, by some miracle, they'd managed to arrange a link, they had no money left to pay for the score. They would have to rob someplace. Or someone.

Simba fell into the sofa, took a half-smoked rollie from the ash tray, and re-lit it. Daisy stared at the floor, arms folded across her chest.

'This is fucked up, man.' She glanced at the grey TV screen, and Simba found himself staring there too.

He didn't want to see, he didn't want to know, but he had to.

He snatched up the remote and turned on the TV. On a black background was only the white BBC logo and the text: 'This channel is currently unavailable.'

BBC2 showed the same screen, but ITV1 blinked to life. A young male reporter stood before Piccadilly Circus, but the scene was like something out of a movie. A red TFL bus lay on its side in the box junction and the road behind it was blocked with abandoned black cabs and other cars. The iconic Piccadilly Lights screen was blacked out. Half a dozen figures walked briskly across the street, a couple of which dragged suitcases behind them.

A car alarm or fire alarm rang in the background.

'There is no comment yet from the government, Met police, or the army,' the reporter said, 'but I can confirm that streets have cleared of hosts - if that's what we're calling these people - for the time being. The sunlight seems to have driven them inside, like something out of a gothic horror movie. We've had reports of houses, shops, tube stations, and other public buildings broken into by large groups of hosts. Those who were stranded outside have all died, but they seem to have been in the minority.'

The camera panned slowly left to Shaftesbury Memorial, on whose steps a body lay, surrounded by half a dozen feasting birds.

Simba shivered.

'Many more have died at sunrise from frenzied and violent domestic invasions. We might have some respite until dusk, but this is far from over. Once again, we implore you all to stay in your homes, block all windows and doors, and await further instruction.'

Yes, thanks for the damning judgement, ITV. That just about summed it up.

The feed cut back to the newsreader's studio. 'Thank you, Dan. We've also received reports of incidents in Ireland, France, and Belgium in the early hours of this morning, despite the UN's efforts to lock down all borders.'

It was a fever dream, surely, or psychosis. Everything had been building up in Simba's mind his whole life, and finally, he'd lost it.

But no. This was real, and looking back, part of him felt like he'd always known this was going to happen. The technology, the nuclear armament, the reckless disregard for the environment. Humanity had played God and now it would suffer the consequences. It had only been a matter of time before civilisation blew out at its weakest point. And he was as guilty as the rest; even now, he cared less about the total annihilation of the world than he did about a small wrap of off-white powder.

He'd be okay. Somehow he always was. The hunger was

a fully-formed beast within, and the more desperate it grew, the more cunning and resourceful it became too. London was in a state of chaos, and their supply was disrupted. Well, fuck it, they'd just have to find another supply line.

'You know any other dealers' numbers?' he asked. 'Or where they live?'

Daisy sighed. 'Nah, man. I know where Sam lives obviously, but he's off the junk.'

'Alright, we just gotta think about this. I need to clear my head.' He scanned the room. 'Terry got any painkillers around here?'

'I dunno. Try the bathroom, innit.'

Simba jumped up and headed to the bathroom. He found some paracetamol in the cupboard over the sink, which looked about a decade old, but he popped four tablets into his palm and swallowed them with tap water nonetheless. It wasn't codeine or oxycodone, but maybe it would keep the shakes at bay long enough for him to figure his shit out. Of course, Terry was a recovering junky himself; he would know better than to keep opioids lying around the place.

He took the paracetamol back to Daisy and collapsed on the sofa. She'd switched the TV off - thank God - but the silence rang louder.

'That's all he has?'

'Looks like it.'

She looked around for a drink, then dry-swallowed a few tabs with a grimace.

'That was some good fucking shit last night, as well,' she sighed.

Simba raised his eyebrows, nodded. And thanks for the reminder too.

The paracetamol would do little to alleviate his symptoms, compared to a strip of codeine. Or the real deal. That was the only thing that could really silence the voice.

He wasn't really running from his pain anymore. He was just stewing in it like a cold, murky bath. He just needed the junk to keep the shakes and the itches and the diarrhoea and the crippling nausea away.

To keep the devil away.

'We're gonna need something stronger than paracetamol before tonight,' Daisy said, scratching at both arms crossed over her chest.

'Yeah.'

Where could they find a dealer now?

'There'll be a pharmacy on the main road,' Daisy said. 'It'll be easy to loot.'

He nodded slowly. They would not be the only opportunists raiding shops across London. It would be easy enough to loot a rucksack full of prescription-grade painkillers. Methadone if they were lucky. Codeine and oxy, if they were not.

Fuck the child's play, Simba. We need the real shit, straight in the vein. It's your job to feed us.

The empty space in his stomach swelled; the hunger screamed.

'Fuck it. Let's do it,' he said.

'Now?' Daisy asked.

'No time like the present.'

'Safe,' she said, jumping up. She patted her jeans down, then slipped into her trainers and pulled on a hoody.

Simba emptied his rucksack onto the sofa and slung it over his shoulders. He wrapped the kitchen knife's blade in a t-shirt and stowed it in his waistband.

'Ready?' Daisy asked, snatching up the house key from the coffee table.

'Yeah.'

Daisy led the way through the tight hallway. Light blinded him as she opened the door, opened the portal to the outside world. A shiver ran down his back like clawed fingers, and he was gripped by the sudden urge to slam the door shut, run back into the bedroom, and barricade the door.

Daisy raised her hood as she stepped out. He exhaled

and followed suit.

The sound of the door closing was like a falling gavel condemning him to whatever fate lay ahead.

He touched the knife handle at his hip and followed Daisy up the street.

It was quiet, with no sign of life, but as his senses sharpened, he noticed sounds beyond the street. An alarm. A dog barking. Voices?

They walked quickly, the force of every footstep coursing through his legs. It was like re-inhabiting his body after two months in a coma.

They passed the courtyard where they'd been followed by the group of youths last night, but now it was empty. He scanned the windows of the apartments around them, feeling the same sensation of being watched, but he saw no one.

They turned out of the estate and emerged onto the main street towards Aldgate. The road was mostly blocked by empty cars, but a motorcyclist was riding down the pavement, a few pedestrians. The shutter of a corner shop ahead had been battered and bent up from the ground, and other shop windows had been smashed in. Suddenly, the chaos of the city was not some distant reality on a TV screen; it was the world around them opening its jaws to swallow them.

He touched the knife handle. Was this the work of looters or crazed hosts escaping the first light of dawn?

They walked on, past takeaways, ethnic stores, and off-licences, until Daisy let out a yelp and grabbed at his arm.

'Over there.'

His fingers gripped the knife handle instinctively. He would have drawn the blade if he hadn't spotted the Boots Pharmacy Daisy was pointing at.

They picked up the pace. The pharmacy's blue shutter was fully intact, which meant no hosts were inside - thank fuck - but which also meant they would have to smash their way through it.

They stopped outside the shop. Daisy gave the shutter an ineffectual kick, which rippled vaguely up the slats. It was locked to the ground with a thick padlock. There was no getting through the lock without an angle grinder or maybe a sledge hammer.

How did people usually break through? Even with strong, calculated kicks, it would take a lot of brute force to get through. Something Simba didn't have in him.

'We need a car,' Daisy said, scanning the street.

'You want to drive into it?' he asked. That wasn't a bad idea.

'Mmm,' Daisy said, approaching a silver Golf and trying the door.

The third car she tried, a white Ford van, was open with its keys in the ignition.

'Bingo.' She climbed into the driver's seat, then reached over and opened the passenger's door. 'Come on, then.'

He sighed and climbed up. 'Can you drive?'

'I never did a test, but I know enough. You?'

'I used to. But not for fifteen years or something.'

'You're so old, man,' she laughed, and started the engine.

He pulled his seatbelt to as Daisy manoeuvred the van up the pavement to the Boots. She backed it up into the road as far as she could, and stopped.

'Ready?'

He sighed. 'Fuck it. Do it.'

She shifted into first, revved the engine, and released the handbrake in one fluid motion. The van lurched forwards, seemed about to stall, before Daisy shifted gear and floored the accelerator.

The blue shutter rushed towards them. He gripped the armrest, turned away just as they smashed into the shop. The impact jerked him forwards against his seatbelt and threw him back again.

Daisy let out a manic laugh as the shop alarm screamed into life.

The van's bumper had indented its shape in the blue

shutter, but it had not broken through yet.

Daisy re-ignited the engine and backed up the van again.

Simba tensed every muscle as they crashed into the shutter once more. This time, something definitely gave way. The shutter had crumpled inwards, away from its frame.

'Yes, mate,' Daisy yelled over the shop alarm, raising her hand. Simba high-fived her, and they climbed out.

Daisy went first, squeezing past the broken shutter. He followed.

Inside, the alarm was much louder - a physical force on his ear drums - and it seemed his heart was beating in time with the oscillating notes.

It took his eyes a moment to adjust to the dimness. Glass crunched under his feet as he looked around the shop.

Daisy's form dissolved into the shadows.

'Wait,' he called, feeling his way along the shelves. The lights flickered on: a brief preliminary glow, before their full, blinding presence.

He navigated past the shelves for hair care, dental hygiene, sexual health, to the counter Daisy had already vaulted.

She tried the 'Staff Only' door to the right. 'Locked,' she called. 'Do us a favour, will you, mate?'

Simba climbed over the counter, took a deep breath in and out, then gripped the counters on both sides and kicked.

Come on, Simba, stop fucking about. Get in there and get the goods.

Simba growled and put all of his strength into the next kick. The door sprang inwards.

His calf burned - he'd pay for that later - but he didn't care. They were in now.

He reached around for the light switch and illuminated the stock room.

The screaming alarm faded away as he looked around the shelves upon shelves of pharmaceuticals.

He was a child in a sweet shop for the first time.

Thousands of neatly packaged pills to cure or at least relieve almost any ailment he could conceive of. Hundreds of different drugs, which, in various combinations, could alter and distort his mood, physical experience, even his very thoughts. It was the world's greatest pick 'n' mix and his sweet tooth was stinging. But that was okay; there was enough novocaine here to kill a horse.

He scanned the shelves. Where to begin? All of the boxes were almost identical: predominantly white, with splashes of blues and greens mostly, but some pinks and yellows. Regulated, he assumed, to not be too attractive to their users.

He did not need antibiotics, antipyretics, or anti-diarrhoeals, although, on second thought, they would be useful to have on-hand.

His gaze was drawn magnetically to the shelf marked 'analgesics'. Seeing the word was almost as sedating as the onset of the drugs themselves. A whispered promise.

Soon you won't feel a thing.

'Oh, shit.' Daisy's voices brought the world rushing back in. He felt the relentless alarm resounding in his skull. Why did it have to be so fucking loud?

He shrugged off his rucksack and dropped in half a dozen boxes each of codeine, oxycodone, and tramadol. Daisy added her own stock as he scanned the shelves for the methadone. After some panic, he found the drug under the brand name Dolophine and dropped the shelf's entire stock into his bag.

'Okay, let's get out of here,' he called, gesturing to the door.

Daisy nodded and led the way out.

'I'll catch you up,' she shouted as he made for the exit. He hesitated, then slipped out of the shop.

He leaned against the van and looked around the street.

Only a few people walked by, giving only cursory glances towards the shop. The alarm was a little fainter outside, but its presence lingered in his head. It wasn't just his head that ached, though. It was his whole body.

He was about to reach inside his rucksack for the methadone when he heard a nearby whimper. Was it Daisy or was he imagining things? He had almost convinced himself that it was just the echoing alarm playing tricks on him, like how people naturally listened for familiar patterns in repeated sounds, when he heard it again.

It wasn't human, that he knew instinctively. A prickle of fear set his heart racing again. His whole body tensed as his fingers closed around his knife and drew it.

He could see no motion in the immediate vicinity, but he noticed with a shiver that the day was greyer than when they'd entered the shop; the sun was hidden by storm clouds.

He stepped back into the street, pinning his gaze on the adjacent shop's corner. If something rounded the corner and made for him, he'd only have seconds to react.

He'd always known, deep down, that his addiction would kill him, one way or another. Beneath the panic and the adrenaline, his survival instinct battled to subdue the following trail of relief.

He circled the corner, bringing the side road further into view with each step.

The whimper hadn't been from a host. It wasn't even from a human.

It was a husky, sniffing around a bin. The fur around its neck was stained crimson. It whined again, a private sound of pain. When it registered his presence, it sunk low to the ground, fixing Simba with a stare and baring its teeth.

'It's okay,' Simba said, raising his hands. 'I'm not gonna hurt you.' Not unless it went for him, in which case he could only hope to stick it in the throat before it got its teeth in him.

They stared into each other's eyes as time melted away in stalemate. Then the husky relaxed its jaws, and took a tentative step towards him.

He lowered his free hand, slowly and deliberately, and

the dog allowed him to stroke its head.

'Sim?' Daisy called behind him. The husky shrank back a step as she rounded the corner. 'Oh, shit.'

'It's okay,' he said. He took a slow step towards the dog and stroked it again. There was a collar with a bone-shaped pendant around its neck, on which was inscribed a phone number, Holloway address, and its name: Byron.

Daisy slowly approached, and stroked his fur.

'He's beautiful,' she said. 'Can we keep him?'

MAC

He swam out of sleep to face only more darkness.

He reached for Charlotte, but the bed was empty. With a numb shot of panic, he fumbled for the bedside lamp.

There was no sign in the bland hotel-like room that Charlotte and Luke had ever inhabited it. For all he knew, he had woken in limbo.

He checked his watch: half-past-nine. In the morning, he assumed, but without a window, he had no way of knowing. Surely, if he'd slept through the whole day, he wouldn't feel so fucking exhausted.

He found Charlotte and Luke on the living room sofa. She was cradling him and humming a tune.

'Hey,' he said.

'Hey, how are you feeling?'

'Knackered, but better. You?'

She nodded unconvincingly. 'Okay.'

'What about you, mate?' Mac asked Luke, falling into the armchair.

Luke shrugged.

Charlotte held his eye a moment, conveying concern. 'I told him we'd get some breakfast when you were up. They serve until half-ten.'

'Sounds good. I'm starving. You ready to go now?'

Luke buried his face in Charlotte's shoulder.

'Come on, love,' she said. 'We'll get you some nice food, and then after, we can look around this library, see if they have any good films to watch.'

Luke nodded in acquiescence and Charlotte helped him to his feet.

Mac frowned deliberately as she guided him towards the door. Charlotte pointed to her mouth and shook her head: Luke didn't want to speak. Come to think of it, Mac couldn't recall Luke saying anything last night either. It was the shock still setting in, surely. There was no natural reaction to all of this. If Luke had been chatting away about *Star Wars* or video games like nothing had happened, Mac would have been more worried.

'Do we need to put our shoes on?' Charlotte asked in the hallway.

'I… I don't know,' he said. 'I guess we should.'

He laced his own work shoes, thinking he might have to wear them for the rest of his life, or until the soles wore away to nothing, unless Charlotte had packed some trainers for him.

He led the way through the teal corridors, following signs for the dining hall.

The sedating smell of fried food hit him like a wall as he pushed through the double doors. Hunger swelled in his stomach.

The dining hall was populated by a couple of dozen people talking animatedly: the strangers who would become their extended family. The room was buzzing with an energy he could not put his finger on.

They joined the end of the service line and filled their plates from the buffet. Mac piled his with a full English, and added a side plate of toast, orange juice, and coffee to the tray.

He wondered how many sausages and bacon rashers were stockpiled in the Ark, how many cartons of orange juice. They'd have stored enough food to last them years, probably even decades, but everything was limited. Everything had an expiration date.

Mac led them to a table at the back of the room, near Grant and his daughter, Lucy. Mac shot him a smile, and looked around for Andrew and his family. No sign. That was probably for the best. He didn't fancy mediating another argument between the two. Hopefully they'd both had time to calm down since the early morning.

The small TV screens mounted on the walls displayed the news. Christ, what had happened now? He could barely hear the newscaster over the din of conversation, but the reality washed over him within seconds.

'Oh, shit,' he breathed.

The hosts had gone from the streets, driven inside by the daylight. He had to pay close attention to his senses to convince himself that he was still not dreaming. This shit just got crazier and crazier. What would happen next, the army would drop garlic-gas on the city and erect giant crosses in the street to keep the hosts away?

He wished they were vampires. That would simplify things. At least that way he'd have some feeble grasp on the virus, instead of whatever the fuck was happening here. Could the outbreak really have been caused by Apollo Pharmaceuticals after all? He could just about wrap his head around the defective antipsychotics causing frenzied mass murder across the city, maybe even the spread of primitive rage to new hosts, but this… This was something else. The world was playing Buckaroo with his reason. There was only so much it could load on before the horse bucked.

Things were too strange to be an accident. Wasn't it more likely that this virus had been manufactured in a lab by the Chinese or Russians or some extra-national terrorist group?

This was all hurting his head. When would the backdrop fall to the floor with a whisper and reveal the great deception of his senses? Would some cosmic audience ripple with hysterical laughter at his naiveté?

Charlotte and Luke watched dumbly. He needed to cut those kind of thoughts off at the stems; he needed to be strong and support his family, and he could not do that if he was questioning his reality every five minutes. Even if it was all a dream or simulation or some sick joke, what could he possibly lose by playing his role?

'Maybe we'll get out of here before too long,' Charlotte said. Before she died, he was sure she meant.

'Maybe,' he said, trying to inject a little optimism into his voice, but not too much. Even if the virus was eradicated or cured, they would be down here for months at the least.

Charlotte shrugged to herself and ruffled Luke's hair. 'I'm going to get some more orange juice. You want a re-fill?'

Luke shook his head, set his fork down.

'Not hungry?' Mac asked as Charlotte walked away.

Luke shrugged, looked back at the TV.

'Meesa so hungry,' Mac said in his best Jar Jar Binks impression and stabbed a sausage with his fork. 'Meesa need energy.'

Luke glanced at him with a wan expression.

'It's okay. I get it,' he said. 'You don't need to talk if you don't want to.'

Mac heaped some beans and sausage onto his fork but as he raised it to his mouth, a yell from across the room froze his hand.

He turned to the source of the noise. Charlotte. Where was Charlotte?

A few people had gathered around the serving line, but he could not spot her. That was, until a man stepped forwards and revealed a woman crouching by the juice station beside another body.

'Stay here,' Mac said, already on his feet. He cleared the hall in several running strides, his heart thumping, as though he'd crossed a football field already.

He elbowed through the gormless spectators and fell to

his knees.

'Charlotte, honey, are you okay?'

Her drunken gaze drifted slowly up, tried to place him, before her eyes closed again.

'What happened?' he asked the older woman beside them.

'I don't know,' she said. 'One second she was there, the next she was on the ground.'

Charlotte half-opened her eyes and looked around lazily. She was pale, her cheek cold to the touch.

'Did you hit your head?'

She shook her head, tried to sit up.

'It's okay, just take your time.'

'I'm fine,' she murmured, some of the focus bleeding back into her eyes.

'Can someone get her a glass of water, please?' Mac asked, looking around. Luke stood on the edge of the crowd, watching intently.

Jesus Christ, that was the last thing he needed. As if Luke hadn't seen enough over the last twenty-four hours, he'd now witnessed his mum collapse for the second time.

Mac had the image of sitting in a flooded rowing boat, the sea pouring in faster than he could drain it with a tin bucket.

A glass of water was handed down to them.

'Can we have some space, please, guys?' Kamal appeared through the bodies and lowered himself to his haunches.

'Did she fall?'

'Yeah,' Mac said.

'I'm just tired,' Charlotte said. 'Just fell asleep on my feet.' She let out a laugh she'd probably meant to sound blasé, but instead came across a little manic.

'Happens to the best of us,' Kamal said with an occupational smile. 'But I'd like to check you over quickly, just to be sure. Can you walk?'

'Yes, but it's alright. I'm fine now,' Charlotte said, forcing a smile.

'Of course, but that's what I'm here for. It'll take two seconds.'

She spotted Luke then, and closed her eyes in despair. 'Oh honey, I'm sorry.'

'He'll be fine - he didn't see anything,' Mac muttered more quietly, stroking her back. 'Come on. Let's get you checked over.'

Daggers flashed in her eyes, as though it were all Mac's fault that she had fallen, that she was slowly dying, that the world had gone to shit. And then she nodded in defeat and allowed Mac to help her up.

'I can watch your boy if you'd like,' said the woman who'd been first to Charlotte. 'Stick some TV on in the common room.'

Did he want to leave Luke with a stranger? Perhaps it was better than sitting in the sterile hospital ward. It would also give them a chance to explain Charlotte's situation, and Mac wasn't sure when they'd get another chance.

'That okay with you?' Mac asked Luke. He shrugged, nodded. 'Okay,' he told the woman. 'Thank you.'

She had a calming demeanour, the way some older women had. Luke would be safe with her.

'Thank you,' Charlotte muttered. 'I'll be right back, honey,' she told Luke and allowed Mac and Kamal to lead her out of the dining hall.

She shook off Mac's supporting arm as they entered the corridor, but brushed his hand and allowed him to hold it instead.

'Just up here,' Kamal said, leading them around the corner. He held the door for them and gestured them inside his office.

'How do you feel?' Kamal asked.

'Just tired, like I said.'

'Does anything hurt? Did you hit your head?'

'I don't know. I just fell asleep for a second.'

'You passed out?'

'No. I... maybe.'

'I'd like to check your head, if that's okay,' Kamal said. 'Just to be sure.'

Kamal pulled on a pair of latex gloves and examined Charlotte's head. 'No visible signs of trauma. Is this the first time you've fainted?'

Charlotte sighed and lowered her gaze. 'No.'

'She fell down yesterday,' Mac said. 'Before... well, before all of this.'

'I see,' Kamal said, taking a seat behind his desk. 'Any pre-existing health conditions?'

'I have cancer,' Charlotte said matter-of-factly.

'Ah.' He frowned and turned to his computer, typed into the keyboard. 'Stage 3B breast cancer?' he asked.

Charlotte nodded.

Mac glanced at the monitor. It shouldn't surprise him to hear that they had access to all of their medical records. Had that been in his contract? He was too exhausted to remember.

'And you've had three cycles of chemotherapy already?'

'Two,' Charlotte said. 'And immunotherapy. I was supposed to start my third cycle tomorrow.'

Kamal raised his eyebrows. 'I see. Well, I'm not an oncologist and neither are Adam or Paul, but we will do everything we can to ensure you receive the best treatment.'

Charlotte nodded, unconvinced. She'd been told that before.

Kamal clicked his mouse and typed into the computer again. 'I see that common drugs have been ineffective after your relapse and you were scheduled for early phase experimental chemotherapy at the Royal London hospital.'

'We're getting desperate,' Charlotte said quietly.

Kamal nodded. 'I'll look into your proposed treatment. I can't promise we'll have the necessary drugs, but there are many options we can explore yet. I'll read up on your chemo, check our inventory, and get back to you, hopefully by the end of the day. In the meantime, you should get plenty of rest, drink lots of fluids, and make sure you're eating properly.

Kamal glanced at Mac; this was his job as much as hers.

Mac nodded. 'Thank you.'

'Is there anything else I can help you with?'

'No, that's fine, thank you,' Charlotte said. 'I really do feel better now.'

'Alright, well take it easy for the rest of the day and I'll let you know about treatment.'

As soon as they were in the corridor, Charlotte's composure collapsed like a dam. She broke into sobs, shaking visibly. Mac enveloped her with his arms, his own eyes stinging with tears.

'Hey, it's okay. I've got you. Everything's going to be okay.'

Those familiar, empty lies.

SAFF

Saff fumbled for her mother's phone without taking her eyes off the TV screen. Her heart was trying to jump out of her chest.

The dial tone rang only a few times before Rory came on the line.

'Hey,' he said.

'Hey. Have you seen the news?'

'Not for a while. Why? Has something happened?'

'The streets are clear. It's safe for you to come.'

'What?'

'It was the sun.'

'What are you talking about?'

'Just turn on the news, babe.'

'Okay.' She heard Rory walking through the house. 'It's not working. The channel's dead.'

'Try ITV,' she said.

'Okay, got it.' Over his heavy breathing, she heard the same news report she was watching, delayed half a second over the phone. 'Jesus Christ.'

'So, what do you think? Can you get over here?'

'I don't know, Saff. Mum's in a bad way.'

'What? What's wrong?'

He sighed. 'It's like last Christmas. She won't get out of bed. She keeps talking about my dad.'

'I'm sorry,' she said. 'It's just, they said you can join us as long as you get here by the end of the day. I don't know if they'd turn you away after that, but I can't bear the thought of losing you. It's safe here. We have doctors and a psychiatrist. They can help your mum.'

'Yeah,' he said after a pause. 'I get that. I'll try. But I've never seen her like this, Saff. She won't leave her bed, let alone the house. If I could drive, maybe, but on foot, I don't have much hope.'

Rage gripped her heart like a burning hand. How could he accept defeat so easily? There had to be another way. There had to be something he could do.

'We're supposed to be together,' she said, looking down at her ring through a film of tears.

'I know, and I'll do everything I can, but I can't leave her, Saff. Not like this.'

She nodded to herself, tried to gather her composure. 'Just keep me updated, yeah?'

'I will. I love-' The line went dead. Had he hung up on her? There were still so many things she had to say. She looked down at her phone to see her signal had cut out. Seconds later, the TV feed died too.

'No,' she muttered stupidly.

It was all too much.

Desperation tore at her like razor-winged butterflies skittering around the walls of her gut.

If this was not a dream she could wake from, she needed to escape reality some other way. But there was no escape. Only walls holding her in.

She jumped to her feet and hurried out of the room. She followed the corridors with no idea where she was going, as though she were in a lifeboat caught in white-water rapids.

Her feet led her inevitably to the giant metal door through which they'd entered the Ark. The hand wheel stood out in the centre like a submarine door. She reached out and touched its cold metal, tried to turn it, but the wheel did not budge.

A control panel with a keypad was mounted on the wall to her left. There was no leaving without the pass code, and she had a feeling only Warren knew it. No: the soldiers did too.

She hammered her fist against the metal. It barely rang.

She slid down the wall, pulled her knees into her chest, and buried her face in her hands.

A door opened on the corridor. A woman stepped out, looked down at her.

'You okay, love?'

Saff nodded and forced a smile. 'I'm fine, thanks.'

The woman hesitated a moment, then turned away and followed the corridor out of sight.

She needed to get her shit together. But what the fuck was she supposed to do? She was trapped in a corner. She was starting to understand the panic her father felt in enclosed spaces. All she could do was wait and suffer, but she supposed she could have some dignity about it.

She got to her feet and followed the corridor back, but she did not stop at their apartment. Instead, she kept walking and turned the corner towards the chapel.

It was empty inside, which was fitting. The priest had never made it then.

She walked slowly down the aisle and sat in the front pew.

She'd never believed in God, not like the Bible portrayed Him, but she'd always had a feeling deep down that there was something beyond their immediate awareness. It was this sense of unknown to which she prayed. She wished for this virus to die out, for everything to go back to how it had been before, and most of all, to be reunited with Rory.

She didn't believe that her prayers would achieve anything more than a birthday wish as she blew out the candles on her cake, but they brought her some semblance of serenity all the same. It gave her the feeling that she was actually doing something. For a moment, at least, until the crushing paralysis of her powerlessness returned.

ANDREW

The rise and fall of conversation in the dining hall was like the breathing of some unseen beast. How many whispered rumours had been exchanged about his role in this all? At least Grant had had the balls to ask him to his face, but most were not so upfront.

He was probably just paranoid. Gossip changed like the wind, not that there was any down here. They'd be talking about the latest developments of the outbreak - the hosts clearing the streets to shelter from the daylight - or the fact that they were now cut off from all communication with the outside world.

Still, he had to clear his name somehow. Reputation in this kind of closed group was everything. He needed to start building connections.

'I'm going for a cigarette,' he told Karen, thinking he could kill two birds with one stone.

'Alright. I'll head back to check on Saff when I've finished.'

He deposited his empty coffee mug and mostly untouched English breakfast on the trolley and made for the smoking room.

Callum looked up from the floor as he entered. 'You alright, mate? It's Andrew, right?'

'Yeah. How you doing?'

'I've been worse.'

Andrew put a Mayfair between his lips, and looked around for a lighter. Callum handed him a Bic. 'Thanks.'

'You come in with Mac?'

'Yeah. The man can fucking drive, I'll tell you that.'

A ghost of a smile passed over Callum's lips. 'Aye. Used to drive for the Met, didn't he?'

'I didn't know, but that explains a lot. How about you? How long have you been in service?'

'Forever, man. I was a wee shit growing up, to tell you the truth, fucking about with birds and drugs. So, my parents sent me to cadets to teach me some discipline, and I never looked back. Cut my teeth on the Troubles and just worked my way up command. I was supposed to leave for Afghanistan in a couple of weeks, before all of this shit.' He laughed with genuine humour, and toked on his cigarette.

Andrew wondered whether Callum had got the short or long end of the stick. Perhaps it was too early to tell.

'And you?' Callum asked. 'You're a CEO, right? Must have seen your fair share of corporate warfare.'

Was Callum testing him? He'd helped defuse the situation when Grant had accused him but offered no opinion of his own.

'Something like that. I mostly keep the directors from each other's throats and butter up foreign investors. Or did, I guess I should say.'

'Aye. I knew Grant was barking up the wrong tree last night.' Andrew fought to keep the relief from his poker face. 'He's just angry and scared about his lassie.'

'What happened?'

Callum turned away as though the thought caused him physical pain. 'They crashed on the way here. She got hurt in the accident. Nothing serious, I don't think, but it's not nice to see your kid in that state, you know?'

'Of course,' he said. 'You got family yourself?'

'Nah,' Callum said. 'I was engaged once, but the bitch had an affair while I was on tour. Was just lonely and missing me, she said.' He grunted.

'That's fucked up,' Andrew said. 'Hey, do you know when we'll get our bags?'

'Aye. We'll bring them down when John and David are done eating.'

'Great. I've got a bottle of whisky in one of our bags. We could play some cards or something tonight with the others if you fancy it. Take our minds off everything.'

Callum raised his hands palm-up. 'I got nothing better to do,' he said with a grin, although this time Andrew saw the cracks in his mask. He had been hardened by decades of military service but beneath it all, there was a scared little boy like there was inside every man. 'Aye, that sounds good, mate,' Callum said sincerely, stubbing out his cigarette. 'I'll catch you in a bit then.'

'Yeah. See you,' Andrew said.

When the door closed behind Callum and Andrew was alone in the room, he let out a long sigh of relief.

It was a small victory, but wars were won with similar alliances. All he needed was another dozen diplomatic relationships, and he'd command a significant influence over the Ark's residents. It was like carrying any motion in a board meeting or convincing a jury in a corporate trial; most people were sheep, who followed those with half an idea what was actually going on. You just had to get the outliers on board and the flock was yours.

If he could get the three soldiers, Mac, and one or two others in for a game of cards, get them a little inebriated, he'd be two steps ahead. His charming but witty routine never failed in business meetings; he'd just have to adapt it a little for the everyman. Then, when gossip inevitably circulated, the outliers would sing his praises and the others would swallow it down like good sheep.

He'd leave it to mature like an asset, for a time when he'd

need it. This was a long game he was playing, and he didn't want to overstep the mark or draw attention to himself if he could avoid it.

I see the monster you bury within. You might fool the world, but you'll never fool me, Andy.

And then there was Warren. He would be the hardest to ingratiate himself with. He hadn't been chosen as director for his naiveté. He'd smell a power play from a mile off.

He lit another cigarette and started pacing back and forth over the Victorian rug. His head was still a mess - a few hours of shallow sleep hadn't done much to alleviate his drink and drug hangover - but he had a goal now. The more power and influence he earned, the less he and the girls would suffer.

He paused in his tracks. Was that really why he was doing this? He'd been lying to himself for so long, sometimes he almost believed it.

And then the cold, sharp fear stroked his spine like a box cutter. He scanned the walls and ceiling, his breath coming faster, then drew on his cigarette and resumed pacing.

HARRIS

'So, I've just spoken to Commander Perrin,' Julia said, surveying the table. 'We'll have fluid and tissue samples arriving by helicopter within a half hour, and live subjects within two and a half. We have several professors from the school.' She gestured to the new arrivals. 'And a few dozen postgraduate students and technicians. Is that correct?'

'Yes, thirty, maybe thirty-five,' a man said in a gruff French accent.

'Great. And you'll have the parameters set and the analysers ready to go before the samples arrive?'

'I'll see to it myself.'

'Thank you. I think it's best we divide the faculty into groups to support the seven of you. So, if Professor Marcel and…' She gestured to the woman beside him.

'Rodier.'

'Rodier. If you both cover haematology. Rousseau and Kuhn, can you cover histopathology tests for the moment? What else do we need?'

'I'd like to brain-image the live subjects as soon as they arrive, with your permission,' Harris said. 'We'll need FMRI scans and EEGs if we have the equipment on campus.'

'We do,' Marcel said.

'Okay, good,' Julia said. 'Make sure the equipment is ready to go, and in the meantime, you'll need to catch up with the data after your flight.'

'That would be ideal.'

'And Campbell, will you help Professor Harris with the brain-imaging, or do you have another suggestion?'

'I just want to know what our priorities are here. I mean, it's all well and good designating teams to research the virus, but what about the bigger picture? Are we trying to find a vaccine here, which will take weeks, if not months? Or are we trying to suppress the symptoms of the disease? You all heard the Security President. They've cleared a strike on London. Where my wife is and my boy.' He turned away and pressed his hands together in prayer. 'We have twenty-four hours. We don't have time to waste expending our efforts in the wrong places.'

'So, what do you suggest?' Julia asked.

'We set our intent on minimising total deaths, which includes the millions of people stranded in London. If we can demonstrate that there's some way to at least slow the virus's transmission, we can save all of those people too. I suggest we test the subjects for ways to incapacitate them. Maybe playing certain frequencies repels them, like rats. We need to test their photosensitivity. Maybe a big light will subdue them. We should focus on ways of stopping transmission.'

'Okay. I'm happy with that. Can we all agree to keeping the citizens of London in mind throughout our pursuit?'

There was a murmur of assent from the room.

'Okay. I'll come and check on you all but let's try to meet here again in two hours. Any other questions?'

They looked around each others' wan faces.

'Okay, good.' She clapped her hands with finality. 'Thank you, everyone.'

Chair legs scraped and suits rustled as they got to their feet.

'Actually, Julia,' Harris said. 'I'd like to call my wife. Is there a phone I could use somewhere?'

'Of course,' she said with a tight smile. 'Just in the office next door.' She pointed to the left-hand wall.

'Thank you.'

He filed out after the others and slipped into the office. He closed the door behind him, heard the blood pulsing in his ears in the silence. He fell into the desk chair and lifted the phone to his ear. He dialled Laura's mobile and held his breath.

He didn't expect it to connect, but the dialler rang in his ear, and Laura picked up after a few seconds.

'Hello?' There was a lot of interference on the line - probably she was driving - but he could just make her out.

'Hey, it's me.'

'Oh, honey. Thank God. Where are you? Are you okay?'

'I'm okay. We just had the World Health meeting. We're at the university's medical school. Just waiting on samples to come in. What about you? Where are you?'

'Still on the road, as you can probably hear. Just passed Cleveland about a half hour ago. There was heavy traffic in New York, so we went via Pennsylvania.'

'How's Murphy?'

'Sleeping now,' she said. 'I had to let her out near Pittsburgh for a bit, but she's okay now. What happened at the conference? Are you allowed to tell me?'

He considered telling her about the imminent decimation of London, of the impossible task he now faced. The information was strictly classified, although they didn't have the resources to monitor their phone calls. But he couldn't bring himself to tell her anyway.

'It was mostly technicalities. They've given us a load of military personnel, and we have assistance from the medical faculty, and there are other professors from across the world.'

'That's good. You think there's a chance you can cure it?'

170

'It's too early to tell.'

'You are safe though, right? I heard there were reports out in France.'

'We're safe here. I don't think they made it off the coast.' The line rang dead. 'Hello? Laura?'

Harris redialled the number, but it did not connect.

'Fuck,' he breathed.

He waited another couple of minutes and tried again. Nothing. Why hadn't he told Laura he loved her right away? How long until he'd have the chance to tell her again?

He set the receiver back in its cradle and rose to his feet.

He nearly jumped out of his skin when he ran into Campbell around the corner.

'Hey. I thought I'd wait for you. The neuroscience labs are in the East wing.' Campbell pointed.

'After you then.'

SIMBA

It wasn't the same.

He'd tried methadone before, after his second overdose, and lasted less than two weeks before he'd started using again.

His body was relatively relaxed - his muscle tension and crawling skin had reduced to a vague buzz - but he was still inside his body. Inside his mind. Withdrawal was a physiological signal that something was missing, and now the signal was mostly gone, but the something was still missing. He reached beside the sofa and rummaged inside his rucksack.

The first box he came out with was oxycodone: as good as any.

Fuck it.

He popped two fifteen mg tabs out of the blister packet, then a third.

'We shooting it?' Daisy said, still running her fingers absentmindedly through Byron's fur.

'If you want.'

'I can't wait another hour, man. This is bullshit.' The light in her eyes was dull, like a dying star.

'Alright.' He popped out another three tabs, wrapped them in last night's cling film, and crushed them up with the heel of the kitchen knife.

Byron jerked up at the sound, watching him intently.

'It's okay, boy,' Daisy said, stroking his head. She emptied her shooting gear onto the coffee table and carried the syringe to the kitchen.

Byron's alarm turned to curiosity as he watched Simba empty the crushed pills onto two spoons. His big, glassy eyes were like domed mirrors. Simba's warped reflection stared back at him from the Husky's clear blue eyes and for a second, nausea surfaced through the methadone, or perhaps as a result of it.

Daisy returned with the syringe of water, and his attention snapped back to the task at hand.

He squirted a little water into his spoon and mixed the solution with the needle. He felt the sound of scratching metal on metal in his bones and shivered.

He fumbled for a lighter and cooked up his shot. The flame danced in the dog's wide, innocent eyes as it watched Simba's self-destruction. He imagined equal measures of horror and awe in its stare, like the first time he'd found drugs. Or drugs had found him.

Just shoot the fucking oxy, Simba. You can philosophise later, although we both know you'll be too high to give a fuck.

He tied off his arm with his shoelace, bit down on the end to keep it taut as he probed for a vein. Once the needle was in, he released the tourniquet and shot the oxy home.

He stared at the coffee rings on the table for a second before his focus dissolved. A groan fell out of his mouth as warmth spread through his body. He set the syringe down and lay back against the cushions.

The high was foggier than heroin, and a lot of it went to his head, but the voice fell silent all the same.

Waves broke again and again in his mind, but the pull of the moon went deeper. Nausea washed through his stomach, echoed in his head.

'Jesus,' he breathed.

'Is it good?' Daisy asked, tying off her pink plastic belt and probing for a vein.

He drew a breath to tell her no - something was wrong - but his lips would not shape the words. The contents of his stomach were coagulating. Every neuron in his body was like a pixel of TV static. His favourite show had been cut short.

Shooting the oxy had been a mistake, especially on top of the methadone, but it was too late to go back now. He had to ride the wave.

He fumbled for the armrest and got to his feet. His legs barely supported his weight.

'What's up?' Daisy asked drunkenly.

'I just need to…' he started, but he didn't know how to finish the sentence. Did he need to vomit? His stomach was unsettled, but his discomfort didn't stop there.

He needed to lie down.

It was that fucking dog, staring at him, judging him. He just needed to get away from its watchful eyes, and then he would be okay.

He stumbled into the hallway, feeling along the walls for support.

Daisy murmured something, but her voice came from another room, another dimension.

He made it to Terry's bedroom, leaned back against the door to close it, and then staggered the final few steps and collapsed on the bed.

The room wasn't so much swimming as crumbling in on him.

Every breath was laboured, as though if he didn't consciously fill his lungs with air, he might start to asphyxiate. What if he passed out and there was no one to keep him breathing? Would he die? Was he OD'ing?

No. He was just panicking. He probably hadn't dissolved the oxycodone properly, and his body was overreacting.

Currents of euphoria rippled somewhere beneath the

discomfort. There was a place he could shelter from the storm.

He crawled further up the bed, freed the duvet from underneath him, and hugged it around him.

The bed sheets were warm like a womb: the sanctuary he'd spent his whole life searching for. The pre-infantile oblivion before the tunnel had spat him out into a viper's nest. Of all the drugs he'd smoked, snorted, shot into his collapsing veins, heroin was the closest approximation he'd found.

How could she do it? How could she carry him in her belly for nine months, cradle him in her arms, and then leave him alone in this cold, dark world?

For a long time, he'd told himself that she must have believed she was doing the right thing. She was probably a junky herself, with no friends or family around her. She'd probably imagined he would be adopted by some nice, white middle-class family and have a much better life than she could ever give him. Or perhaps, she'd been raped and couldn't bear to look at the baby that was fifty percent of her assailant. But he wasn't sure he believed any of that anymore. It was just a story he told himself to ease the pain. That was how he'd started using junk too: some vague notion of needing the high to escape his suffering.

'Sim? You okay?' Daisy stood in the doorway, Byron behind her.

He shook his head, pulled his knees into his chest. 'Close the door,' he groaned.

She did and sat down on the bed beside him. She seemed fine. Why was she okay when the world was trying to tear him apart like a pack of wolves?

She touched a cool hand to his forehead and then slipped into the covers beside him.

'Don't look at me,' he said, turning over.

'Okay,' she said. 'It'll pass, you know. It always passes.'

'And it always comes back.'

He was done running. It wouldn't be so bad if he did

overdose, if the blackness opened up and swallowed him.

He filled his lungs with as much air as they would permit and exhaled in a slow, wavering breath.

Daisy pressed her body against his back, laid an arm over his torso.

He closed his eyes and followed her warmth towards its source.

The years peeled away like shedding skin.

Yes, that's it, Simba. Follow me to the safe place. Nothing will hurt you down here.

The tension melted away from his limbs and then the rest of his body. The mattress gave way to his weight.

A sigh escaped him.

'It's okay,' Daisy whispered. 'I've got you.'

He opened his eyes and turned over. Daisy smiled, touched his face.

The child who had seen too much and the stoic survivor danced in and out of each other, blurred together. There was pain in her blue-green eyes but also love.

She leaned towards him slightly, and his instinct was to shrink away. He did not deserve her affection or her sympathy, whichever it was. It would only hurt him in the end. But against his will, he found himself leaning towards her.

His eyes pulled sedately shut as their lips met, and a flower bloomed in the void. Warmth filled his entire body like a rush of medical-grade opium.

His hands roamed for her under the covers and found the soft curve of her hip. He felt the heat of her body as though it were diffusing through his own skin. He followed the shape of her torso up to her breast, then her neck. Galaxies glowed wherever he moved his hands, as though they'd mixed morphine with ketamine or maybe LSD. He didn't want to open his eyes in case he lost the feeling forever.

Where his own hands felt warmth, hers were cool against his skin.

She moved down his chest towards his jeans.

'Take them off,' she said.

He opened his eyes.

Daisy pulled her top over her head, and he followed suit.

They kissed again and she lowered herself onto him, but the cosmic theatrics were diminishing. No, that wasn't true. The warmth, the fireworks were still there, but he was drifting away from it all. He felt Daisy moving on him, felt his own body receiving her, but he was not entirely present.

He was dissolving, floating away to the place he visited in his darkest times, when no other dimension of his mind was safe.

All fell dark and silent, and he was only a ghost of a ghost until Daisy rolled away, panting.

He stared up at the clouds of damp on the ceiling. The peak of the high was fleeting now. Even the mix of oxy and methadone couldn't alleviate the discomfort of re-inhabiting his stiff, heavy body.

MAC

'So,' Mac said, stepping into the living room. Charlotte and Luke looked up. 'I've got everyone's favourite ogre.' He produced the *Shrek* DVD from behind his back. 'Or, I've got this other movie, but I don't think you'll care about that.' He paused for dramatic effect, and then held up the *Phantom Menace* box.

He'd expected Luke to beam with delight, or at least give a small smile of relief, but he only nodded and pointed to the *Star Wars* DVD.

Luke had been through a lot. Mac supposed it'd take more than his favourite movie to make him forget everything that had happened.

'Oh, wow,' Charlotte said, playing along. 'Isn't that lucky?'

Luke said nothing.

'They have all the other episodes too. There's a really good selection actually,' Mac said. 'Books, movies, TV, music, some pretty recent stuff. You just have to write it in the book and you can borrow whatever you want.'

'You want to watch it now, honey?' Charlotte asked Luke, who nodded.

Mac knelt before the TV and put the DVD in. As the DVD loaded, he took the folded paper and pen from his back pocket and offered them to Luke.

'I got these too. If you don't want to speak, maybe it's easier to write something.'

Luke shook his head.

'Alright. Well, I'll leave them here on the side if you want them.'

He started the movie and fell into the armchair. He met Charlotte's eye and they exchanged a silent semblance of conversation: *how are you doing? … I'm fine. Don't worry about me… Okay.*

The opening crawl was drifting across the screen to the main theme song when a knock came at the door.

'I'll get it,' Charlotte said, slipping out from under Luke. 'Stay here, honey.'

Mac followed.

It was Kamal, surely. He tried to prepare himself for the news in the meagre steps it took to reach the door. Kamal would either have the drugs Charlotte needed, or he wouldn't. The wide selection of entertainment was promising. They must have an equally broad spectrum of pharmaceuticals too. Right?

He drew a deep breath as Charlotte opened the door.

Callum stood in the corridor.

'We've got your bags down now, if you want to come and collect them.'

Only when the tension drained out of Mac, did he realise how tense he'd made himself, as though he'd been bracing himself in a plane hurtling towards the sea at a thousand miles an hour. But his relief dissipated as soon as it had appeared; the apocalypse had not been diverted, only delayed momentarily, which was probably worse in the long run.

'Thank you,' he told Callum and followed him into the corridor.

'Back in a second,' he told Charlotte, but she was as

unresponsive as a mannequin, leaning against the doorway.

'How you keeping?' Callum asked as they walked. 'I heard about the incident.'

'I'm alright,' he said. 'We're just waiting to hear back from the doctors about Charlotte's treatment.'

'Right. Well, they're world-class specialists. She's in the best hands.'

Yes, that was true, but none of them were specialists in cancer treatment. 'That's what I keep telling myself,' he said, forcing a stoic smile. 'How's things in the Ark? Everything calm?'

'Aye. Relatively. It'll take time for people to settle in.'

They turned a corner. At the end of the corridor, in front of the oversized submarine door, suitcases, rucksacks, and canvas bags were stacked against the wall. Someone had brought a guitar in a hard case.

'I had a wee chat with Andrew before. He's organising a card game tonight. Got a bottle of whisky too. If you fancy it.'

Mac rummaged in the pile for his own bags and slung them over his shoulders. 'I should be with Charlotte. And Luke.' He considered telling Callum about Luke's muteness, but thought better of it. 'But maybe another time.'

'Aye. Sounds good - Let me help with that,' Callum said, taking the holdall for Mac.

'Thanks.'

'Listen, if you ever want to talk, I'm in room eight. Just give me a knock.'

'Thank you. I'll probably see you in the smoking room sooner or later.'

'Aye.' They stopped outside Mac's apartment and Callum handed him the bag. 'Take care, mate.' He slapped Mac on the shoulder and headed back up the corridor.

Mac carried the bags inside and set them on the breakfast bar. 'There we go,' he said.

Did he detect the ghost of a smile on Luke's face? 'You want your things?' he asked, offering Luke his bag.

Luke shook his head, looked back to the TV screen.

Charlotte got to her feet and looked through the bags. 'Any news of Byron?' she whispered.

'I don't know. I didn't ask.'

'Right,' Charlotte said.

Was there a hint of resentment in her tone? He was too tired to tell. The universe had loaded another item onto his horse's back. One more and it would buck. Maybe two if he was lucky.

'I'm sorry.'

'It's not your fault,' she said.

She started to unpack food from one of the bags, lining up the tins and packets of food on the counter.

'You want a biscuit, honey?' she asked Luke. 'I've got bourbons.'

He stared back, shook his head, and returned his eyes to *The Phantom Menace*. Mac was gripped by the sudden urge to grab Luke and shake him, to scream at him to say something. Anything.

'You want a cup of tea?' she asked Mac, taking out a box of Earl Grey. Even in her panic, she'd thought to pack the teabags that only he liked.

'Sure. I'll make it,' he said, hugging her from behind. 'You?'

'Yeah, okay.' She laid her head against his shoulder.

He closed his eyes, drinking her fragrance, feeling her warmth inside his arms. If only he could hold her together, he would never let go.

But she slipped out of his embrace and reached inside the bag again.

He filled the kettle and took down two mugs from the cupboard over the sink.

Another knock on the door. He looked instinctively to Charlotte instead of the source of the noise.

It couldn't be a second false alarm. He saw the same knowledge in Charlotte's eyes.

She made for the door like a soldier walking into gunfire,

and a chill covered him like an icy blanket. He liked to think of himself as the backbone of the family, his shoulders weighed down with all of their loads, but in reality, he was terrified of his own inadequacy. One day, she was going to die, and he had no idea if he could suffer it. The idea that his legs would give out and spill him to the ground terrified him. He could barely support Luke as it was. What the fuck was he supposed to do without her?

When he'd been stabbed, he'd spent weeks in bed, neglecting his world of responsibility to wallow in his own suffering. And that was nothing compared to what was coming.

But this was not his burden alone. Not yet. It wasn't like Charlotte was unaware of the fact. It was not a sweet release at the end of the tunnel for her. It was hell. Yet still she walked into the flames without flinching.

He didn't deserve her - he'd known that since the beginning - but here she was nonetheless. The question was, what was he going to do now?

He followed her into the hallway, and closed the living room door behind him.

Kamal stood in the doorway.

'Can I come in?' he asked.

'Actually, can we do this somewhere else?' she said. 'Our son, he doesn't know.'

Kamal met Mac's eye, suppressing a frown. 'Of course. We can go to my office?'

'Sure,' Charlotte said. She turned back to Mac. 'Stay here with Luke, will you?'

A bolt went through his chest. Was he supposed to let her go alone, now when she needed him more than ever?

Yes. That was exactly what he was supposed to do.

'Okay,' he said.

She took his hand and squeezed it. 'I'll be back soon.'

She turned away and followed Kamal into the corridor. The door swung closed, leaving Mac in the darkness of the tight hallway.

He returned to Luke, sat beside him on the sofa.

On screen, Qui-Gon, Obi-Wan, and Jar Jar navigated an underwater cavern in a futuristic sub, but Luke's gaze lingered on the doorway.

'She'll be back soon,' Mac said. 'She's just gone to-' Fuck. What did he tell Luke? The truth, if it were up to him, but it wasn't. '-Talk to the other mums for a second.' It was a lame excuse, but Luke was fixated on the screen again.

A giant mouth - some kind of alien shark - opened to swallow the sub, but Obi-Wan steered away at the last second.

They watched in uncomfortable silence, although Mac realised the discomfort was more on his part. Luke seemed sedately calm just watching the movie. Perhaps he should just let Luke process things in his own way. If he didn't want to speak, that was okay. If he wanted to lose himself in the same movie again and again, that was okay too.

He tried to watch with Luke, but his mind raced through the corridors to the hospital where, right now, Charlotte was receiving the news about her treatment. If the Ark had the necessary drugs, they would have to start treatment soon. It had been a struggle to keep her most recent treatments from Luke, but at least then they'd been able to time hospital trips around school hours. How the fuck were they going to keep the secret in here? Luke would start to ask questions when Charlotte disappeared for hours and spent days in bed. She wouldn't be happy about it, of course, but he didn't see any conceivable way around it. They would simply have to break the news to him.

And if they didn't have the right drugs down here... well, he didn't even want to think about that. He'd find out soon enough.

He checked his watch, but only minutes had passed. He drummed his fingers on the arm of the sofa. They itched to hold a cigarette, but he could not leave Luke or Charlotte for at least the next hour or two. They needed him more than he needed a cheap nicotine fix.

He laced his fingers in his lap, but they quivered there. Was his whole body shaking?

He crossed the room to the sink and took a glass from the cupboard.

'You want a drink?' he asked Luke, who shook his head. He poured a glass of water, drank it in two swallows, and took a series of deep breaths to calm his nerves.

It was the not knowing. The treading water. That was always the worst fucking part. At least there was some degree of comfort in finality, no matter how dire the future. At least you could attempt to prepare yourself.

The apartment door opened and closed. Mac watched the living room door, waiting.

Slowly, it opened. Charlotte forced a smile but it did not reach her eyes.

He searched for an answer in her face, but she shook her head and moved past him to sit with Luke.

What did she mean? No, they don't have the drugs to treat her, or no, she wouldn't tell him now with Luke around? She had a better poker face than most of his superiors in the Met. Or perhaps she was just too tired.

He returned to the armchair, glanced between the TV and Charlotte, trying to read further into her face until she turned on him with a piercing stare. *Just drop it*, the look said, but beneath the rage he read the despair written in her face.

There were no drugs in the Ark, not the ones she needed at least.

His heart melted like hot wax, dripping down to scald his stomach and intestines, leaking out of his re-opening stab wounds.

He stared at the TV, but he could not focus his gaze. The screen was the only window out of the Ark, out of all of the suffering yet to come, but it was an illusion. There were no windows in the Ark. There was no escape.

He filled his lungs with air, but he still felt like he was suffocating. His veins burned as adrenaline shot through his blood. His fight or flight response was in overdrive, but he had nowhere to run. The greatest threat was the very walls closing him in, and outside of those were only more walls.

The only thing that stopped him from jumping up and withdrawing to the smoking room was the knowledge that Charlotte would perceive his weakness. Somehow, she managed to sit there beside Luke with the knowledge of their impending doom bubbling away within.

Luke extricated himself from Charlotte's arms and made for the door.

'You going to the toilet?' she asked.

Luke nodded and left the room.

Charlotte met Mac's eye, then looked immediately down. He reached for her hand, but she pulled away.

'I'm sorry, I just-' He laced his fingers behind his head and grimaced. 'I don't know what you need.'

She let out a desperate laugh, which threatened to devolve into a sob. 'Me neither.'

'So, no dice then?'

She looked to the door and shook her head. 'They can give me the same chemo as before. Kamal recommends surgery but…' she shrugged. 'I don't know.'

'We need to tell him,' he said.

'Not now.'

'Then when?'

'Soon,' she hissed.

Mac ran his sweaty hands over his face. 'This isn't helping him.'

Charlotte glared at him with more rage than he'd seen her display in the fifteen years they'd been together, as though he were the malign architect of all of their suffering. And then her rage blurred seamlessly into despair. Her face screwed into an infantile bawl.

They'd been close to the edge for so long but here it finally was. The sharp drop-off.

He leaned forwards, and she let him take her hands in his. He squeezed them with force, pressing his forehead against hers.

Their tears dripped down onto the wooden floor.

She gave a deep, shaky exhalation, like he'd only heard from her during Luke's birth. A feeble attempt to gather composure in the face of unprecedented torment.

'Okay,' she said quietly. 'Tell him then.'

He wiped away his tears and looked into her eyes. 'You sure?'

She swallowed and nodded. 'Yeah.'

The toilet flushed and a moment later, Luke walked in. Charlotte clamped down on Mac's hand, and he squeezed back.

Luke stopped in the doorway, clearly perturbed by their intent stares, their tears. He frowned, returned to the sofa.

'Honey, we need to talk to you,' Charlotte said, running a hand through his hair. She looked to Mac, and he took over.

'We know this is going to be hard for you, but we're all in this together, and we think you deserve to know the truth.' He took a deep breath. 'A few months ago, your mother went for a check-up at the hospital and we told you that everything was still fine, but we lied to you. It was the hardest decision we've ever made, but we did what we thought was best for you. After everything you'd been through, and then all of the progress you'd made, we couldn't bear the thought of you being depressed again. So we lied. We told you everything was fine, but your mum's cancer came back. That's why she's been so tired lately. She was due for a new type of chemotherapy next week that had some promising results in America. But now she's going to have to be treated in here, and we don't have access to those new drugs.'

There were tears in Luke's eyes, but his lips curled into a smile. Why was he smiling?

'I know,' Luke said, and wiped his eyes.

'What?' Charlotte asked. 'What do you mean, you know?'

'I heard you on the phone.'

'When?'

Luke shrugged. 'About three weeks ago.'

'Oh, honey.' Charlotte gave a restrained wail and folded him into her chest. 'Why didn't you say something?'

He shrugged as he withdrew from her embrace. 'You seemed happier that way.'

'Jesus Christ,' Mac said in a heavy breath.

Luke met his eye: *see, Dad, I can carry a burden too.*

He reached over and pulled them both into a hug. 'God, I love you both so much. We're going to make it through this, I promise.'

'The important thing is we've got each other,' Charlotte said.

They held each other for what seemed an eternity as *The Phantom Menace* soundtrack played in the background.

His relief was like a cool breeze, and he imagined he stood on a hill, looking down over a tranquil landscape. And then he opened his eyes to the same four walls. The same prison.

For a second, he'd almost forgotten the underlying fact.

Charlotte was going to die, and there was nothing he could do to stop it.

KAREN

Karen jumped at a knock on the apartment door. She'd been staring at the country road painting, but she couldn't recall a single thought or emotion. Perhaps she had drifted off into some space between waking and dreaming.

Andrew went for the door. A brief exchange came from the doorway, but she could not make out any words. She glanced back at the painting. She had been thinking something, something profound maybe, but the more she probed for the recollection, the further it slipped into the oblivion of memory.

She was going mad. It was inevitable, of course, but it was too soon. She needed to occupy her mind with a book or a movie. Anything but staring blankly at walls or paintings. That's what crazy people did.

The apartment was silent. Saff made no noise in the bedroom next door - Karen could only hope she was sleeping - and Andrew was... gone?

She crossed the room and opened the door to the hallway. Yes, Andrew had left again, probably for a cigarette, or to talk to the other men in the facility. She understood it on a rational level, but she was starting to feel like some kind of fugitive. She needed to get out of their apartment and meet people, but at the same time she did not want to leave Saff alone.

She poured a glass of water from the kitchen tap, and closed her eyes to savour its coolness. She imagined the swimming ponds in Hampstead Heath, the sun glistening off the surface on a summer's day.

She needed to remember that image. And dozens more like it. If that life was stolen from her forever, she could at least remember it as clearly as possible. She'd become the crazy old woman of the Ark, sitting alone in an armchair after Andrew and Saff died, but still children would gather to hear her stories of the time before. Like how, on Christmas morning, hundreds of locals would gather to watch the daring brave the icy temperatures of the Highgate men's pond. Or how fireworks of all colours had lit up the city skyline to celebrate the new year, reflecting in the river Thames. How the London Eye had been transformed into a giant neon Catherine wheel in 2001. Although, of course, the children who had been born and raised in the Ark would have no idea what a Catherine wheel was, or any fireworks for that matter, and they would have only seen pictures of the city beneath which they lived. Time would bury them, and all of their best memories too.

The door went again and Andrew returned, burdened with their bags. He dropped his leather holdall and laptop bag onto the counter, slipped out of his rucksack, and fetched the others from the corridor.

A delivery from Father Time himself. Karen peered inside the bags. Relics of their old lives as mundane as tins of food, blouses, and toiletries. But there were also bottles of Scotch and the Bordeaux, her boxes of Prozac, and the photo album.

She clutched the book to her chest, suppressing a sob only for Andrew's sake. He unzipped his holdall and froze, staring inside for a moment, before lifting out the wood axe.

'I guess they didn't search the bags,' he said, weighing

the axe in both hands.

'What are you going to do with it?' she asked.

'Hide it,' he said and headed for their bedroom.

Karen followed him into the hallway and watched him lift up the bottom of the mattress and stow the axe underneath.

She couldn't imagine a scenario where they would have to use it, but she couldn't deny the security it brought her, just knowing it was there.

Andrew turned the light off, closed the door, and went back into the kitchen.

'I'm going to play cards with some of the guys tonight,' he said, setting the bottles of whisky on the counter and taking a glass from the cupboard. 'It'll give me an opportunity to get to know people a little better. To prove myself.'

'Okay,' she said, setting the photo album down on the breakfast bar.

Andrew poured himself a half-glass of whisky and poised over her empty glass. 'You want some?'

She considered, then shook her head. She poured herself a glass of Bordeaux instead.

'Cheers?' Andrew said, raising his glass.

She rang it with a breath of dry humour and drank.

'When did you open it?' Andrew asked.

'Hm?'

'The wine.' He gestured to the half-empty bottle.

'Oh. Last night.'

'Why didn't you tell me about Saff?'

'I just… You had so much on your plate with Apollo. I was going to tell you as soon as things settled down a bit.'

'Right,' he said. She couldn't tell if he was angry or just despondent.

'I'm sorry. We need to be honest with each other, especially now.'

He nodded slowly, knocked his glass back.

'I was thinking of checking out the gym. Just being in

closed spaces, you know, fucks with my head. Do you mind?'

She waved towards the door. 'Of course. I understand.'

He forced a smile. 'Thanks. I won't be too long.'

'Take all the time you need.'

He drained the rest of his whisky in one swallow and headed out.

Just like that, she was alone again. She supposed some things hadn't changed. It had never been in Andrew's nature to sit still, especially not in times of distress, but she couldn't shift the sense of loneliness, the vague emptiness in her stomach. Even when Andrew was with her, his mind always seemed fixed on something else. How long had she felt like this? Months, at least. He'd been particularly busy with the business since Christmas, but perhaps the feeling went back further. When had they last had sex?

She laughed to herself. Their whole lives had been torn away from them, their daughter was distraught in the next room over the likelihood that she would never see her fiancé again, and she was wondering about hers and Andrew's sex life.

Her gaze fell upon the white-and-blue Prozac boxes and she lifted one out of the bag. A clear mind like a clear sky. She popped three pills out of the blister packet and swallowed them with wine.

The perpetual knot in her stomach relaxed a little as the pills slipped down her throat. Soon they would work their magic. They would do little to alleviate the hell all around her, but a little was better than nothing.

She ran her fingers down the cover of the photo album, tracing the distressed leather, the gold embossed wording. She opened it to the first page: a photograph of her and Andrew on Parliament Hill. They had their arms around each other, smiling placidly into the camera. The city sprawled behind them, back before it had been dominated by skyscrapers. She distinctly remembered that day; Andy had taken her for a picnic in the Heath, a welcome departure from the lavish dinner dates of Soho and Shoreditch. She'd felt free from the entrapments of the city, perhaps for the first time in her life, and Andrew had promised her that they would buy a house in Hampstead, away from the constant noise.

They were both so young in the photo. She was almost pretty. Things had been much simpler back then.

She re-filled her wine glass and turned the pages. She relived their wedding day in the Kensington Palace Orangery, their first days in Hampstead, Saff's birth.

A tear landed on the dust sheet, and then another. She wiped them away with her sleeve.

If she'd known during those precious moments that one day she'd be looking back at them from an underground facility beneath the city, would she have done anything differently?

It was surreal that the young Saffron in summer dresses and pig-tails had grown into a woman. Karen had thought, holding Saff in her arms for the first time, that it was her job to mould Saffron, like a piece of clay, into the best possible person, but now it seemed as though she'd blinked and there was a fully-formed woman with hopes and fears of her own. With a ring on her finger and an ache in her heart. How much had she really shaped Saffron in the end? What could she have done better?

She was thinking as though her life were over, but it was not. Everything she needed in life was down here. Andrew and Saff were going nowhere, and they had safety, food, potential friendships. All of that other shit - the cars, the big house, the expensive dinners - that was all just filler. So, why did she still feel like she'd lost everything?

She snapped the album shut and returned it to the bag.

The canvas bag beside it was packed with personal effects from the living room. She lifted out the novels: *Alice in Wonderland*, *Wuthering Heights*, and *Jane Eyre*. There were probably copies of these very books in the library, but these were her copies, well-thumbed and faded with age. She had lost herself in their fictional worlds so many times, their stories were as vivid as her greatest memories.

On the cover, the Cheshire Cat grinned down at Alice from a branch as if to say, *I know, my dear. I've always known.* If she was going to go mad, at least she could go mad alongside Alice, Jane, and Cathy.

Also inside the bag were her iPod and headphones. She took them out, revealing the Eiffel Tower ornament hidden beneath. She held it up to the light, her heart sinking like an anchor through a bottomless sea.

Twenty-four hours ago, she'd been dreaming of spreading her wings and flying away from London, of seeing the vast world beyond her confines. And now she found herself in an even smaller cage with little to no hope of escape. She was not a believer, but it was hard to reject the feeling that she was being punished or mocked by some sadistic deity.

She squeezed the Eiffel Tower tight in her palm, its jagged edges digging into her flesh. Tears welled in her eyes, but she swiped them away and got to her feet. Her body was charged, ready to run, to flee, but there was nowhere to go. This was all there was now.

She crossed the room to the TV cabinet and placed the gunmetal ornament there. It looked out of place in the sterile, hotel-like environment. She stacked the photo album and novels on the coffee table, draped a sweater over the back of the armchair, and scattered tins and packets of food across the counter.

That was better. A bit. This place would never be home, but at least it could remind them of home.

She snatched up her iPod, pulled the headphones on and fell into the sofa. She selected Dido's *Life for Rent*, closed her eyes, and let the music carry her out of the Ark, out of London, out of the existential prison that had contained her since girlhood. The Prozac was starting to take effect, and for the briefest of moments, the storm clouds cleared and there was only sky.

ANDREW

Andrew stared into the bathroom mirror. A blank, waxen face stared back, wrinkles carved into the skin around his mouth and eyes years too soon. The mask sagged. His salt-and-pepper stubble was more salt than pepper.

He shut off the growling electric razor and set it down on the sink shelf.

He retrieved his keys and the baggy from his wallet and shot a dusting up his left nostril. He stared at the remaining powder for a second, then did a second key.

His left nostril glowed numbly. Electricity straightened his spine.

He smiled, a warm, gregarious grin that could tame a lion.

Show your teeth, baby.

He straightened his collar, turned his head to observe himself from every angle, and nodded.

Karen looked up from her book as he entered the living room. 'You look nice.'

'Yeah, well, I need to make a good impression.'

'Of course,' she said.

He took four glasses down from the cupboard, wiped them with a tea towel, and set them beside the bottles of whisky.

'Are you high?' she asked.

He glanced deliberately at the Prozac boxes on the counter, before looking into her eyes. 'Are you?'

She looked away. 'It's not the same.'

'Isn't it?' He sighed. 'Look, this is a difficult time for all of us. You do what you need to do, and I'll do what I need to do, okay?'

'Fine.' She stared at the blacked-out TV screen. 'I just thought we were supposed to be in this together.'

She had him there.

He glanced slyly at his Patek Philippe. He'd wanted to be the first one there, but he couldn't leave Karen like this. He knew what happened when he left things on bad terms. The negativity would fester, and she'd come back with a sharper argument later.

'We are, honey. That's not what I meant.' He sat down beside her and laid a hand on her knee. 'I just need to get through these few days, and I can't function under this kind of stress without it. Just a few days, that's all I ask. Let me clear my name and establish a reputation for all our sakes. I only have enough for a few days anyway.'

She ran her hands over her face, formed praying hands under her chin. 'Okay.'

'Thank you,' he said and kissed her cheek.

She closed her eyes but did not turn away.

'I'll be back in an hour or so, then.'

'Alright.'

He nested the bottle of Dalmore under his arm and carried the poker set and glasses out.

You're not fooling her, Andy. You're not fooling anyone.

The clap of his heels and the jingle of glasses echoed back from the corridor. He had the feeling someone was following him and glanced back. It was just the paranoia, the claustrophobia.

The smoking room's only occupant was Grant. Fucking hell. That was just his luck.

'You alright?' Andrew said, setting the bottle and glasses on the table, fell into a chair.

'I've been worse,' Grant said. 'You?'

'Something similar.' Andrew reached for a Mayfair and lit up.

'Listen, I wanted to apologise for this morning,' Grant said. 'I was angry and I took it out on you. I saw on the news before the TV died that they don't think it's related to your company. And even if it was, it's not on your conscience.'

This was too fucking easy. Andrew had to suppress a manic laugh.

'I completely understand. I would have jumped to the same conclusion myself. Hey, I don't know if you heard but a few of us are playing some cards. Why don't you join us?'

'I'd love to, but I don't want to leave Lucy alone. Maybe another time, though. It'd be nice to take my mind off things for a couple of hours.'

'Yeah, of course. I'm sure we can make a regular thing of it. How is your daughter, by the way? I heard you were in a collision on the way here.'

'She's okay, yeah. We were worried that her appendix might have ruptured from the impact, but it's just a little bruising. Kamal's given her some painkillers. I think they're putting a movie on the projector, so that should be nice. You have a daughter too, right?'

Andrew started to speak, but the door opened and Callum walked in, followed by one of the other soldiers.

'Not started without us, have you?' Callum asked, gesturing to the whisky bottle.

'Wouldn't dream of it,' Andrew said with a smile.

'This is John. John, this is Andrew.'

'Pleasure,' Andrew said, standing to shake the man's hand. He poured the Dalmore while the soldiers lit cigarettes. 'Can I tempt you with a quick drink?' he asked Grant.

'Thanks, but I should be getting back. Glad we cleared the air, mate,' he said, offering his hand.

'Of course. Take it easy.'

Andrew passed the glasses around and raised a toast. 'To our new lives,' he said.

Callum and John echoed his toast, and they all drank deeply.

'Oh, man, that hits the spot,' Callum said.

'Yeah, that's good fucking whisky,' John said. 'What is that, fifteen?'

'Eighteen,' Andrew said.

'Oh, aye, those three extra years make all the difference,' Callum laughed.

You wouldn't know, Andrew thought, but he humoured him with a smile. 'Is anyone else joining us or should we make a start?'

'Ian said he'll come for a few hands,' Callum said.

'Great. What we playing, hold 'em?'

'Sounds good to me,' John said. 'What are we playing for? Money's not much good down here.'

Loyalty, Andrew thought. 'I don't know. Just for fun, I suppose.'

'Fun it is then,' Callum said. He knocked back his glass and chased it with a long pull of his cigarette.

Silence lingered for a moment as the three of them smoked and drank, before John asked, 'So, you were the Apollo CEO, right?'

'Yeah. Was.'

He'd gone to bed last night a CEO, and by morning, Apollo Pharmaceuticals had been only a memory. How much were their stocks worth now? How much was anything worth? Perhaps he should gamble his individual shares on the poker game.

'You must have had a hell of a week, man,' John said, and drained his whisky.

'Yeah, you could say that,' Andrew laughed, filling John's glass. 'But the worst is over now.'

197

'Aye,' Callum said. 'We're the lucky ones, believe it or not.'

The door opened, and Ian walked in. 'Alright, guys? Fucking hell, there's a party in here.'

'There is now,' Andrew said, pouring him a glass of whisky.

'Thanks.'

Andrew counted and distributed the chips as Ian made small talk with the soldiers.

'So, what's your role down here exactly?' Andrew asked.

'I'm a technician. Engineer. Handyman. I'm not sure I have an exact job title, but I monitor all of the electrics in the Ark, make sure all of the generators and ventilators are maintained properly. That kind of thing.'

'I see. Any family with you?'

'No. My wife died a few years ago. We never had kids.'

'I'm sorry to hear that,' Andrew said.

Ian shrugged as if to say, *what can you do?* 'How about yourself?'

'Yeah, I have a wife and daughter in here. My daughter's fiancé is supposed to be joining us, but his mother's sick, and he obviously won't leave her. And then the phones went dead, and it looks like she's not going to see him again, so obviously she's distraught.'

'That's rough,' Ian said.

'How old is she?' John asked.

'Nearly eighteen.'

'Fucking hell,' Callum said. 'Poor lass.'

'Well, if they can make it here,' John said. 'Warren will probably let them in.'

'He gave us twenty-four hours from this morning, so considering it'll be getting dark outside already, I'd say that window's closed.'

'Even so,' Callum said. 'If they're engaged, I'm sure he'll make an exception.'

'Why is that?' Andrew asked.

'Well, the Ark's designed to accommodate several

generations. There's piles of baby supplies in the stockrooms. I can't see Warren passing on the opportunity of a new bairn, you know.'

'Yeah, there is that,' Andrew said. The idea had occurred to him from the get-go - they'd been specially selected for their genetic value, Warren had said - but to hear someone else speak it filled him with protective rage. His mind flashed with thoughts of an authoritarian dystopia. Was Saff just a means to an end, a pawn in this game of chess? He supposed they all were in the end, but what if she didn't want to have children?

His own position in the Ark wasn't just about power. This wasn't just a Hobbesian dominance competition. It was their very standard of living he was playing for here. That was something Karen had never understood.

'Anyway,' he said, waving the notion away. 'Let's play, shall we?' He knocked back his whisky and dealt the cards. His own pair comprised a seven of clubs and a jack of diamonds. A strong enough hand for now.

He scanned the others' blank faces. John played the small blind, Ian the big. Callum folded.

Andrew and John matched. Andrew dealt the three shared cards, glancing at the others' expressions, but they revealed nothing.

He had a high pair of jacks now, although there were two spades on the table. A moderate chance of someone forming a flush. He raised the pot two hundred when it came around.

After a few hands and a few more glasses of Dalmore, he would home in on the real prize: the men's confidence.

Another spade came up on the fifth shared card but no further face cards. Andrew gambled on the pair of jacks and won a sizeable pot.

'I should have known better than to play Poker with a CEO,' Ian laughed.

Andrew was dealing the next hand when a tap came at the door. He looked up, froze. Someone had probably just walked by. He finished dealing and looked at his cards. Eight of hearts and four of hearts.

A heavier knock at the door. Why didn't they just fucking enter?

'Come in,' he called. The others looked at him, puzzled, and he knew instantly that no one else had heard anything. 'I thought someone knocked.'

Ian leaned over and opened the door. There was no one.

'Never mind,' Andrew laughed. He matched the bet and dealt the shared cards.

Another soft tap at the door.

Andy, baby.

Fuck. He'd thought he was over the comedown, but here the bitch was again. Unless it wasn't the drugs at all. Perhaps he was suffering from some kind of post-traumatic stress disorder, exacerbated by the coke.

You hadn't forgotten about me, had you, Andy? I'm lonely out here.

She wasn't real. She was just a voice in his head. If he ignored it, it would soon pass.

Andrew lit another cigarette with trembling fingers and tried to focus on the game.

He folded and watched the showdown between Callum and John, his leg rocking up and down under the table.

The door opened and Andrew started, nearly spilling his whisky.

Mac looked around. 'Not interrupting anything, am I?'

'Not at all,' Callum said. 'Have a seat.'

Mac seated himself in the corner and lit a cigarette.

'How you doing, mate?' Callum asked.

Mac leaned his head back to stare at the ceiling. 'I've been better, to be honest.'

'What's happened?' Andrew asked.

'Charlotte talked to Kamal about her cancer treatment. It turns out they don't have the right drugs she needs. So they can either give her another round of chemo that did nothing in the past, or give her surgery, which is a big risk in itself.'

'Shit, man,' Callum said. 'I'm sorry.'

Mac nodded to himself as he fumbled for a cigarette and lit it. 'The worst part is, the hospital where she was due for treatment is only up the road.'

'The Royal London?' John asked.

'Yeah,' Mac said.

'Fuck. Well, if there's anything we can do, mate,' Callum said with a tender smile.

Mac looked up quickly. 'Could you open the door? Do you know the code?'

Callum sighed. 'Aye. We know it. But it'd be too dangerous, if that's what you're thinking. The hospital will be full of hosts.'

'So give me the Glock back,' Mac said. 'I'll only need to find the stockroom. I can be back in an hour. First thing tomorrow.'

Callum ruminated on it, and lit another cigarette himself. 'I suggest you really think it through, but fuck, man, if that's what you want to do, then I'll come with you. You'll need the fire power.'

Mac closed his eyes and when he opened them again, tears spilled out. 'Thank you. I just don't know what else to do. We told Luke and it turns out, he's known for weeks. What kid is supposed to shoulder that kind of burden? And now all this.'

'I'm sorry,' Andrew said. 'I've never fired a gun before, but I'll come with you too. I owe you my life.'

'Surely your family need you more,' Mac said.

'We're all family now.'

'Okay. Thank you.'

Andrew smiled.

Anything for half an hour outside of these walls. He could almost feel the breeze on his skin, smell the rain-slicked streets.

HARRIS

Harris looked between the blood results of each sample and the normal ranges. By all measures, the sample appeared to be taken from a deceased subject. Its haemoglobin, cortisol, and testosterone levels were unprecedented. No human could sustain these kinds of levels for more than fifteen minutes without something giving out. Their heart, usually.

He wondered how many hosts had died simply from the excess pressure on their bodies. Perhaps the virus would kill its hosts within days. That way, the UN would not need to strike London at all. Once the live hosts arrived on campus, they would monitor changes to their vitals and blood levels, while Campbell ran his tests.

He swallowed a mouthful of coffee and scanned the faces of the medical students. It was his job to direct them in researching the virus, but he could barely direct his own attention. He'd never been in a position with so little to work with, and what they did have was nonsensical.

The hosts should be dead. The catecholamine levels indicated those of a patient in fight-or-flight mode. If it were only one sample, he might have deduced an anomaly, but all eight blood samples showed the same soaring levels of adrenal hormones. The males exhibited higher total levels of testosterone, but the females were proportionally high too: high enough to elicit a fight-or-flight response. Levels of dopamine, cortisol, ACTH, norepinephrine, and epinephrine were consistently high.

The lab door opened, and Campbell leaned around the doorway. Every head turned as he looked for Harris.

'They're here,' Campbell said.

Already?

A sickening lurch went through Harris's stomach. Until now, the hosts had been something fantastical, something hypothetical that he could analyse from a distance, but now they were a very real threat he would have to stare in the face.

'Okay,' he said, getting to his feet.

'We'll need a couple of technicians too,' Campbell said. 'Anyone experienced with EEGs and MRIs.'

Three hands raised reluctantly.

'And you all speak English?' Campbell asked. 'Perfect. We'll take you two ladies.'

Harris gathered his laptop and papers into his bag and followed Campbell and the two women into the corridor.

'We've got five subjects,' Campbell said. He led the way as soon as Harris had closed the door behind him. 'One died in transit. They're all under general anaesthetic and securely restrained. We'll have soldiers with us at all times.'

'Have you seen them?' Harris asked.

After a moment's hesitation, Campbell said, 'Yes. It's hard to believe they're still human but… well, you'll see for yourself.'

Their footsteps echoed around the stairwell as they headed down. A police truck was parked outside, like the kind they used to transport inmates. Police and military stood around, smoking.

Harris would have killed for a cigarette, but Campbell led them away from the exit and stopped in front of a lab door, guarded by armed soldiers.

'None of you need to go near the hosts, if you don't want to,' Campbell said, mostly to the women. 'I just need you to help me locate and use equipment. That okay?'

They nodded.

'Alright. Just remember what's at stake here.' He exhaled through his mouth. 'Let's do it then.'

Campbell pushed into the lab.

Harris followed. At first the room was too bright and there were too many bodies in the way to make anything out, but then two more soldiers stepped aside and Harris saw the five trolleys with their pale patients.

'Here.' Campbell was thrusting a surgical mask at him, another at the technicians. 'We should wear these. Just as a precaution.' He snapped one over his own face and gestured to the hosts.

'As I said, they're all under sedation and strapped and handcuffed to their trolleys. I think -' He looked around. 'Hey, Rousseau, right? Can we get some IVs in them ASAP?'

They fumbled about to get the hosts on drips, but Harris could not take his eyes off them. Their skin was as pale as albinos, but their veins stood out like purple ink on their arms and faces. If he didn't know they were sedated, he would have assumed the bodies had been dead for days. But otherwise, they seemed human. He could imagine them hugging their families for the last time or whispering a final prayer.

He touched the chain around his neck, squeezed Laura's crucifix.

How long had they been under? More importantly, how long until they opened their eyes again? Writhed against their restraints?

Every time he saw the first victim of a new disease, he felt the same ice cold chill. It snapped him into fight-or-flight response himself to see a new danger with his own eyes. At least he'd be meeting the hosts on similar terms.

'Harris.'

He snapped out of his reverie.

Campbell stood beside him, frowning. 'You good?'

'Fine. We should get an EEG headset on one of them before they wake.'

'Yes. Can you cover that?'

'Of course.' He looked around for a technician.

'Hey. Do you know where the EEGs are kept around here?'

The woman nodded. 'Follow me.' She walked quickly away from the hosts, led him to the store room. He lifted the headset from its polystyrene bust and carried it back to the hosts.

He chose the left-most host, a mid-forties balding male, and attached the electrodes to his skull, bracing himself for the man to jerk around at any second. But the host was out cold. They all were.

For now.

He hooked up the EEG to his laptop and opened the programme.

Unsurprisingly, the EEG displayed entirely delta waves. The host was in a deep, dreamless sleep.

He'd have to wait until the host woke up for the real testing to begin.

'Can we wake them any quicker?' he asked Rousseau as she put in the host's IV.

'They should wake within about ten minutes of shutting off the anaesthesia, but we can administer caffeine or Ritalin to try and boost that.'

'What do you think?' he asked Campbell.

'I'd say let them come around naturally to eliminate variables, but it's your call.'

'Okay. I agree. And can we keep all but one sedated for the time being?'

'Yes,' Campbell said. 'Rousseau, can you see to that?'

She nodded and hurried to the store room.

When Harris looked back to his laptop, he saw the peak in brain activity, the first theta waves amongst the delta. A jolt went through his chest. He glanced at the host, but he showed no sign of waking.

Was he dreaming?

But the theta waves gave way to beta. A faint moan escaped the host's throat.

'Campbell,' he called. 'He's waking.'

'Shit. It's okay. Just-'

The host's eyes snapped open. It stared directly at Harris, pupils wide like black holes, and let out a guttural snarl. Its rage was directed solely at him, as though Harris were the one who had put him in this state to begin with.

'Can you hear me?' he asked. 'What's your name?'

But the host tipped its head back, screamed without language. Or with the most primitive of languages.

Its brainwaves on the screen were short and narrow.

The host was in pain. It took Harris a second to figure out why.

'It's the lights. Kill the lights,' he told Campbell.

Campbell hesitated a second, then crossed the room and hit the switch.

Darkness.

The host breathed heavily, low whining noises in its throat, but it had stopped screaming. If Harris didn't know differently, he would have thought there was a dying wolf on the trolley.

'Everyone stay where you are,' Campbell ordered.

Footsteps crossed the room towards Harris and a flashlight blinked on. Campbell aimed it at the host. It fought against its restraints, leaning out to try and bite him. All of Harris's empathy was gone. There was an animal inside this man, and it would kill in an instant, given the chance. It wasn't so much that the virus had injected the host with some foreign emotion. Rather, it had stripped away every mechanism beyond its base survival instinct.

'This is going to be a fucking problem,' Campbell said, killing the flashlight. He stared at the laptop for a moment. 'I suggest we get the techs out of here. This is beyond their level.'

It was beyond all of their levels. 'I agree. The soldiers, they must have night-vision goggles.'

'Yes,' Campbell said emphatically. 'Good thinking.'

'Are all of the other hosts hooked up to sedatives?' Harris asked the darkness. The last thing they needed was other hosts coming to.

'Yes,' came Rousseau's voice.

'Okay. Can we get the technicians outside for the time being? And can you ask the soldiers for their night-vision goggles?'

Rousseau spoke in French. A soldier replied.

The door opened, bathing the room in light. The host screamed again, forcing against its restraints. Harris wondered how much pressure the straps could take. Surely they could not break out of the handcuffs.

The technicians left, and a soldier returned, carrying two helmets mounted with night-vision goggles. He used the flashlight mounted on his rifle to light the way across the room.

'Thank you,' Harris said, taking his. He strapped it onto his head, drew a deep breath, and lowered the goggles.

The lab was transformed into a negative nightmare, painted in shades of vivid green. The host's eyes were like pencil flashlight beams set into its pale, green face. It looked like some trick, some special effect from a Hollywood movie. But Harris's skin crawled and his heart raced all the same.

The host was still breathing heavily, as though it had just run a block.

Harris glanced back to the EEG recording. The host was in a state of distress, that was for sure, but its brain waves were not as sharp as when they had shone the light on it.

'What now?' Harris asked.

But the answer came from the host: a sustained cry echoing off the walls. That same clicking, like a socket wrench deep in its throat. Had the infection damaged its throat like rabies often did? He figured they'd have to wait for an autopsy to see for certain. There was something different about this vocalisation. It wasn't necessarily prompted by rage, or even fear. It seemed to Harris as though it were trying to communicate with them somehow.

'They should have cut its fucking vocal cords,' Campbell muttered. He sighed. 'Well, looks like it takes a lot of light to incapacitate it. A torch beam just makes it angrier - Rousseau, do we have a variable frequency oscillator? I want to try sound.'

'I will look for you.' The door opened again and Rousseau headed out amidst the host's revitalised screams.

What if sound didn't work? Did they try different fragrances? Would the smell of garlic deter them?

'What about water?' Harris asked. 'That works for rabies. Maybe a fire hose will deter them.'

'Shit,' Campbell said. He crossed the room to the doorway and yelled after Rousseau to bring water.

The host screamed.

SAFF

Saff tried to imagine what Rory was doing at that moment. Was he sitting alone in the darkness of his room as hell opened and spilled onto the streets? Or had they tried to make the journey to the Ark and got stranded somewhere? She thought not, but still she could not stop the slideshow of Rory's possible deaths, like a View-Master reel in her mind's eye.

Click.

Rory slumped in the road, his cold eyes staring up at the starless sky.

Click.

A crazed man standing over Rory's corpse in his kitchen, foaming blood dripping from his mouth.

Click.

Rory was fine. She'd panicked like this before he'd made contact and he'd been fine then.

Shavings of red nail paint covered the white sheet in front of her. She brushed them away and balled her hands into fists.

He should have been here, spooning her in their bed, stroking her back and whispering sweet nothings in her ear. Instead, he was on the outside, and she was alone in this prison.

She could always take a knife from the kitchen, slit her wrists in the bathtub. What would they do with her body? Open the Ark door and toss it out into the chamber to decay in the cold darkness?

No. She would never do that. Where had that thought come from?

She crawled inside the covers, drew them up to her chin.

She could do nothing but lie there with the stone in her stomach and the thoughts eating away at her, like insects feasting on a corpse, and hope to sleep. Everything was okay in the darkness of dreams, until she woke up, of course. If only she could slip into a deep sleep, like Princess Aurora, only to be woken by Rory, or else to drift on the seas of oblivion for eternity.

A child's fantasy, of course. There was no escape from this lucid hell. She'd slept too long during the day to drift off again.

Her head ached. She needed to drink some water. It wouldn't hurt to eat something either, even though she had zero appetite. The window for dinner had probably closed by now, but they had some snacks in the kitchen.

The apartment door banged. Footsteps went past the hallway. Her parents' voices in the living room.

She let out a slow breath and sat up. She could not be bothered with their questions, their attempts to reassure her, but what was the alternative? Lying here alone and wallowing in her misery?

She re-tied her pony tail, tried to emotionally compose herself, and wandered into the living room.

Her parents fell silent and turned to face her.

'Hey,' she said, walking to the sink and pouring a glass of water.

'How are you doing?' her father asked. He'd been drinking, unsurprisingly.

'Alright,' she said. She drank half of her glass, re-filled it, and carried it over to the sofa.

'I just talked to some of the guys,' he said, falling into the armchair beside her. 'We're leaving in the morning to find medicine for Mac's wife.'

'What?' She looked into her father's eyes. He wasn't lying.

'Yeah. She needs drugs for her chemo that they don't have here. There's a hospital up the road. We're going first thing in the morning. The soldiers are sympathetic to his cause, you see, at least two of the three. They know the code to get in and out, so, you know, if Rory and his mother do manage to make it here, I can probably pull some strings.'

She couldn't believe what she was hearing. Somehow, after all that had happened, this detail was hardest to process. This prison had seemed so final, so unyielding, but her father was leaving tomorrow.

'What about the director? Is he okay with it?'

'He doesn't know,' her father said. 'We're hoping we can be out and back in before anyone realises. And if he does find out, he's just one man. His power depends on the loyalty of the people, of the soldiers. If they don't recognise his authority, he has no power.'

'Okay,' she said. 'But I can't get through to Rory to tell him that. We need to go to him.'

'That's not possible,' her father said. 'It's one thing to ask the soldiers to walk up the road and collect drugs for Mac's dying wife, and another to ask them to trek across London to escort your boyfriend.'

She opened her mouth to protest.

'I'm just telling you how they'll see it. And besides, Mac didn't ask. Callum offered to go with him. But it's a start. There's hope, okay?'

She nodded slowly. If her father really cared, if he really loved her, he'd go himself, go with Saff to find Rory and his mother and bring them back safely. But she couldn't say that. It wouldn't help her cause in the slightest.

In the end, she said, 'Okay. Thank you.'

But inside, an idea was unravelling like a ball of string. If no one would help her, then she would have to act herself.

PART THREE

ANDREW

Andy.

He opened his eyes only to higher resolution darkness. But as his vision adjusted, he made out a thin beam of light slicing diagonally through the black. Dust motes fell like snow.

He tried to turn his hips but his knees were locked in place by walls on both sides.

So were his shoulders.

Nor could he stretch out his legs or push his arms out in front of him.

He was boxed in at all angles. A square coffin.

A boot under his bare foot. He was in the shoe cupboard of his mother's home.

Clap.

He homed in on the sound, calculating its exact location.

His breath had been shut off for focus. There was danger nearby, or at least the strong possibility of it.

Silence, then, another clap. A stiletto on the floor, echoing around the hallway.

Clap. Clap. Getting nearer now.

A shadow passed over the beam of light.

Andy.

The voice was female. Delicate. Curious.

A shiver went up his spine like a razor on glass. She wouldn't hurt him. She never hurt him.

I thought you loved me, Andy. Don't you love me?

'I do,' he moaned. 'You know I do.'

He sniffled, grating his sinuses like sand paper. Something wet slipped down the bridge of his nose. In the dark, he couldn't tell if it was snot or blood.

'Then why-' A weight slammed into the cupboard door. '-did you upset me?' Her tone wavered between rage and hysterics.

'I'm sorry.' He needed to get out of the cupboard, but she was out there. 'I didn't mean for this to happen.'

'Oh, you didn't mean for this to happen?' she laughed. 'But you fucking did it, didn't you? It's the same thing time and time again with you.'

He shook his head against the accusations, although she could not see him. Not yet.

'I'm sorry,' was all he could manage.

She stamped a heel on the floor. 'Then show me.'

She fumbled with the cupboard latch and tore the door open.

Light blinded him as his eyes focused. Her scent was sweet and sharp.

Her fingers gripped his arm like a vice, the long acrylic nails digging into his skin.

Andrew's eyes snapped open as he jerked away from the shape in front of him. He fumbled for the lamp switch.

He was not in the cupboard anymore; he was in bed in the Ark. Where he'd drawn the covers aside was a bare, pale back. Red lingerie.

'Baby?' he asked, reaching for her arm. Her body rolled effortlessly under his hand. Selina's empty, glassy eyes stared into him. Her face was bloated, turning blue in places.

He yelled and pushed her body away. It rolled off the bed and hit the floor with a thump.

He was dreaming. He could feel his body in the waking dimension, stiff, unyielding.

For a moment, he was stretched over both realities simultaneously, and then the dream released him.

He stared up at Karen's frown. She had a cool hand on his chest.

'You were dreaming,' she said. 'It's over.'

His back was slicked with sweat.

'Jesus.' he moaned. 'That was horrible.'

Karen nodded. Her concern slowly drained away. 'Who's Selina?' she asked, staring at the wall ahead.

Fuck.

'What?'

'You were mumbling in your sleep. Who's Selina?' She turned to face him, her stare paralysing.

'I-' He searched for the words, but he had no response ready.

His hesitation alone was a confession.

His head stung like a sharp, electric pulse. He ran a hand through his hair. 'I don't know. A journalist maybe. It was just a dream.'

'Did you cheat on me, Andrew? Before?'

Her stare was unwavering. She knew. Every passing moment only twisted the knife.

'Yes.' The word fell out of him.

Karen got to her feet, and panic filled his stomach. She couldn't go. There was nowhere to go.

'I'm sorry. It meant nothing. I was just so stressed with work and - God, I was a fucking mess. I still am, but I'm trying to make things right.'

She started to pace in front of the bed, looking anywhere but at him.

'I would give anything to go back and change it. I love you, Karen.'

She stopped in her tracks, staring down at the cupboard. 'Who was she?'

'No one. Just some girl I met at a bar.'

Karen scoffed, looked as though she were about to be sick. 'How many times?'

He could lie, but his resolve was weakened by the vivid nightmares. 'Three,' he said. 'But it was over. I called it off. It was eating me inside.'

She laughed to herself, the kind of manic laugh that precedes a breakdown. Then she looked him dead in the eyes, looked into all that he hid from the world, all that he hid from himself.

'Why? Just tell me that, Andrew. Why did you do it? Wasn't I good enough for you?'

'You were. You were too good for me. I-'

'Oh, give me a fucking break,' she said, raising her voice. 'I got too old for you and you wanted some tight, young whore.'

'It wasn't like that.' *It wasn't about you*, he didn't add.

'So, what the fuck was it like?'

He winced. She would wake Saff, if she hadn't already. Jesus, what was the time? He was supposed to be meeting Mac and Callum at seven.

'I just wanted - I needed to feel some kind of affection. Like I never had growing up.'

'So, why didn't you come to me, your wife?' she cried.

'Because I didn't want you to see how broken I was,' he yelled back. 'So I found someone fucked up like me. Is that what you want to hear?'

She closed her eyes, took a deep breath. 'None of this is what I want to hear.'

'I know. I'm sorry, Karen. I'm so sorry.' Tears stung his eyes, but he could not bring himself to wipe them away. It was what he deserved.

His fingers trembled. They needed to hold a cigarette or a glass of whisky. He closed them into fists, squeezed his nails into his palms.

Silence. She had nothing to say. She could not even look at him. She'd stared right into his heart of darkness and she knew exactly what was there.

He reached for his watch. Five-to-seven.

'I have to go soon,' he said. 'I don't have to come back, if that's what you want.'

She snorted to herself. 'Please. I'm not some bimbo you can smooth-talk. You do what you want.'

Did she want him to go? Probably, considering she could not stand the sight of him. She needed time to process the news, naturally. On the other hand, he felt so dirty delivering the blow and scarpering away from the scene of the crime.

The silence was deafening, echoing off the closing walls.

He jumped up and dressed in silence, in shame, just as he'd done after each night with Selina.

He looked at Karen, who still stood in the middle of the floor. 'I'm gonna go then. Give you some space.'

She nodded.

He opened his mouth and closed it again. There was nothing more to say. Not now.

He lifted the edge of the mattress up, took the axe out, and left without looking back.

He carried his shoes into the living room, where Saff was sitting on the sofa. She stared blankly up at him.

She'd heard. She might not have made out every word, but she definitely knew. He couldn't begin to explain anything to her, so he laced his shoes on a stool, swallowed a mouthful of whisky from the bottle, and left.

Maybe he shouldn't come back. Maybe that was the honourable thing to do, to rid them both of his poison. To run away and never look back.

It'd be so easy.

MAC

He woke with a shudder from dreams of dying: pale faces and glistening blades in the shadows. Unseen mouths grinning, lips pulled back from teeth.

Charlotte was still sleeping. He watched her chest rise and fall beneath the sheets in the dim light. Her expression gave no sign of the distress awaiting her in waking life.

He was gripped by a sudden panic about leaving. His chest was tight, as though restricted by a straitjacket. He filled his lungs with each breath, but still he felt always a breath behind.

What if he never returned, and Charlotte was faced not only with her own impending death but his as well? What if Luke grew up alone in this godforsaken place?

He stared up at the painting. The boy leaned over the river to launch his toy ship. A second ship had crashed on the bank.

If he didn't go, it would haunt him for the rest of his life. As he watched Charlotte deteriorate and Luke withdraw further into himself with each passing day, the walls would whisper louder: *you had the chance to avoid this and you shrank away*.

He had the Glock after all and a decorated soldier at his back. If it was too risky, he would turn around, yes, but he had to at least try.

He took his watch from the bedside table and checked the time.

Five-to-seven.

It would be light outside already.

He slipped his watch over his wrist and fastened it. The cold metal and the weight of it, like a gun, comforted him.

He slid out of bed and dressed as quietly as a shadow: jeans, a crew neck sweater, and his black work shoes. They would provide better grip than the plimsolls they'd all been given, if he needed to run.

He stood over Charlotte, watching her tranquil expression.

What if this was the last time he saw her?

He reached out to touch her, then withdrew his hand again. He could not risk waking her.

He trod carefully to the door and slipped out.

In the open-plan living room, he poured himself half a glass of cool water and drained it in one. The sheet of paper and pen he'd taken from the library laid on the TV cabinet. He brought them over to the breakfast bar and poised with his pen over the paper.

What did he write that would cause her the least possible distress?

He considered, then wrote: *Just gone with Callum to look for Byron. I didn't want to tell you because you'd worry. Should be back in an hour or so. All my love, Mac.*

With any luck, he'd be back with the drugs before she woke. She could start her treatment today and everything would be okay. Perhaps they'd even bump into Byron on the way and bring him home. It was wishful thinking, he knew, but there was a chance.

He closed the apartment door carefully behind him and followed the corridor to Callum's.

Callum opened the door, wearing camo trousers and a

tank top. He glanced up and down the corridor, as though they were about to conduct a drug deal, and stepped aside to let Mac in.

The apartment was identical to Mac's own, save for the meagre personal effects scattered around the room. Andrew and John were sitting on stools at the breakfast bar.

'You're sure about this then?' Callum asked.

'Yes.'

'Did you tell her?'

'I left a note.'

'Alright.' Callum pulled on his jacket, holstered his sidearm, and pocketed a flashlight. 'And you know which drugs you need?'

He nodded.

'Okay.' He handed Mac the Glock and shrugged into the assault rifle sling as Mac attached the holster to his belt.

'You ready?' Callum asked Andrew.

Andrew took his axe from the surface and got to his feet. 'Yeah.'

'Alright then.' Callum led them to the door, peered out, and scanned the corridor again. 'We're clear.'

They filed into the corridor and followed it down to the entrance door. Callum punched the code into the keypad, grasped the hand wheel, and turned to face Mac.

'Do it,' he said, before Callum could ask him again.

Callum nodded. He and John turned the wheel until a hollow clunk came from inside the door and pulled it inwards. The door opened slowly, releasing a wave of cool air.

'After you,' Andrew said, gesturing to the chamber.

Mac stepped over the threshold and looked back. Over Andrew's shoulder, a woman was approaching them. For a second, Mac thought it was Charlotte and his spine tingled, but it was not.

It was Andrew's daughter.

As Andrew walked through the door, she broke into a run, pushed him out of the way with both hands, and broke for the elevator.

'What the-' Andrew wheeled around, raising his axe. 'Saff!'

In a flash, she was at the elevator, but she did not waste time waiting for the doors to open; she jumped onto the ladder and scrambled up the rungs.

Andrew ran after her, but she was already a couple of meters up by the time he reached the ladder.

'Ah, shit,' Callum growled, pulling the door closed behind them.

Mac pressed the call lift button, trying to remember how long it had taken them to reach the bottom on the way down. Would it be faster to climb after Andrew?

The doors opened. He and Callum stepped inside, and he punched the ground floor button.

The doors drew closed, and the car rose up the shaft.

'Man, this is fucked up,' Mac breathed, touching the Glock's grip.

'Aye,' Callum said without taking his eyes from the elevator doors. 'That it is.'

Mac counted the seconds as the lift ascended. It was definitely further than he remembered.

Eventually, the lift slowed, and the doors opened with a chime.

Mac stepped out and scanned the lobby in time to see Andrew disappear from view.

SIMBA

Simba woke to the smell of cigarette smoke. Daisy was sitting on the windowsill, smoking out the window.

A cool breeze blew through the room, kissing his face and neck. He drew the covers up to his chin, shuddering, as though the bed were directly above grating tectonic plates. His body felt brittle, like it could shatter at any moment. A rodent turned in his stomach, scratched at his throat.

He groaned. Daisy turned to face him, and only then did he remember the events of last night.

'Hey,' she said. 'How you feel?'

'Like shit. You?'

'The same.'

A blister packet of methadone lay on the bedside table. Simba was torn between the necessity of alleviating his current suffering and the risk of making it worse. As long as he didn't inject the pills again, he should be fine, but memories of his intense anxiety, of his dissociation plagued him.

He hadn't dreamed it all, had he?

He popped out two tabs and swallowed them with water. Daisy snuffed out her cigarette and slid back into bed with him. Her bare legs were cool against his.

She laid her head on his shoulder, a hand on his chest. The scent of smoke was repugnantly stale and soothing at once.

They lay in silence for a long time. He could only surrender to the constantly shifting discomfort of his body, wait for the methadone to kick in and bring him some semblance of normality again.

'About last night,' Daisy said. Here it came. 'Like, how do you feel about it?'

'It was good. I just...' he sighed. 'I felt weird after a while. I kind of disappeared inside myself, you know? Like I didn't know how to deal with the feeling.'

'Yeah, I get you, man. Mostly I just zone out with men, but with you, I don't know, it's different, innit. Like you understand me. You actually care about me.'

'Yeah.' He stroked her arm under the sheets. 'We can try it again sometime.'

'Only if you want to,' she said.

He parted his lips to reply but his stomach convulsed. This was no false alarm. He jumped up, ran to the bathroom on legs of sand, and vomited into the toilet.

He'd have to re-dose on the methadone. Back to zero. Was there some sadistic puppet master pulling his strings, intent on watching him squirm?

He wiped his face on a stretch of toilet roll and rinsed his mouth under the tap.

When he straightened up, his reflection stared accusingly back.

We had a deal, Simba.

Was this what other people saw when they looked at him? The cold, hard stare, the waxen skin like a Madame Tussauds model. No wonder strangers couldn't stand to look at him.

You keep us fed and we take the pain away. You haven't kept your side of the bargain.

And what the fuck was he supposed to do? He'd already

looted the Boots for methadone and opiates. Where was he supposed to magic up smack from?

Use your fucking head, Simba.

He stared back at his reflection, itching to reach through and claw out his eyes. Why didn't the voice just tell him, if everything was so simple?

Because I am you.

He shuddered. Behind the cold, monstrous eyes was a terrified child desperate for shelter from the hell he'd been spat into. He could almost hear the sirens of ambulances pulling into the emergency department where he'd been found.

And then it struck him.

Surely they kept morphine in ambulances. They wouldn't need to risk their lives breaking into a hospital or doctor's surgery; they could simply smash the back window of an ambulance and raid the medical supplies.

He tore away from the mirror and stumbled back to Daisy.

'You okay?' she asked, sitting up.

He smiled. 'I will be.'

She frowned.

He told her his plan.

'Yeah, man. That's a good idea. Where's the nearest hospital to here?'

'Not far. We could walk there in ten minutes.'

'Shit.' An exhausted smile washed over her face. 'Well, what we waiting for?'

KAREN

Karen paced the width of the bedroom, four strides from wall to wall.

Her mind's eye painted an image of Selina: long, blonde hair; doe-eyed with fluttering lashes; delicate, red lips like the mouth of a sex doll; firm tits and a round arse. She bet the slut had sucked his cock on her knees, taken it from behind. One flash of Andrew's wealth and she was his play thing for all of his darkest fantasies.

How many times had they fucked? Three, he'd said, but did he really expect her to believe that? Or that Selina had been the only one? He'd lied all this time. Why would he tell the truth now?

But she did believe it. Maybe she was an even bigger fool than she knew, but she'd seen the terror in his eyes when he woke. Even Hollywood actors would have a hard time performing that. It was the look of someone who had been chased through hell, haunted by unimaginable demons.

And now they'd found Karen too.

Part of her had known all along. On the lonely nights

when he'd worked late for the third time in a week, she'd imagined him flirting with his secretary, fucking her on his desk. She'd even dreamed about his infidelity on numerous occasions. But she'd told herself she was being stupid, jealous. It was almost funny, how naive she'd been.

The evidence had been there all along. Why had she thought that his lack of self-control ended with the coke or the spirits? Or with his insatiable need for wealth and status? Was it her own arrogance to assume that she'd fulfilled him as a wife?

He was a child in a designer suit, chasing a lollipop on a string. He was never happy, only placated momentarily before he started running again.

It wasn't her. She tried to tell herself that it was Andrew who was broken - he'd said so himself - that she could have been the perfect housewife, and he still would have fooled around behind her back. But that didn't make her feel any better. The reasons almost didn't matter. The fact was he'd betrayed her. He'd taken her heart with both hands and torn it in two.

And now she had to live with that, trapped down here of all places. She could not pack her bags and leave, take Saff with her. She would have to see his face every day and be reminded of his infidelity. Maybe he should stay outside the Ark, spare them both the shame.

She collapsed onto the bed, hugged her knees to her chest, and pressed her face into the duvet.

Tears leaked from her eyes; her nose ran. Who would hold her now and tell her that everything would be alright? She yearned for her own mother's arms, but she was lost to the outside. She had no friends in here, and Saff had her own shit to deal with.

That was the child in her, the longing for comfort and security. The same part that had allowed Andrew to play her like a fool. There was no shelter to find in this dark world. She had to fight in the storm.

She got to her feet again, resumed pacing. The rage and

desperation filled her like molten lava. She had so much energy and nothing to do with it. Nowhere to run. Nothing to fight.

Her face contorted and a sob heaved out of her. She heard it almost as a spectator above herself. Such a pathetic, infantile noise. She disgusted herself almost as much as Andrew did, as much as his little blonde slut did, and that only made her bawl harder.

Her hair had fallen out of its bun, her fringe dangling in front of her face. She tore out the hairband and threw it across the room.

She needed to get her shit together. Saff must have already heard her yelling; she could not hear her crying as well.

The Bordeaux was still on the kitchen counter. She could drown her misery with the rest of the bottle, but that was exactly what Andrew did, running from his problems to the next bottle, the next line, the next slut. How many failures could he justify with the abuse his mother had inflicted on him?

Fuck that. It was not the same thing.

She wiped her eyes and walked into the living room. It was dim inside, the only light the corner lamp. The personal effects she'd laid out to make the place homelier only reminded her of her naiveté now: the clothes draped over the armchair, the books stacked on the coffee table, the Eiffel Tower ornament. The domestic life she'd mourned was a lie. A pantomime. When had Andrew first betrayed her? Months ago? Years? How many times had he kissed her cheek, held her in his arms, told her that he loved her, all the while burying the knowledge of his disloyalty inside himself?

She walked to the breakfast bar, poured the rest of the Bordeaux into a pint glass, and tipped it back. She popped out a couple of Prozacs and swallowed them too, took a few deep breaths to collect herself.

She spotted the photo album in the open rucksack,

withdrew it with shaking hands. She opened it to the first page: the photograph on Parliament Hill. Her young, innocent face smiled back at her. If only she'd known back then what Andrew would become. She would have run for her life and never looked back.

Tears filmed her eyes. She peeled back the dust sheet, took the photograph out, and tore it in two. She stacked the two halves, and tore them again and again until the photo was in a dozen pieces on the counter.

She tipped back her glass and turned the page.

Why was she doing this to herself? It was self-flagellation. Nothing else. But somehow, she felt it was necessary, to punish herself for being played, or at least to brand it into her memory as a reminder never again to make herself so vulnerable. She may as well have taken out a kitchen knife and carved the words *I was a fool* down her arm.

She lifted the album with both hands and flung it at the wall. It landed with a resonant thud. Photos rained down like heavy confetti.

Shit. Saff must have heard that. The whole Ark had probably heard it.

Karen walked to the hallway, stood before Saffron's door. There was no light underneath. She turned the handle and peered around the door.

The bed was cloaked in shadow, and Karen could not make out a body. She turned the dimmer switch slowly. The glow illuminated the empty bed.

Saff was gone.

The door to the bathroom was ajar. Saff was not in the apartment. When had Karen last seen her? She'd gone to bed shortly after Andrew had returned from poker, and she seemed to recall hearing her go to the bathroom an hour or so later.

Perhaps she'd gone to breakfast early, or else she'd heard them arguing and escaped to the common room or somewhere.

Karen went back to the bedroom, pulled on a cardigan, and stepped into her plimsolls. She wiped her eyes in the bathroom mirror and fixed her hair before she left the apartment.

There were only half a dozen occupants in the dining hall and Saff was not one of them. Nor was she in the common room or the games room at the back. There were only so many places she could be, as labyrinthine as the Ark first appeared.

Karen tried the smoking room next. She startled its only resident, one of the soldiers, out of reverie.

'Sorry,' she said. 'You haven't seen a seventeen-year-old girl around, have you?'

'No, I haven't,' the man said with a hint of suspicion. 'Is everything okay?'

'Yeah. She must be in the gym or something. Thanks anyway.'

She followed the corridor back down, peered inside the library, but it was deserted.

When she rounded the next corner towards the chapel and gym, she nearly ran into a man coming the other way.

'Jesus.'

'Sorry,' he said. 'It's Karen, right?'

'Yeah. You're...'

'Ian,' he said, as though this was inconsequential. 'You're looking for your daughter.' It wasn't a question.

'Yes. How do you - Have you seen her?'

He nodded his head slowly with a frown. Her heart jumped into her throat. Something had happened to Saff.

'Where? Where is she?'

Ian swallowed. 'I think it's best if I show you.' He gestured for her to follow, and started back down the way he'd come.

They walked past Karen's own apartment to a door marked 'Maintenance' a few down from the metal entrance door. Why would Saff be in here?

But inside was only another soldier, seated in one of the

desk chairs in front of a three-monitor setup. The screens displayed grainy black-and-white CCTV footage of the entire Ark. There were views of the corridors, all of the communal rooms, and even shots of the Gherkin lobby and the street above.

Ian fell into the second chair and hit a few keys.

The footage scrubbed back in time. Karen saw herself and Ian flit back up the corridor and break apart. She watched herself walk in and out of the rooms, and then finally return to her apartment.

Everything was still for a moment as the minutes ticked away in the top right corner of each screen. A few strangers flickered down the corridor: those going for breakfast early, the other soldier entering the smoking room.

Ghosts raced up the street. At the end of the corridor, the metal door opened. Bodies flashed across the screen and the door closed again.

Ian hit another key, and the footage slowed to real time.

Andrew, Mac, and the bald, ginger-bearded soldier stood before the metal door. On another screen, Saff peered around the edge of the corridor, waiting. As the soldier opened the door, Saff rounded the corner, walking briskly towards them. Mac went through first, and by the time Andrew walked through, Saff was running at the gap. She pushed Andrew aside and ran out.

She was gone from view now, in the dead zone where no cameras could detect her.

Karen stood in silence, watching as the real seconds melted away. Eventually, Saff reappeared, sprinting out of the Gherkin lobby. Andrew chased her into the street, but he was too far behind. They ran past the parked cars and out of view again.

Into the abyss.

SAFF

Her lungs heaved like bellows. She was growing lightheaded as her muscles drank oxygen from her brain.

She needed to stop.

She could maybe have pushed herself a little further if it were not for the sudden sting in her stomach, like shrapnel.

She bent over, leaning against a post box. She glanced back over her shoulder, but her father was nowhere near. Why had he ever thought he could catch up to her? She jogged regularly and took care of her figure, while he shovelled cocaine into his nostrils and drank like a sailor in a tempest.

And cheated on her mum. She couldn't forget that one.

She'd known his business and personal habits were far from clean, but she never thought he would stoop that low. Her own father. Her own mother.

Convulsions tickled her stomach. She turned aside, but nothing came up. Oxygen was more important.

She was in Hoxton now. Central lay behind her, but there was a long way to go yet, and it wasn't like she could jump in a cab or on the tube. She would have to pace herself. She'd won the sprint, but now she needed endurance.

Rory's house in Harringay was forty, maybe forty-five minutes away at a brisk walk, and that was probably all she could manage from here on, unless she stumbled across an unchained bicycle, but that wasn't too likely.

Her insides were so dry, it was like she'd been breathing in sand. She needed a drink - water or a Lucozade - but she couldn't risk going into an off-licence. She hadn't forgotten about the hosts lurking in the darkness.

She pressed a hand to her stomach and walked slowly on. Her legs burned with every step, but that soon started to fade.

Her father must have headed back, or else he was streets behind. He knew where she was going, of course, but that didn't matter. He'd had his chance. She didn't need his help now.

If it wasn't for her mother, she would have run and never looked back, barricaded Rory's house and waited until the army or the police or someone saved them.

But she could not leave her mother. Her sobs still rang in Saff's ears. Had she realised Saff was gone yet or was she still crying alone in her room? It didn't matter. There was nothing Saff could do for her now. She needed to focus on getting to Rory as quickly as possible.

She made her way north, glancing all around for signs of movement. There were voices nearby, but she could see no one. An alarm was echoing somewhere behind in central. She'd expected London to be either in a state of pandemonium, like they'd seen en route to the Ark, or a ghost town, but apart from the streets clotted with cars and the occasional body, it seemed so...normal. Birds sang in the trees. The wind carried leaves down the street. The sun shone through a relatively clear sky.

Everything was still so bright. Either her eyes had not fully adjusted yet, or the Ark was much darker than she'd first realised.

And now that her stitch was fading, it felt good to breathe the cool, natural air. She almost hoped it rained soon, just so she could feel it kiss her skin.

She dug her Nokia out of her jeans pocket and checked the signal. Still nothing. Were all of the phone masts in London down, or had something gone wrong at the source?

Fuck. If only she could call Rory, tell him she was coming. That was assuming he was still alive, of course. Yes. He was alive. She couldn't let these kind of thoughts affect her. She knew he was okay. She just had to reach him.

A shout behind her as she walked past the Essex Road Overground station.

A Middle Eastern man had run into the street behind, but he seemed to be headed the other way. Maybe.

She broke into a jog, feeling her stomach tense, leak adrenaline.

She could not take much more. She could not afford to run for her life a second time.

Thankfully, the man didn't follow her towards Holloway. She dashed into an off-licence up the road, whose drink fridge she could see clearly through the window. She was in and out in two seconds, and she heard no noise from the shop.

The water was still cool. She drank most of the bottle and poured the rest over her head.

She wasn't far now. Maybe another twenty minutes at a light jog.

She picked up her pace, ignoring the pain tracing from her ankles up to the back of her thighs. She could rest once she knew Rory was safe.

ANDREW

A stone was growing in his stomach, and his feet felt as though they'd been skinned. His socks were sodden with sweat, but it could easily be blood. His entire body pleaded for rest. His heart thumped against his ribcage, like a manic claustrophobic, but he refused to stop. Not yet, at least.

Saff had her youth and physical health. He had determination.

He fumbled for the last of his coke, shot it up his left nostril, and kept running.

He knew where she was going. He'd dropped Saff off at Rory's enough times to navigate there on foot.

If only the streets weren't so fucking packed, he could take a car with its keys left in and drive there. A motorcycle would be even better, but he wouldn't be able to handle it even if he found one.

She knew. There was no doubt in his mind that she'd heard him and Karen arguing. She'd probably heard everything through the thin walls. Was that what had motivated her to escape, or had she been planning it all night? He should have seen this coming. As if Karen needed another reason to hate him, he'd let their daughter slip through his fingers. He could only pray that Saff intended to bring Rory back to the Ark instead of running away with him somewhere.

A bolt of pain went through his heart. The axe slipped from his grasp, and he clutched at his chest.

His legs slowed under him, and he fell against a bus stop, heaving for breath. A poster for *We Will Rock You: the Queen Musical* urged him to get his tickets from the box office before it was too late.

A cold numbness traced down his trembling fingers. He shouldn't have done the coke. He'd pushed his body too far and now he was going to pay the price.

He slid down the bus stop and hugged his knees to his chest. Shudders surged through his body in slow waves, like a slow-motion seizure.

His mind was spacing out from oxygen deprivation. He closed his eyes and prayed not to pass out.

The wind lifted his hair, kissed his sweat-slicked skin.

He drew deep breaths in through his nose and out through his mouth. He felt almost weightless for a second, as though he were drifting in and out of his body.

He looked up at the infinite blue sky.

If he was going to die, let it be now, out in the open rather than trapped inside the oppressive confines of the Ark. Karen and Saff were probably better off without him.

But no, his tremors were slowing. He felt the cold, hard pavement beneath him.

He pushed himself to his feet, clutching at his chest. When he got back to the Ark, he'd have to see Kamal about his health, explain his addictions. If there was a path to redemption, it started there. He'd talk to the psychiatrist, try to dig deep inside himself and fix the broken, twisted roots. If Karen couldn't stand to be around him, he'd ask Warren for a separate room, give her the time and space she needed to come to terms with it. Fuck it, if she really wanted, he'd leave the Ark and fend for himself in this diseased new world. But first he had to find Saff and ensure she got back safely.

He just needed to take it slowly. He'd catch Saff on the way back, if not before she reached Rory's. He walked on, paying close attention to his heart. If it started to hurt him or beat too fast, he'd stop again.

He was nearly in Hackney now; a sign for the Dalston Junction Overground pointed ahead.

An idea arrived fully formed in his mind. He stopped, staring at the Overground sign with disbelief. It was too simple. It would never work. But if it did...

He hated himself more than he'd imagined was possible, but he had to admit, sometimes he was a fucking genius.

MAC

A man with a grey hood stopped in his tracks on the other side of the road, staring.

'Just keep walking,' Callum said, gripping the handle of his rifle.

They continued down Whitechapel Road. Just forty-eight hours ago, the street would have been bloated with traffic, with shoppers and commuters going about their days. Now the street had been gutted. Driverless cars filled the road, and the crowds were sporadic, many of whom carried baseball bats or knives and heavy rucksacks.

Mac glanced back up the road as they passed the Whitechapel Underground station. The bulbous Gherkin loomed over the street, its glass finish covering only the lower half.

'There it is,' Callum said, pointing ahead to the stone facade of the Royal London Hospital.

They crossed the street and stopped before the entrance. Mac touched the grip of the Glock in its holster.

It was not too late to turn back, but that brought him little reassurance. The only thing scarier than going inside the hospital was going back empty handed.

A dog barked somewhere close. Mac knew that bark.

Byron rounded the corner and shot towards him.

Callum raised his rifle, trained his sights on him.

'Don't,' Mac yelled, throwing out an arm to block Callum's aim. 'He's mine.'

Mac dropped to his knees as Byron crashed into him, nearly knocking him over backwards. 'Jesus, boy.' A laugh escaped him as he threw his arms around the husky. His fur was dirty, dried like glue in some places, but Mac pressed his face into his coat.

'Hey,' came a shout from up the street.

Mac looked up. At the corner where Byron had appeared stood a tall black man and a younger woman, who held a claw hammer at her side. They were both dishevelled and dressed in baggy, dirty clothes. They looked as though they'd been living in an apocalyptic world for years rather than days.

Callum aimed down his sights again. 'Stop where you are.'

'We don't want any trouble,' the man called. 'We just want our dog, and then we'll be on our way.'

'Your dog?' Mac asked, straightening up. 'This is my dog.'

The couple frowned, exchanged a look. The man stepped forwards. 'We found him yesterday. Just down the street.' He gestured back the way they'd come, towards the Gherkin.

'Hey, that's enough,' Callum called.

'You're welcome,' the young woman called.

Mac walked out a couple of steps to meet them. 'Thank you,' he said. 'For taking care of him. We can't be too careful out here, you know.'

'He with the army?' the woman asked, nodding to Callum. 'He's not too friendly.'

'He was,' Mac said. 'Not anymore. What are you guys doing out here, anyway? The streets aren't safe.'

'We're junkies,' the woman said with an ironic grin. 'In

case you couldn't tell. Just looking for a fix like always.'

'You find what you're looking for?'

She regarded him suspiciously for a second before shaking her head. 'Nah. We thought we'd find some morphine in the ambulances, but someone got there before us. What about you? You don't live around here.'

Mac sighed. He didn't want to disclose any personal information to two homeless strangers, but they had been honest with him. And they had taken care of Byron.

'My wife has cancer. The drugs she needs are inside that hospital.' He pointed.

'Shit,' the man said. 'We'll come with you.'

'Out of the question,' Callum said. 'They'll only be a liability.'

'Hey, we might not have guns,' the woman said, 'but we can handle ourselves, man. What about safety in numbers and all that?'

She had a point. They were hardly military trained, but both of them had a hard stare that told him they'd survived worse than most. And weapons.

Mac looked to Callum, who gave the slightest of shrugs. 'It's your call.'

'Alright,' Mac sighed. 'But you do everything we say, and we're not responsible for your lives.'

'Whatever,' the woman said, shrugging.

'What are your names?' Mac asked.

'I'm Simba,' the man said. 'This is Daisy.'

'I'm Mac,' he said.

'Callum,' Callum grunted. 'Now that we're all acquainted, shall we make a move?'

Mac nodded, fastened Byron's lead to the bus stop. 'We'll be back soon,' he muttered, stroking Byron's coat.

'Alright,' Callum said and led the way to the hospital entrance.

Mac drew his Glock and chambered a round. This was it. No going back now.

They walked into an open, brightly lit lobby. It was

deserted save for a body lying in a pool of blood before the receptionist desk. A pungent, infectious smell was already coming off it.

Callum scanned the lobby's angles, nodded to Mac. Clear. He led them through the lobby to the stairway, and they all filed down to the basement floor.

A 'Staff Only' door blocked their entrance, but Callum broke through with a single kick. The corridor was completely dark. Without windows, the only light came from Mac's torch and the one mounted to Callum's rifle. The walls were painted a mint-green only a few shades lighter than the Ark's teal corridors. Christ, he hated corridors.

Mac scanned both directions, and then shone the torchlight on a wall sign. It pointed left for staff locker rooms, medical records, and CSSD; right for the morgue, doctors' offices, and store room.

'This way,' Mac said, pulling away to the right.

'Let me go first,' Callum said, taking over. 'Watch your six.'

They followed the corridor to the double doors of the store room. Through the glass windows, was a space at least the size of the Ark's dining hall. Shelves upon shelves of medical supplies.

A plaque mounted on the door read, 'Staff Only. Alarmed Door.'

'You think the alarm is active?' Mac asked Callum.

'Shouldn't be if the power's out,' Callum said. 'Unless it's on some kind of back up circuit.'

'Should I kick it in?' Mac asked.

Callum considered it, nodded, and stepped back.

Mac drew in a breath and channelled all of his strength into the kick. The door swung inwards and crashed against the wall.

'Okay, go,' Callum said, gesturing Mac inside.

He stepped in, scanning the darkness with his Glock, finger on the cold metal trigger. No safety. If anything lunged out of the shadows, he would not hesitate.

Simba and Daisy followed him in. Callum closed the door behind them.

Mac scanned the room: hospital beds, electrical equipment, gas canisters, and shelves upon shelves. He hurried to the shelves but could see no medicine. There were only hospital gowns, bandages, and boxes of latex gloves.

His leg burned as he walked to the doors at the end of the room. The door ahead was labelled 'Pharmacy.'

'This is it,' he said. He tried the handle. Locked. *Here we go again*, he thought, and kicked the door in.

The room was like a mini-warehouse in itself. It must house hundreds, maybe thousands, of different drugs.

'What is it we're looking for?' Callum asked.

'Eribulin,' Mac said. 'It should be under the brand name Halaven.'

'Alright,' Callum said, unconvinced.

'The aisles are labelled,' Simba said. 'Look. These are all oral drugs.' He crossed the room to the far wall. 'Here. Injectables.'

Mac followed.

'I think they're in alphabetical order,' Simba said.

Mac shone his torch along the shelves. Bupivacaine. Chloroprocaine. Epinephrine. He ran his fingers along the plastic boxes filled with vials.

There was no Eribulin.

'Fuck,' he breathed. It had to be there. Charlotte had been due for chemotherapy in this very hospital in just over twenty-four hours.

'There we go,' Daisy muttered. Mac shone his torch on her as she lifted a vial up.

'You found it?' he asked.

'Just morphine. Sorry.' She shrugged out of her rucksack and emptied the box of vials inside.

Mac scanned the names again. It should be right here. He strode down the aisle, searched for it under Halaven, but found nothing.

'Fuck,' he said again. Perhaps the drug was not stored in the warehouse with all of the other commonly administered pharmaceuticals. Perhaps it was only stored on the chemo ward. He would have to take the stairs up, navigate to the right area, and break into another storage room. And what if there were hosts in the building? It was hard to imagine there wouldn't be. The news had shown outbreaks in other hospitals around London.

Time was running out. Charlotte would be waking soon, if she hadn't already, and it was only a matter of time before Warren discovered that four of the Ark's residents were missing.

'Over here,' Callum called. Mac followed to another aisle labelled *infusions*. 'What was it called again?'

'Eribulin.'

'There,' Callum said, pointing. A half dozen vials in a plastic basket.

Mac picked one up, pressed it to his chest. 'Thank God.' He pocketed four of the vials, handed two to Callum. 'Just in case.'

'Alright, let's get the fuck out of here,' Callum said.

He started towards the door, then threw out his hand and froze. Mac stopped, listening. Had he heard something amidst the echo of their footsteps?

Callum turned, pressed a finger to his lips, and crept forwards. The vials jangled together in Mac's pocket. He pressed a hand against his thigh to silence them.

A voice in the corridor. Something like a grunt.

An icy hand gripped his heart.

Was it human? Host?

'Slowly,' Callum whispered and inched forwards. They crossed the warehouse in slow steps.

The voice came again, and this time, Mac knew it wasn't human. Not anymore.

It was a high-pitched whine, like that of a big cat, underpinned by a clicking sound like a socket wrench in its throat.

The voice echoed around the basement corridor. Or perhaps there were more than one of them.

Mac pressed his face to the door's glass, but could see nothing. It was too dark.

They had two options, the way he saw it. They could wait until the host moved on and make a break for the stairwell. Or they could get the jump on it, and empty a clip into it, but if there were any more down here, the gunfire would bring them running.

'What do we do?' Mac asked.

Callum held up a finger. Wait.

Slow footsteps echoed down the corridor, but Mac couldn't locate the source over his own heart thumping in his ears.

'Alright,' Callum whispered. 'On my count, we move quick and quiet. If anything comes for you - human, host - shoot to kill.'

Mac nodded.

'Alright, Three, two, one, *now*.'

The door whined as Callum pulled it open and stepped out. Mac winced, following him into the corridor, and shone his torch down both ends.

He could only see about ten feet ahead of them and fifteen behind before the corridor bent around.

They'd taken three steps when a scream filled the corridor. A host rounded the corner ahead and sprinted towards them.

A flash of light, the sound of thunder, and the body hit the ground with a wet slap.

'Go,' Callum called, running for the stairwell.

Mac glanced back. Two hosts were running for them. Simba and Daisy were completely unaware.

Mac aimed his Glock and fired off three rounds. One of the hosts fell, but the other kept coming. It snatched hold of Simba's arm as he turned.

Mac tried to line up the shot but Daisy and Simba were

in the way.

Daisy swung her hammer and buried its claw end in the host's head.

He sprinted up the stairs after Callum, through the lobby, and spilled onto the street.

Byron was barking, pulling against his lead.

Simba and Daisy came out behind him.

Mac pressed a hand to his pocket. That had been way too close for comfort, but he had the vials.

He looked up at the sky and filled his lungs with air.

He'd done it.

'Oh my God,' Daisy cried.

She stared at Simba, who was clutching his shoulder, blood dripping between his fingers.

Simba smiled sadly, gave a defeated shrug.

SAFF

She broke into a jog as she left Holloway behind. She would have run, but she was worried her legs might buckle if she tried. It felt like industrial vices were clamped to her bones, threatening to snap them at any moment.

Rory's house was about ten minutes away, on the other side of Finsbury Park.

A motorcycle engine echoed from the street behind her. A police bike filtered between the cars with two youths riding it. She ducked behind a car on the pavement until it disappeared under the Seven Sisters bridges and then followed.

When the motorcycle had faded away, the underpass was dead silent. The sun played hide and seek, blocked out by each railway bridge, and blinding her in the spaces between.

She was passing the final bridge when her father rounded the corner at a jog.

'Saff.'

What the fuck? How was he here already?

She crossed the street to avoid him. She didn't have the strength to run, but she could at least outpace him at a brisk walk.

'Saff, wait. I'm trying to help you.'

'I don't want your fucking help.'

'I've got a car on the tracks.'

She froze in place, looked to the Finsbury Park station to which he pointed.

'We can reach Harringay in minutes.'

He touched a hand to his abdomen, panting. His shirt was patched with sweat under the armpits. She could barely look at him, the man who had cheated on her mother. If she had the energy, she probably would have run, but she could use the help. He might only save her a few minutes en route to Rory's, but if they could drive back to the Ark, it would make everything easier.

'You're fucking crazy,' she said.

He shrugged. There was light in his eyes, as though he were proud of her insult.

She sighed. 'Okay. Fine. Let's go.'

Her father led them into the Finsbury Park station, glancing back every few steps to check she was still following. He vaulted the ticket barrier and offered Saff his hand, but she waved it away.

A black Land Rover was parked on the tracks. She jumped down from the platform and climbed into the passenger seat.

'It's not the smoothest of rides, I'll warn you,' he said, keying the ignition.

None of this has been a smooth ride, she thought but nodded.

Her father put the car into gear, released the handbrake, and pulled away. Gravel crunched under the tires.

She watched the speedometer creep up to twenty-five, thirty. The platforms ran out and the station grew smaller and smaller in the rear-view mirror.

The railway track converged with the other six to form one wide path. Her father drifted into the centre, changed gear, and flattened his foot to the floor. Gravel rang off the tracks on both sides of the wheels, and the Land Rover shook underneath them. The green swathes of Finsbury

Park gave way to residential estates on the right - the same journey she'd made dozens of times in an actual train carriage - and before she knew it, they were approaching Harringay Overground.

Rory's place was only a few minutes' walk from here, even less at a jog if her calves allowed it.

Before her father had even killed the engine, she was out of the car, scrambling up the platform.

'Saff, for fuck's sake, slow down,' her father called as she jogged up the steps to the bridge.

She wheeled around and glared down at him, barely restrained from letting the torrent of hatred pour out of her. Did he think because she'd allowed him to help, she'd forgive him just like that? But if she gave him a piece of her mind, she wasn't sure she'd be able to stop herself, and she didn't have time to waste.

She tore away and followed the bridge to street level. She passed corner shops, restaurants, and pubs at a brisk walk, all closed, some boarded over. An old woman peered out of her front room window, didn't look away when Saff spotted her.

Halfway down Wightman Road, a man crossed the street towards her.

'Hey, do you guys have phone signal?'

'No, sorry,' Saff said.

'Please. I just need to make a call.' He fell into step with her.

'She said we don't have any signal,' her father called from a few feet back.

She broke into a jog again, turning onto Rory's road, counting down the numbers. Four, six, eight, ten.

'Saff,' her father yelled.

She pumped her legs, her vision a shaking blur. There it was, his cream painted house with the brown door. She rounded the corner into his front yard and hammered on the door.

'Rory,' she called.

Her heart thumped in her ears. She waited two seconds, three, four, hammered on the door again, then walked around to the living room window and knocked there too.

'Rory, it's me.'

She pressed her ear to the door. Footsteps thundered down the stairs.

The door opened.

Rory stood in the doorway, staring down at her with disbelief. A second passed, long enough for her to think something was wrong, before he folded her into his arms, squeezing so tight, she couldn't breathe. But that was okay. She didn't need to breathe. Not when his warmth cascaded over her in slow, sedating waves. Not when his sweet, intoxicating scent filled her nostrils.

'What are you doing here?' he asked, finally withdrawing. He sounded almost annoyed.

'I came back for you,' she said defensively.

Only then did Rory seem to notice her father standing behind her.

'You'd better come inside,' Rory said, stepping back to let her past. 'It's not safe out there.'

They filed into his tight hallway, and Rory bolted the door behind them. He led them into the living room, where the sofa had been turned on its side and moved in front of the bay window beside the wooden shelving unit.

She leaned against Rory, and he put an arm around her. 'How's your mum?'

Rory sighed. 'Not good. I tried to convince her to come and join you, but she won't leave her bed. She's just… disappeared inside herself, you know?'

'I'm sorry,' she said, rubbing his back.

'Maybe we can help,' her father said, perching himself on the arm of the armchair. 'We have doctors in the Ark, nurses, a psychiatrist. And it's safe.'

Rory sighed again. 'You haven't seen the state she's in. There's no way she'll walk over an hour through the city.'

'We don't have to walk,' her father said. 'We have a car

on the train tracks. We can drive it right down the Overground line into central. We just need to get her to the station.'

Rory thought in silence for a moment. 'It's possible. Let me talk to her.'

'You want me to come with you?' Saff asked.

'If you want,' Rory said and opened the door to leave.

'Oh, congratulations, by the way,' her father called. He gestured to the two of them. Was there a shadow of sarcasm in his tone or was she just paranoid?

'Thanks,' Rory said, and led the way upstairs. 'You told him then?'

'When they made me leave. I tried to refuse, to come find you, but-'

'It's okay. I wanted you to be safe.'

She nodded. She wanted to tell Rory what she'd overheard this morning, to tell him what kind of man her father really was, if Rory hadn't come to the conclusion on his own, but he had too much on his plate right now. She could tell him once they were all safely back in the Ark.

Rory stopped outside his mother's room, took a second to compose himself. She took his hand and squeezed it. He put an arm around her and pulled her into a hug.

She wanted to savour the moment, to lose herself in his warmth, the strength of his arms, his rich fragrance, but she was still so afraid.

'Alright,' he said, cleared his throat, and knocked gently on the door. 'Mum?'

Silence.

'Mum, it's just me. I'm coming in.'

Rory opened the door slowly, stepped inside.

It was dark in the room. There was a shape in the bed, but it did not move.

'How are you feeling?' he asked.

No response. Surely she could not be asleep. Saff stood awkwardly in the doorway, unsure whether to step inside and close the door or leave Rory to it.

'I brought someone to see you,' Rory said, sitting down on the bed.

Now his mother sat up quickly, looking straight at Saff. She could not see his mother's eyes, but she could feel them boring into her.

'It's just Saff. She's come to help us.'

'Hey,' Saff said, her voice as small as a mouse. She took a tentative step into the room. She could just about make out Jane's face, expressionless, like a wax model. Or a corpse.

Jane made a small grunt of acknowledgement and then laid back against the pillows again.

'Can I get you anything?' Rory asked. 'Some food or something to drink?'

Jane shook her head fervently, as though he'd asked something demanding.

'Okay.'

Now the gravity sank in. Saff had no idea how they were going to get Jane out of bed, let alone across London to the Ark.

Silence descended over them like a parachute in those games she'd used to play at school. She was trapped underneath, and something was hunting her from above, but she could not see from where.

Rory rose from the bed, walked slowly to the window, and pinched the venetian blinds apart. It was still morning. They had a few hours to cross the city, but that was the easy part.

Had Saff's mother noticed her absence yet? Had anyone else? What if Warren found out and refused to let them back in?

Rory opened the blinds. His mother winced, pulled the bedsheets up to her chin.

Panic flooded Saff's stomach. What if Jane was infected? But she wasn't; she would have turned by now, and her symptoms were closer to those of PTSD than some rabies-like virus. She looked like a child who had just seen her whole family butchered in front of her.

What had Rory said? She'd disappeared inside herself. That was exactly it. She was there in the room, but at the same time, she was gone.

Rory walked back to her bedside and took a blister packet out of the top drawer.

'It's time for your medicine, Mum.'

Jane shook her head.

'It'll make you feel better,' he said. 'I promise.'

Jane turned to Saff, an infantile suspicion in her eyes. Why was Jane consulting her?

Saff nodded, tried a reassuring smile.

Jane allowed Rory to place the pills in her palm, watched them for a moment, as though at any moment they might explode in her face, and then swallowed them with a glass of water.

'There, you'll feel better before you know it,' he said. 'Why don't I get my Walkman, put on some nice music?'

She shook her head.

'Or I can read to you?'

Jane considered this, looked at Saff, then nodded to her.

'You want me to read to you?' Saff asked.

She nodded again.

'Wouldn't you rather-' Rory started.

'I don't mind,' Saff said. 'Anything I can do to help.'

'Alright,' Rory said. 'Let me find a book.' He touched Saff's shoulder as he crossed to the door.

She was alone with Jane now. Silence held the room with the tension of a taut wire. She wouldn't have been surprised if Jane suddenly screamed or broke down in hysterics. Saff hadn't been far from it herself the past couple of days. Perhaps what they both needed more than anything was to hold each other and howl at their suffering.

Rory returned, sat down on the bed, and gestured for Saff to sit beside him. He showed his mother the books in his lap: *The Great Gatsby, Mrs Dalloway*, and collections of poems by Keats and Hardy.

Jane took the Hardy book and handed it to Saff.

'She likes her poetry, don't you, Mum?'

She shrugged, looked away.

'Any one in particular?' Saff asked.

Jane didn't respond.

Several pages were folded over in the corners. Saff opened the book at the first mark.

'The Darkling Thrush?' she asked, but again Rory's mother said nothing.

Rory rested a hand at the small of her back. 'That's fine,' he said softly.

'Alright.' She cleared her throat, and read. 'I leant upon a coppice gate, when frost was spectre-grey, and winter's dregs made desolate, the weakening eye of day.'

Was it not too dark and depressing for Jane?

Saff paused, looked up. Jane watched her like a curious child.

She read on. 'The tangled bine-stems scored the sky, like strings of broken lyres, and all mankind that haunted nigh, had sought their household fires.'

When she'd finished, she looked up. Jane's eyes were closed, and Saff thought she saw the ghost of a smile on her lips.

'You want me to read another one?' she asked.

Rory's mother opened her eyes, nodded.

'Okay.' She turned to the next bookmarked poem and read 'The Voice'.

When she'd finished, a tear ran down Jane's face. She wiped it away and looked at the book in Saff's hands.

'Another?' she asked.

Jane reached out, but instead of the book, she took Saff's hand, turned it over. She ran her fingers along Saff's engagement ring.

'It's beautiful, isn't it?' Saff said. 'Rory chose well.'

Jane nodded, more to herself, then withdrew her hand and folded her arms over her stomach. She squeezed her eyes shut and when she opened them again, tears streamed out.

She gave a sniff, as though to try and compose herself, but it had the opposite effect. Her face contorted with the effort of holding the pain back, and a low moan started in her throat.

'Hey, hey, it's okay,' Rory said, putting his arm around his mother. She buried her face in his shoulder and wept.

Is this what they wanted? The real Jane was starting to bleed into the empty shell, but how far would it go?

'It's okay,' Rory said again. 'We're gonna take you somewhere safe. We're all gonna take care of each other.'

Jane nodded against Rory's shoulder, and relief escaped Saff in a sob of her own. Rory found her hand on the mattress and squeezed it. The three of them sat there crying together until a cloud passed over the sun, and the room turned dark again.

SIMBA

The panic was leaving him almost as quickly as his blood.

This was it. The end of the line.

It was the point where his final dregs of survival instinct should surface to rage in the face of death, but he'd already accepted that there was no hope. If he didn't bleed out from the bite wound, he would lose his mind and turn into…one of them.

It had started to rain, but he could not feel it on his face. No, it was not raining. The flickering overlay he saw, like a grainy VHS, was only in his mind.

Even the pain in his shoulder, which at first had felt like an acid burn, had started to fade.

'I'm sorry,' Mac said. None of them knew what to say. They just stared fixedly.

'Let me ask one favour,' Simba said. 'Leave me your gun.'

Mac looked back and forth between Simba and the pistol in his hand. He nodded. 'Alright.' He drew the handgun out of its holster and offered it to Simba. 'There's one in the chamber.'

'Thank you,' he managed, taking the Glock. Its weight

sent cold shivers down his muscles. 'You should go.'

Mac swallowed, nodded. 'I'm sorry,' he said again. He took a step backwards. Byron pulled against his lead, rubbed his face against Simba's leg. Mac turned, followed Callum down the street.

'Sim,' Daisy said, pressing her forehead to his and folding her arms around him.

'Don't touch me,' he said, trying to push her away but he did not have the energy. 'It's too dangerous.'

'I don't care,' she said. 'I'm leaving with you.'

'Don't say that.' He wasn't just getting on a train somewhere; the train was about to derail, to crash in a colossal cloud of smoke. And then after that... only blackness.

'Why? I've been alone for enough of my life. I don't want to be alone again.'

'You'll find a way to keep going. You're stronger than anyone I've ever met.'

Daisy let out a desperate breath of laughter. 'And what do I got left to live for? This?' She held up a vial of morphine.

Even now, his stomach growled.

Feed us, Simba. Come on. One for the road.

'Please,' he said. 'Just go. You don't need to-'

Daisy kissed her teeth. 'Shut up, man. I've made my decision, alright?'

'Alright.'

His legs were growing weak, or his body was growing too heavy. He needed to sit down, but he could not die here on the street.

He looked up at the Royal London hospital. He supposed it would be poetic, in a way, to leave where he'd come from.

'This is where they found me,' he said, gesturing to the hospital steps. 'Where she left me.'

'Shit,' Daisy said. 'Well, I'm not leaving you.' She took his hand, wet with blood, and he squeezed hers.

'There's a green just round the corner,' he said. 'We should do it there.'

'Alright. Let me help you.' She slipped under his right arm to support his weight. Together, they walked slowly up Whitechapel Road towards the looming skeleton of the Gherkin.

He squeezed the Glock, his ticket out of this world of pain. Just a blink, a flash, and it would all be over.

That's all, folks.

And yet... he was afraid.

Tears stung his eyes, but he wiped them away with his free arm.

They crossed the street, and Simba guided them down Vallance Road. He hadn't been down here in months - years, maybe - but other than the frozen traffic, it looked just the same. They walked through the green, where Simba had slept rough more than a couple of nights. That had been during his teens and early twenties, when he'd come to Whitechapel like a lost pilgrim, searching for some great revelation that would make sense of his tangled string of memories.

He'd stopped looking a long time ago.

'There,' he said, pointing to the largest tree. Its leaves were all dead, clinging to skeletal branches.

Daisy helped him to the tree. He fell against its trunk, lay his head back, and closed his eyes. Even in the darkness behind his lids, static flickered. His senses were fading, but at the same time, they were sharper than he'd ever known.

He could hear voices spilling over from Whitechapel Road, birds singing in the trees above. He opened his eyes and gazed into the endless blue. The clouds looked like cotton wool drifting in the wind.

In the grand scheme of things, his own suffering seemed so insignificant.

'You want a shot?' Daisy said, sitting beside him and taking the morphine from her pocket.

He touched his shoulder, and his hand came back

shining with blood. His head was growing light, like a balloon that would float off into the sky at any moment.

It was coming fast.

'Yeah.'

He set the Glock on the ground between them. Daisy took two syringes from her rucksack, handed him one and a vial of morphine. The liquid was as clear as water. Pure, unlike the murky bog water he'd been shooting into his veins for half of his life.

Daisy drew out her pink, plastic belt from her jeans and fastened it around his bicep. Simba loaded the syringe with morphine and probed for a vein. He left bloody streaks with each tap, like a child finger-painting.

He wiped the blood away with his sleeve, found a vein, but when he went to insert the needle, his hand was shaking too much.

'Let me help, man,' Daisy said, taking the syringe.

She pierced his vein and pushed the plunger.

The sterile coldness traced up his vein like the path of a scalpel, and right behind it came the wave of warm bliss, sunlight filling every inch of his body.

He opened his mouth to moan, but the sound didn't make the journey from his diaphragm. Instead, his lungs relaxed, and the breath escaped him in a sigh.

Daisy unfastened his tourniquet and tied it around her own arm. 'Good?' she asked.

He could only nod.

The birds were singing something about another world, and for a second, he could think of nothing else.

And then his body shuddered. Nausea filled his stomach. Symptoms from the corporeal world.

He was slipping away. The great tide was pulling him, and he had no strength to hold on.

He took up the Glock, and pressed the cold barrel flat against his forehead.

It'll be quick. Painless.

He closed his eyes for a second, and when he opened

259

them again, Daisy had already finished her shot. Her belt and syringe lay in the grass at their feet. She was watching him with drowsy concern.

'You okay?' she asked.

He nodded, barely had the energy to move his head.

He was running out of time.

'It has to be now,' he said. 'You want to go first?'

Daisy shook her head. 'I'll go after you.'

Images flashed of his own mangled skull, of blood pooling in his lap as Daisy pried the Glock from his cold, dead fingers, and pressed it to her own head. But he didn't have time to argue.

She took his hand and squeezed it tightly.

'I wouldn't want to leave with anyone else, you know?' he said.

Daisy smiled. 'Me too, man.'

He opened his mouth to say something else - some final speech that might encapsulate his gratitude, his love for her - to express the existential revelations dancing on the edge of conception. Then he put the cold barrel into his mouth and squeezed the trigger.

HARRIS

Harris knocked back his glass of water, closed his eyes. He tried to burrow deep inside himself, to syphon the last of his reserve energy.

They had just less than an hour until the UN meeting, and they had little to nothing to show.

Where had the time gone?

Save for a wink on the flight, he hadn't slept in over forty-eight hours. His body was like a sack of potatoes in the desk chair, the weight spilling over the table. His head pounded, as though his brain were another swollen heart pressing against his skull. He needed to wake himself up, but caffeine only made things worse and splashing water into his face only revitalised him for a few minutes at a time.

If it weren't for the steady stream of cool air blowing in through the open window, probably he would have nodded off already.

The FMRI visualisations on his laptop screen didn't look real anymore. The sound of the Euronews broadcast on TV seemed to come from across an empty auditorium rather than the far end of the lab.

Come on, Harris, focus.

He could sleep a few hours after the meeting, but he needed to channel all his remaining energy into the task at hand.

He looked over his notes again. What did they have to show for their tests? The hosts were in a constant state of primitive alertness, their brain activity dominated by high-range beta waves; according to the MRIs, the limbic system was constantly activated, the amygdala glowing incessantly like a red-hot coal, but the cortex showed severely decreased activity. Antipsychotics and SSRIs decreased the emotional response in all hosts - it seemed to numb their murderous rage - but that gave them little leverage in the long run. Administering pharmaceuticals to millions of hosts at the same time was just not feasible, and it was a solution that lasted a few hours at best.

If there was any hope of convincing the Security Council to hold fire on the London strike, they needed to present a clear case for hindering transmission of the virus, especially since it had spread further into France during the night.

Light seemed their best bet for keeping the hosts at bay, but the military knew this already. They'd mounted floodlights around the campus perimeter, but they would not have enough to protect the whole border. Tear gas would slow the hosts down, but again the military must have figured this out already. They needed something new to present.

The biologists among them had isolated the infective agent, but they were no closer to manufacturing a vaccine than the hosts were to controlling their rage.

Perhaps the strongest evidence they had that the virus could be slowed was the fact that eventually, the hosts would die of fatigue or cardiac arrest. They did not seem to eat or drink, and the human body could only take so much adrenaline before it crashed. If the virus had been bio-chemically designed, as many of their team believed, it had not been designed to keep individual hosts alive; it had been designed simply to wipe across the populace as quickly as possible.

They'd lost three of their five subjects already, all from heart failure. Two broke into full-body convulsions first, the other simply nodded off in its trolley.

If they had accurate data, they could potentially simulate a transmission map, accounting for the short life span of the hosts and the hours of daylight that prohibited their movements. With the narrow window of transmission, he was sure that any further attempt to slow it would have exponential results. If the military could erect floodlights across a national border, for example, the hosts would probably die before they got across. This was good news for the States and for the other continents, but it was little consolation for mainland Europe, which was already infected.

It took only one host to infect a city.

Campbell got to his feet so quickly that Harris started. Had he been drifting towards sleep again? Campbell started to pace back and forth in front of the window, his hands pressed together in prayer.

'What are you thinking?' Harris asked.

'I'm not. That's the fucking problem. We're just going around in circles. Tell me we're missing something here.' Campbell's tone grew more desperate with each sentence. He was close to the edge.

'I don't know,' Harris sighed. 'If we group the preventative measures together, we've got, what? Pharmaceuticals and light stimulation.'

'Which are both dead ends. Fuck,' Campbell yelled, thumping his fist on the table. He fell into a chair, rested both elbows on the table, and covered his face with his hands.

'I'm sorry,' was all Harris could manage. They'd been fighting an impossible battle from the beginning, but he thought better than to tell Campbell this. The infection was simply too quick, on an individual and collective level. If it had taken days to infect the host, like rabies, they might have had a chance of saving London, but it was not rabies.

'Did your family manage to get out?' Harris asked.

'I don't know,' Campbell said through his fingers. 'The phone lines went dead after hours.'

A knock on the door. Julia leaned in. She looked between them both with a blank expression.

'It's time,' she said eventually. 'I'm sorry.'

Campbell stared at the table top for a long moment, before slowly rising to his feet and packing his laptop into its bag.

'I need someone to speak to the UN, to report on our progress,' Julia said. 'I'd like you to do it, Harris.'

He glanced at Campbell, who didn't look happy about being overlooked. It was his city on the line.

'Sure,' Harris said.

'Thank you.'

They walked out of the building in silence and climbed into the SUV with Rousseau and Kuhn. The drive to the World Health Organization headquarters was like the drive to a funeral. Julia tried to consolidate them, ignite them with a little passion, but it was a lost cause. They all knew they'd failed. Their only hope was that the Security Council would hold off the strike for a little longer.

They filed into the chamber and took their seats at the front. There were only around half of the people present in the first meeting, but still the murmur of conversation filled the room like running water. Julia took her seat on the stage and spoke in whispers with the man beside her.

A wave of nausea went through Harris's stomach, and the blood in his head pulsed violently in response. He needed water, but he'd left his flask in the medical school.

A couple dozen more people trickled in before Julia rose to the podium and called for silence.

'Welcome back, everyone. For those of you who missed the first meeting, my name is Julia West. I'm the Director-General here at the World Health Organization, and I've been overseeing the team at the university's medical school.

Despite the limited time frame, our team has worked tirelessly to research the prognosis of the currently unnamed virus. To tell you more about our findings, allow me to introduce Nobel prize winner and Harvard Professor of Pathology, Richard Harris.'

He rose on stiff legs and walked up to the podium. He held the podium with both hands to steady himself and surveyed the sea of dignitaries. He had no speech prepared, was probably too tired to formulate coherent sentences, but if there was any hope of saving London's surviving population, it rested on his shoulders alone.

A breeze echoed around the chamber. No: it was his own breathing coming through the speakers.

'I think it's safe to say that the world has never seen anything like the last forty-eight hours. My colleagues and I have tested extensively on both fluid and tissue samples taken from dead and living hosts. The biological mechanisms with which the virus infects its hosts seem too efficient to be real. Professors Campbell, Rousseau, and myself have put live hosts through a series of tests over the last twenty-four hours.

'We've documented the hosts' major symptoms, the most significant of which is murderous rage, as I'm sure you have all seen footage of yourself. Many have likened this to the rabies virus, with which I have extensive experience, and although this virus shares many similarities, it is far more complex. The virus forces hosts to produce inordinate amounts of adrenal hormones, including cortisol, testosterone, noradrenaline, and, of course, adrenaline. The hosts are frozen in a primitive fight-or-flight response, which causes them to attack others on sight, chiefly through biting. This seems to be the mode of transmission in the majority of cases, although the virus can surely be spread through any interaction with infected blood or saliva.

'As well as murderous rage, hosts suffer intense photophobia, primarily from sunlight but also from artificial light. A strong flashlight beam, car headlights, or, better still, floodlights will cause them enough pain to keep them at bay. Further testing is necessary, but this seems to be a result of damage to the occipital lobe of the brain. In fact, aside from the lightening of the skin and the deoxygenation of the blood, the major symptoms are all neurological. We have tested a variety of antipsychotics and antidepressants on living hosts, which seem to subdue their aggressive tendencies, although, the persisting brain damage leaves them in an unresponsive, dissociated state.

'Our evidence shows that these are at least two methods of slowing the transmission of the virus, but I would like to argue that the virus is slowing naturally. The physiological changes are too great for the hosts to survive more than a few days at best. Of our five subjects, three died within twenty-four hours, and we've had reports from across Europe of hosts falling dead in the streets.

'With a little more time, I'm confident that we can slow the virus long enough that the hosts die from cardiac arrest and fatigue. Thank you.'

He returned to his seat amidst an echo of applause.

Campbell stared blankly past him, nodding slowly to himself.

'Thank you for your insight, Professor,' Julia said. 'I believe Director Garcia also has an update from the security council.'

Garcia took to the podium and scanned the room with a hard, measured stare. 'We have also worked tirelessly for twenty-four hours to slow the transmission of the virus. As Professor Harris mentioned, our best defence against the hosts is light. During the night, it's possible to stop the hosts' movement with artificial lights, but we do not have the resources to illuminate a perimeter around them, especially since they are spreading further with each night. Just last night, hosts managed to spread to the outskirts of Paris. Many of our resources were directed to protecting the capital and we have managed to keep them at bay for now, but every hour more and more civilians are crossing the channel into France. After much consideration, it is still the will of the security council to strike the south of England with immediate effect.'

A mix of cheers and cries filled the chamber. More cheers than cries this time.

Garcia sat back down, and Julia slowly took her place again. 'The final decision will now be voted on anonymously by the general assembly. In the absence of the United Kingdom's ambassador, their vote will default to negative.'

A hundred voices talked at once as the vote was conducted on stage. Campbell shouted beside him, but Harris could focus on nothing but Julia. She collected the vote slips, counted them, and then passed them to someone else to recount. From the second she took the ballots back, Harris knew from the look on her face that they'd failed.

She stepped up to the podium. Silence held for a long moment before she spoke.

'The vote rules ten to five in favour of the strike.'

Harris's stomach turned to water.

KAREN

A sharp knock on the door.

They were back.

She jumped up from the sofa and hurried to the door.

Andrew must have caught up with Saff in the end and brought her back to the Ark.

But when she opened the door, it was Charlotte who stood in the corridor.

'Hi. Sorry, I know it's early, but I need to speak to Andrew,' she said. She was breathing heavily, as though she'd just run a mile on the treadmill. There were dark bags under her eyes, as though she hadn't slept since they'd arrived at the Ark. Maybe she hadn't.

'He's sleeping right now,' Karen said, trying to mask her disappointment. 'Maybe I can help you.'

'I just really need to talk to him about Mac. I don't know if you heard about their, um, plan.'

Karen looked both ways down the corridor, searching for what? Spies?

'Come in,' she said, stepping back.

Charlotte glanced back up the corridor herself and reluctantly crossed the threshold.

'Andrew's not here,' Karen said, closing the door. She felt dirty just saying his name. 'He went with Mac. So did Saffron. Well, she ran out after them.' She led Charlotte into the living room.

'Oh. I'm sorry.'

Karen swallowed and nodded.

Charlotte was looking quizzically around the room, as though trying to place some peculiar aspect.

'Can I get you a drink? Tea? Coffee?'

'No. Thank you,' Charlotte said. 'I can't leave Luke for long.'

Karen perched on the edge of the sofa, and Charlotte, after a moment's hesitation, sat down in the armchair.

'Do you know what their plans are?' Charlotte asked. 'Out there?'

Did Charlotte not know herself? Or was she probing to see how much Karen already knew? Maybe it was too painful to explain the situation again.

'Yeah,' Karen said. 'They went to get your... medicine?'

Charlotte looked up, and as she held Karen's gaze, a tear rolled down her cheek. 'I knew it,' she sniffled, wiping her eyes. 'Mac told me he'd gone to look for our dog.'

She produced a folded note from her jeans pocket and handed it to Karen.

It read: *Just gone with Callum to look for Byron. I didn't want to tell you because you'd worry. Should be back in an hour or so. All my love, Mac.*

'Do you know when they left?' Charlotte asked.

'I don't know. About an hour ago. Maybe less.

'Oh,' Charlotte said despondently. Her gaze rested on the photo album on the floor, the scattered photos.

Karen wanted to tell her about Andrew's infidelity - she needed to say it out loud to know it was real - but Charlotte had her own problems to deal with.

'Can they get back in on their own?' Charlotte asked.

'I don't think so. But the soldiers know the door code. John's watching the CCTV with Ian. He's the technician

269

down here, or something. He told me he'd come find me as soon as they returned.'

'Where are they? Ian and the soldier?'

'There's a maintenance room at the end of the corridor.'

'I need to speak to them,' Charlotte said, rising to her feet.

'Okay. I'll come with you,' Karen said.

She led Charlotte back into the corridor and down to the maintenance room.

She made sure no one else was around before she knocked on the door.

It fell back to reveal the soldier she'd met in the smoking room. He had a handgun pointed at the doorway. Ian and John sat in front of the monitors.

Behind them, stood Warren.

He smiled politely. 'Karen. Charlotte. Why don't you come in for a little chat and clear some things up for me?'

ANDREW

Andrew lit a cigarette as he walked. His lungs had barely recovered from running across London, but… well, he needed the fucking thing. He had no other defence, just like he had no defence for his portfolio of vices. Smoking a cigarette was nothing compared to the coke or the cheating, but it all came from the same place, didn't it?

That black vacuum within.

It brought him some relief that there was a chance he could shrink the emptiness with a little medication and therapy. Maybe if he just explained everything to the psychiatrist, told him about his mother's episodes, about those days when she vacated her earthly form and let something else take over, maybe then he could start to heal.

Perhaps, if he really committed to getting clean, weathered the storm to come, the wound would scab over, and eventually heal. He didn't have a choice anyway. He'd snorted the last of his powder, and he could not call a dealer to the Ark. He had a little whisky left, but with every sip, he would advertise his lack of inhibition. If he had any hope of placating Karen, and Saff, for that matter, he would need to steer well clear of the booze.

He'd allow himself a cigarette a day, or maybe two, for social benefits. After all the work he'd put in to establish a reputation for himself with Mac and the others, he could not afford to lose touch with them.

What if Karen told people? What if she told Charlotte or one of the other women and the gossip spread throughout the Ark? She would ruin his reputation.

He had a rough few weeks ahead of him, whichever way he looked at it. He was walking naked into the flames of hell, and it terrified him, but there was no other way.

The nicotine rose to his head like a grey fog. He snuffed the cigarette out prematurely and glanced back down the street.

Saff, Rory, and his mother were about thirty feet behind. Andrew slowed his pace to allow them to close some of the distance.

Why don't you walk in front, just to give Jane some space? Saff had said, but he had no doubt the real reason she'd asked was because she wanted to avoid him as much as possible.

Your own daughter can't stand the sight of you. How does that feel?

The street faded away. His vision clouded for a second, and when it cleared, he was sitting in the road with his back against a car. His head throbbed dully. Had he fallen?

Saff jogged up, leaned over him.

Her lips seemed to move ahead of her voice, like an out-of-sync DVD. 'Are you okay?'

'Fine,' he said, pushing himself to his feet with an aching wrist. 'Just lost my footing.'

Saff opened her rucksack and offered him a water bottle.

'Thanks,' he said. His head was clearing now - maybe a good knock would do him some good - but he drank deeply.

Rory was a couple of cars back, guiding his mother by the hand.

He was a good kid, as far as Andrew could judge. He hadn't wanted to see it before, but he saw it now.

'Come on,' Saff said. 'We may as well walk together.'

They walked the final stretch of Wightman Road and joined the bridge down to the Overground station.

'I need to turn the car around,' he said. He slow-jogged down the stairs and dropped down onto the platform. The railway was wider than he remembered, and he managed to turn the Land Rover in three points.

In the rear-view mirror, Saff and Rory helped his mother down the final steps. If he didn't know better, he'd assume she'd drunk herself into a stupor.

It was reassuring to know that he wasn't the only one fucked in the head.

A plastic bag blew along the tracks and flattened against the windscreen before drifting on.

Saff dropped down from the platform and took out a CD case. He unwound the window and took it.

'What's this?'

Dido's *No Angel*. The same record he'd bought Karen for her birthday a couple of years ago. He'd gotten it imported from the States before its UK release after she'd fallen in love with 'Thank You' on the radio.

'You've got to be kidding me,' he muttered.

'It's her favourite album,' Saff said. 'Rory thinks it'll keep her calm.'

'Alright,' Andrew said, and loaded it into the car stereo.

The sombre electronic intro played from the Land Rover's speakers. He shifted his seat and gripped the steering wheel with white knuckles.

This was going to be a long drive.

The back door opened. Rory got in and then Jane. She met Andrew's eye through heavy lids and gave the slightest of frowns. Saff got in the passenger seat and turned to him.

'Okay.' She looked away quickly.

He inhaled, exhaled, then put the Land Rover in gear and slowly pulled away.

Jane gave a small noise, as though she'd been startled out of reverie. 'Where are we going, Rory?'

'Somewhere safe. In the city. We're going to stay with Saff's family.'

Jane met Andrew's eye again when he glanced into the rear-view. He gave a nod of reassurance, turned the stereo up a hair.

He kept the speed at twenty for the time being. When she settled down, he could take it up to thirty, thirty-five.

Soon, Harringay was behind them, and then Finsbury Park too. The Seven Sisters fractured, converged again. Dido sang on about heartbreak and moving on.

As they approached Drayton Park, he slowed back to twenty and checked the road map. This was the hard part: one wrong turn would cost them dearly. Jane was relatively calm, but he could not afford to backtrack.

When they passed Canonbury, he knew they were on the right track. They split off again towards London Fields, which, without any unforeseen complications, should carry them right to Liverpool Street station. From there, the Gherkin was only a five-minute walk.

The tracks rose above street level. The roads were like winding rivers beneath, bloated with driftwood. The lines upon lines of cars stretched as far as he could see. Pedestrians stared as they drove by.

As they passed another intersecting Overground line, the Gherkin's skeletal head emerged between a couple of council blocks and then disappeared again as the tracks descended.

They were heading for a tunnel now. A big dark mouth to swallow them.

He glanced in the rear-view. Jane was slumped sideways against Rory's shoulder.

This must be the final stretch now. The tunnel would spit them out in Liverpool Street.

The light grew smaller and smaller in the rear-view. He could see the tracks by the Land Rover's headlights but little else.

The darkness pressed against both sides like a car

crusher. He gripped the wheel tighter and held a breath.

The front-left wheel dragged against the wall with a grinding sound. He pulled it back.

'Where are we?' Jane asked.

'Just going through a tunnel, Mum,' Rory said. 'We'll be out soon. Just listen to the music.'

Something slammed against the passenger door. Saff gasped.

He had not hit the wall again. It seemed as though someone had kicked the car, but no one would be in the tube tunnels, would they?

Over Dido's lamenting chorus, a scream of rage.

His heart jumped into his throat. He pressed his foot down on the accelerator.

A figure rushed out of the darkness, was flattened by the Land Rover's front bumper. Andrew stole a glance in the rear-view. The body writhed on the tracks in the red headlight glow.

Hosts.

Why hadn't he considered this? They should have gotten off at Bethnal Green and walked the rest of the way, but there was no going back now.

At least the hosts couldn't break through the metal and glass construction of the Land Rover.

No, but he couldn't get out either.

'I don't like this,' Jane muttered. 'Please, Rory, make it stop.'

'It'll be over soon. I promise.'

More screams echoed around the shaft. Were they behind or ahead of them?

A weight dropped onto the roof.

Andrew changed down a gear and floored the accelerator. The host landed on the tracks behind them.

He was driving too fast. If there was a sharp bend, he wasn't sure he could turn the car in time, especially not on gravel.

There was light at the end of the tunnel. The end was

near. As the daylight filled the tunnel again, he saw the hosts running on the maintenance platforms alongside the track. Did humans usually run that fast?

Just as he thought they were in the clear, a host leaped down from the tunnel and somehow managed to cling onto the windscreen wiper. It stared into his eyes with such hate, it turned Andrew's stomach to ice water.

He fumbled to turn on the wiper and hit the horn instead. Jane moaned. The host held on.

They were emerging into Liverpool Street station now. With its high glass roof, the host had no escape from the daylight.

It started to growl over Dido with an almost feline undulation.

'Hold on,' Andrew called. He waited a second until they were fully out of the tunnel and then pumped the brakes. Not an emergency stop, but fast enough that the host bounced off the bonnet and landed on the tracks.

It convulsed there like some expressive dance routine, roaring in agony. It clawed at the gravel, pulled itself to its feet. It stumbled a few steps back towards the tunnel, before its legs buckled again. Steam rose from its skin, or perhaps that was just the light.

There was nothing to do but watch it die in agony as Dido sang that she was no angel.

Andrew stared blankly for a moment, waiting to make sure it was really dead and then killed the engine and the music with it.

He threw open the door and jumped down to the tracks. The stench hit him instantly: the unmistakable smell of burning flesh. He walked slowly to the host, nudged it with his foot. Two days ago, it had been a man, probably with a wife and kids. Well, it was probably better off dead now.

'Alright, it's safe,' he called. The cries of the dead still echoed in the tunnel, but none would dare emerge into the station. Not unless they wanted to face the same fate as their friend on the tracks.

Saff and Rory climbed out, helped Jane down.

Jane stared back into the tunnel, her arms hugged around her middle.

'Don't worry about that,' Rory said, taking their bags from the back seat. 'We're nearly there.'

'Let me take something,' Andrew said.

'You sure?' Saff asked, regarding him.

'Yeah.' He took a rucksack from Rory and slipped it onto his back.

He dropped to one knee by the platform and laced his fingers together. Saff stepped into his hands and climbed up to the platform.

'After you,' Rory said. He boosted Andrew up and then his mother. Saff helped Rory up.

Their footsteps echoed around the high ceiling, the only sound in a building usually bustling with travellers.

The platform ran out, and they emerged into the station lobby.

Andrew smelled the bodies before he saw them, slumped across the floor beneath the blank departure boards. Blood had dried in smears between the bodies, a browning, burgundy colour.

'I don't like this,' Jane murmured. 'Can we go home, Rory?'

'It's okay. We're nearly there. Then everything will be okay.'

They had to step over another heap of bodies in the entrance, but then they were out in the street again.

Andrew led the way, past franchise outlets and office complexes. The Gherkin was hidden from view behind other buildings, but he knew it was only around the corner.

He wondered if Canary Wharf was overrun. Probably. But what did it matter anyway?

He saw the Gherkin's reflection in the windows across the street before he saw the building itself.

He led them past Mac's Range Rover and the other cars in which the Ark's residents had arrived. He allowed himself a breath of relief only once he'd closed the construction gate behind them.

Mac must have returned some time before them, assuming they had returned at all. Had they found the medicine they were looking for?

They walked through the Gherkin's lobby and stopped before the elevator shaft.

Saff called the lift.

'Where are we going?' Jane asked.

'We're going to stay with Saff's family, remember? Her mum's waiting downstairs.'

'Down?' she asked.

The elevator doors opened with a chime.

They filed in, and Andrew pressed the button for the basement.

What would Karen say when she saw him? What would Warren do when he found out they'd left the Ark and brought back two new inhabitants? If Warren kicked off, would the soldiers back him or Andrew? A game of poker and a few glasses of whisky were enough to establish a good impression, but was it enough to change their allegiance? They had only helped Mac because Charlotte was dying. But Andrew had never asked for this. He had not planned for Saff to slip through his fingers and trek across London for Rory.

Before he could outline any kind of projection as to what would happen, the elevator car slowed to a stop. The doors opened.

Andrew stepped out to see Mac and Callum rise from the chamber floor. Mac's dog was curled up at his feet.

'Shit, you found him,' Andrew laughed. 'Did you find the drugs?'

Mac nodded heavily. 'Yeah, we got them.'

'Why are you still out here?' Andrew asked.

'Something's happened inside. They won't open the door.'

KAREN

There was complete silence as Karen watched the CCTV footage for a second time.

As Mac and Callum walked off screen, Warren looked around the room. 'Would someone like to explain what the fuck is going on here?'

'I have cancer,' Charlotte said. 'Stage four. The chemo did nothing for me, so I was scheduled for some new experimental treatment tomorrow at the Royal London hospital in Whitechapel. We spoke to Kamal, but you don't have the right drugs here. Mac...' She closed her eyes to gather her composure. 'Mac seems to have taken it upon himself to try to get the drugs.'

'And the girl? Saffron?' Warren directed this part at Karen.

'She was distraught about her fiancé. She must have run off to find him. Andrew told us last night about his plan to go with Mac.'

'And where does he live, her fiancé?'

'Harringay.'

Warren raised his eyebrows. 'Jesus Christ. And you were all in on this?' He turned to the others.

Ian and John nodded silently.

'I wasn't,' Charlotte said. 'The first I heard of it, they were already gone.'

'The plan was to be back before anyone noticed,' John said.

But how did Warren know? Had the other soldier, David, tipped him off?

'And when they returned,' Warren said, 'did you plan on re-screening them for infectious agents?'

John swallowed, exchanged a look with Ian. 'No.'

Warren ran a hand through his hair. 'If you'd asked me in the first place, I would have said just that. Do you understand how fucking dangerous this is? If one trace of blood or saliva was brought inside these walls, the whole Ark could be infected. The future of the human race would be jeopardised.'

'But you will let them back in, won't you?' Charlotte asked.

'If they're clean, yes, but I'll have to quarantine them first. I'll need to get the medical team to screen them.' Warren took a deep breath. 'One woman already knows that people have left the Ark. When everyone else finds out, there's going to be chaos.'

'How?' Ian asked.

'She heard it. Her apartment's right by the door.'

'Fuck,' John muttered. 'Warren, I'm sorry.'

'Save it. Right now, I need your help. Go for breakfast. I need you to be my eyes and ears on the ground. Make sure things stay calm.'

John nodded, got to his feet, and squeezed past Karen to the door.

'Oh, and John?'

He turned.

'Give me your gun.'

John took his handgun out of its holster and passed it to Warren.

'Thank you.'

Warren set the gun down on the desk as John left.

Karen glanced at the monitors, expecting to see them appear onscreen, but the CCTV feed was still playing the moments after the others had left the Ark. Ian seemed to remember this at the same time and hit a button.

The feed switched to real-time playback.

'What the fuck?' Ian muttered.

The bottom-left box of the central monitor displayed a view of the chamber outside the Ark's security door. Mac and Callum had returned, and with them was the dog that had run off in the street.

'Oh my God,' Charlotte said. Her eyes shone with tears.

Warren stared for a moment, then fell into the seat John had left. He clicked and typed into the computer to bring up a spreadsheet.

'David, I need you to wake Kamal for me. He's in room eleven. Explain the situation and ask him to get ready to screen them.'

'Of course,' David said and left them.

'This facility was not designed for a dog,' he told Charlotte, as though she were the one who had brought it here.

She nodded, defeated, tears streaming.

Karen put a hand on her shoulder.

Warren sighed. 'You'll have to keep it in your own apartment, for the time being at least. And it'll have to make do with human food.'

'You'll let him in?' she asked.

'If he's clean.'

Charlotte sniffled. 'Thank you. When do you think they'll be able to come back inside? It's just I left my son alone.'

'I couldn't say,' Warren said. 'Half an hour. Maybe longer. If you need to be with your son, you should go.'

'Okay.'

'I'll come find you when,' Karen said.

'Thank you.' With a final, lingering look back at Karen, Charlotte left.

Now it was only her, Warren, and Ian. They all watched the monitors silently: Charlotte walking back to her apartment; Mac pacing in and out of view in the chamber not ten metres away from where they were sitting.

The longer she stared, the greater her discomfort grew. Her skin was too taut, her body too heavy. They were living in a grid, in a series of boxes from which they could never escape. They were battery hens in an industrial chicken coop. With every day, every week, every year that passed, her memory of the outside world would fade until all she knew was this prison.

There was no video feed for the maintenance room, but Karen imagined watching herself from a bird's eye view.

Part of her wished that Saff never came back, that she remained free in the outside world, but that thought was soon replaced by a sharp abdominal fear. It was daylight for now. The world was quiet and safe, but in several hours, it would devolve into a new kind of hell. There were worse fates than imprisonment, especially when she had her family around her.

'Your daughter's fiancé,' Warren said, as though he'd read her mind. She shivered at the thought. 'He'll be joining us in the Ark, I take it?'

'Yes, with his mother.'

'His mother?'

'He won't leave her on her own out there. We have space for her, don't we?'

She met Warren's eye, saw the conflict in him. 'That's not the issue.'

'What is the issue? If we don't have the food, I can miss some meals to make up for it. Or, I don't know, whatever it takes.'

Warren regarded her with a tentative smile. 'It's not that either. Look, the Ark has been over fifty years in the making. Every little detail has been orchestrated, cross-referenced, and simulated where possible to construct the safest conditions we can. Locking fifty to sixty strangers together

282

in a confined space is a very fragile operation. I've studied every inhabitant of the Ark carefully. Introducing an anomaly into the Ark is risky enough. Introducing two…' Warren sighed, as though he were struggling to convince even himself with the argument.

So, they *had* been watching her. Did they have cameras like these in her Hampstead home? The prison had always been there. She was only now becoming aware of its dimensions. On the other hand, Warren couldn't have studied them all too accurately, or he would have known about Andrew's infidelity, his addictive personality. Was that not part of their criteria for living in harmony?

'Rory's a good kid,' she said, 'and his mother seems like a lovely woman. What's the worst that could happen?'

Warren smiled to himself as though remembering a distasteful joke. 'That's not a question you want to know the answer to, Karen. The stability of society within the Ark already balances on a knife-edge. You introduce one personality disorder or one genetic defect to the mix, the whole thing collapses.'

'She's not a psychopath, if that's what you mean, and she's had her children. You said yourself, the people here were chosen partially for their genetics. The Ark's designed not just for us now, but for generations to come, right?'

Warren nodded slowly.

'Rory and Saff are a good match. They love each other - hear me out, please - they chose each other the same way our ancestors chose their partners for millions of years of evolution. Surely our evolutionary drives are just as accurate as whatever algorithms or tests you put us through. Rory won't leave his mother behind - what kind of son would? - and Saff won't return to the Ark without him. So, it comes down to that: do you let one mother into the Ark, or do you lose a young couple who have chosen each other naturally and who could well be the future of the Ark? And Andrew and me, because I'm not staying in here without my daughter.'

Warren raised his eyebrows silently, considered, then nodded. 'Okay.'

Tears filled Karen's eyes. 'Thank you.'

'No. You're right.'

She dried her eyes and looked back to the monitor. David was heading back along the corridor. Karen watched him walk through the door as he appeared in her peripheral vision.

'Kamal says, give him fifteen minutes and he'll be ready to go.'

'Good,' Warren said. 'Thank you.'

'Oh, shit,' Ian said.

Karen turned to face him. Ian was staring at the left-hand monitor in front of him.

Her heart somersaulted in her chest. In the road outside, Andrew, Saff, Rory, and his mother came filtering through the line of cars.

She stared at the apparitions, expecting them to flicker out of existence with each frame.

They could not have walked to Harringay and back so quickly. She must be hallucinating. Unless the streets had cleared up during the day and they had driven here. In any case, she could not be hallucinating if Ian, Warren, and David could see them too.

'We'll have to get them in without coming into contact with anyone else,' Warren said. 'Find a face mask, please, David. I'd like you to escort them all to the chapel again when we're clear. And then you'll take them to the hospital one by one for screening, just like we did on day zero.'

'Got it.'

The others were moving through the Gherkin's construction gate now. In a minute or two, they'd be right outside. The relief was almost painful as it flooded her stomach, washed away the stone lodged there. But she would have to face Andrew too. Could she look at him, speak to him, without wanting to throw up? She supposed she could cage her emotions until they'd settled into the Ark and Andrew could disappear again, like he did best.

The elevator doors closed, and they were gone from the CCTV feed. Panic gnawed at her intestines, as though Saff had disappeared forever. Karen had imagined it after all. Or the video feed had played some kind of trick on her.

She held her breath until they appeared again in the chamber with Mac and Callum. They all congregated in front of the door. The door that would not open for another ten minutes at least.

'I should tell them what's happening,' Karen said, moving towards the door.

'They won't hear you,' Warren said. 'Not through that door.'

Well, they were safe. That was the important thing. Soon they'd be inside with her and her main stress would be avoiding Andrew. Oh God, the photos were still scattered across the living room floor. What would Saff think when she saw them? Had Andrew even told her about his confession? She supposed it would be easier if he hadn't, for the time being at least.

A low rumble went through Karen's stomach, her feet. The room vibrated. It was going to collapse in on her, and she would wake up in her bed back home.

A deeper wave shook the room. On the left-hand monitor, the cars on St Mary Axe went up in smoke. Glass exploded from the Gherkin's base, and the whole structure slowly started to lean.

'Open the door,' she said. Her voice was distant, as though coming out of some tinny speaker across the room. She turned to face Warren, and her vision pulled in slow motion. Warren stared fixedly at the monitor. He had a scar under his left eye that she hadn't noticed before.

'Warren, open the door,' she yelled.

Through a cloud of white smoke, the Gherkin was tipping sideways into the street.

Warren stared back at her with black-hole pupils, frozen in place.

Karen turned to David, but the soldier, too, stared in disbelief at the monitor. It was like time had stopped. Her own movements were thick and slow like wading through syrup.

She snatched the handgun from the desk and aimed it at both men in an arc. 'Open the fucking door.'

Like a pin popping her balloon, they were back.

Warren lunged for the door and ran into the corridor. She followed on his heels, still aiming the gun redundantly at his back.

He punched the door code into the keypad and reached for the hand wheel. Karen grabbed a spoke with her free hand, and together they turned the wheel until it stopped.

She pulled with all her strength, and the door swung slowly inwards.

A cloud of smoke billowed through the gap, blinding her, but there were footsteps moving. The dog's bark echoed endlessly around the chamber.

Shadows moved past her as the smoke and dust filled her lungs, made her cough. She tried to count them, but she couldn't see properly.

'That's it,' someone yelled. 'Close the door.'

She heaved the slab of metal until it thudded home, turned the hand wheel to secure it.

The smoke slowly dissipated, and Karen saw Rory, and then his mother, and then Saff.

Karen threw herself at her daughter and enveloped her in her arms. She just needed to keep her there, by her chest, where nothing could harm her.

'What the fuck?' Andrew yelled, materialising out of the fog. 'What the fuck was that?'

They all looked around each other, as though one of them might have the answer.

Doors were opening all along the corridor and more people were arriving from the other end.

'Stay back,' David called, holding out both arms. 'Everyone stay where you are.'

Charlotte was at the forefront of the crowd. She spotted Mac and closed her eyes on the spot, as though freezing to savour the relief.

The walls and floor continued to shake, but faintly now. The final explosions rippled out.

'Alright, I need everyone back in their rooms or wherever they were,' Warren called. 'I'll call a meeting in the common room shortly. And all of you,' he said, turning to those who had just come through, 'I need in the chapel. Just follow David, and I will come and speak to you in a minute.' He held out his hand to Karen. Only then did she remember she was still holding the handgun. 'I'm going to need that back now.'

She handed it over, glad to be rid of it, and hugged Saff again.

'God, I'm so glad you're okay. All of you.' She met Rory's eye, folded him into an embrace as well. 'My son-in-law.'

She didn't hug Rory's mother. She seemed to still be processing whatever had just happened.

'How did you make it so quickly?' Karen asked.

Saff nodded to Andrew, who turned around.

'He drove us on the Overground tracks,' she said matter-of-factly, as though she did not want to give him too much credit.

So, Saff did know about Andrew. Even though they had nearly died on the other side of that door, she still did not want to look her father in the face.

As they filed through the corridor after David, Andrew fell in beside her.

'How are you doing?'

'I've had better days,' she said, facing ahead.

'Mmm.'

'Thank you, for bringing them back.'

Andrew winced, as though her gratitude caused him physical pain, and nodded.

'Listen, I've been thinking -'

287

'Not now,' she said. 'Later, we'll talk, but for now, let's just focus on getting everyone settled.'

'Okay,' he said.

'Did he find the medicine?' she asked, nodding to Mac's back.

'Yeah.'

'Thank God.'

They filed into the dim chapel.

Charlotte fell into a pew and sobbed into Byron's fur. Rory and Saff sat beside his mother, consoling her. Andrew and Mac conversed in the aisle. Callum sat in the pew closest to the door, stared up at the artificially illuminated stained-glass window.

Karen scanned the chapel's walls, its ceiling. She could not spot a camera, but she knew it was there. She could feel its cold gaze freezing her in place, chopping her up into slow, fuzzy frames.

She imagined her pixelated body on screen beside a dozen other boxes filled with the strangers that would become her extended family, her tribe.

What did London look like half a mile above them? Piles of stone, glass, and metal rubble. Skyscrapers fallen like trees in the wind. If the elevator shaft hadn't caved in, the Gherkin had surely collapsed on top of it.

They couldn't get out now if they'd wanted to.

What had happened anyway? Those had been bombs or missiles. Either the British military had friendly fired on the streets of London, or some external nation or terrorist group had targeted them.

She would never know. Not unless the news networks recovered themselves and started broadcasting again, or the phone networks came back online and she managed to get hold of her parents.

She'd have to settle into this isolation, and perhaps they would adapt. That's what people were good at, wasn't it? Adapting to their suffering, one day at a time.

EPILOGUE

MAC

Mac peered around the bedroom door. At first he thought Charlotte was sleeping. He was about to back out when she twisted around to face him.

'Hey,' he said, stepping into the room. 'I brought you some food if you feel up to eating.' He set the plate down on the bedside table and sat down on the bed.

'Thanks, honey.' She stared at the plate for a moment before taking a triangle of toast and biting into it.

On the TV he'd moved into the bedroom, a Julia Roberts rom-com played.

Charlotte returned the toast to the plate and shrank down into the pillows. She hugged the washing-up bowl to her chest, closed her eyes.

'Feeling sick again?' he asked.

Charlotte shook her head, frowning as though the very effort of communication caused her intense pain. 'Just faint, I think... I don't know.'

Mac took her hand from the bed sheets and squeezed it. She squeezed back.

He checked his watch. Quarter-to-eight.

'You know, I can ask the others to postpone the

meeting. It doesn't need to be tonight. I don't want to leave you feeling like this.'

'It's fine,' she said, forcing a faint smile. 'I'll probably just sleep. Is Luke still out?'

'Yeah.'

'Will you check on him first?'

'Sure.' He stretched his legs out on the bed and settled next to Charlotte. On screen, a heated argument was brewing between Julia Roberts and her supposed love interest.

'What if he starts to withdraw again, Mac?'

'Then we'll talk to him about it, encourage him to communicate with us. Or with the psychiatrist. He'll be okay.'

She nodded, closed her eyes. 'I've still not forgiven you, you know.'

'For what?'

'For lying to me.'

'About leaving? You'd never have let me go.'

'I know,' she said. She opened her eyes, smiled weakly.

He laughed to himself, checked his watch. 'I should go then, if you're sure you'll be okay.'

'Yeah, yeah.'

'You need anything before I go?'

She shook her head.

'Alright.' He kissed her forehead. 'I love you.'

'I love you too.'

He slipped out of the room and nearly tripped over Byron in the dim hallway.

'Jesus,' he whispered. 'Sorry, mate.'

Byron whined and padded into the living room.

He patted his pockets to check for his phone, wallet, and keys, then realised he needed none of those things.

He followed the corridors down to the common room. The lights had started to grow dimmer and warmer in colour to simulate the setting sun. He yawned. How much sleep had he lost over the last few days? He had plenty of time to catch up, but not yet.

A sitcom was playing in the common room. A dozen or so people were gathered around to watch. He caught Ian and Andrew's eyes as he walked through, gave them a nod.

He heard the noise from the games room before he pushed through the doors at the back of the common room.

Inside, Luke and another boy were perched on the edge of the sofa, controlling two skateboarders on the PlayStation. Neither of them turned around.

A girl and a boy were playing a noisy game of table football on the other side of the room.

On TV, one of the skateboarders pulled an impressive display of tricks in the air before landing on their head, leaving a pixelated smear of blood down the half pipe.

'Oh shit, did you see that?' Luke asked the other kid.

'I saw it,' Mac said.

Luke spun around.

'Some of these games are so violent,' Mac said and laughed at how much of a parent he sounded. 'You guys having fun?'

'Yeah,' Luke said, as though there were some caveat. Or perhaps it wasn't deemed cool to enjoy yourself too much.

'Hey, Dad?' Luke said, taking control of his skateboarder again and grinding down a handrail.

'What's up?'

'Can Michael come see Byron?'

'Not now. I have to go for this meeting, and your mother will be sleeping. But probably tomorrow. We can play fetch in the garden together.'

'Okay, thanks.'

Mac checked his watch. Three-minutes-to-eight. 'Alright, I've got to make a move, but I should be done in an hour or so. Have fun.'

'See you,' Luke said, not taking his eyes off the TV.

Mac lingered in the doorway, thinking for the first time in too long that Luke seemed just like a normal kid. He smiled.

Andrew and Ian got to their feet and fell in beside him as he walked back through the common room.

They went next door to the smoking room, where Warren, Kamal, and the three soldiers were already sitting.

'How are you doing, guys?' Warren said. 'Please, take a seat.'

The side tables had been put together, around which all the chairs were arranged.

'Alright, that's everyone, so we'll make a start,' Warren said. 'I called you here for a preliminary meeting about the future management of the Ark. It's become clear to me that, despite the careful calculation of all aspects of the facility, the majority of residents are not comfortable with an authoritarian management. Essentially, people want a say in how things are run down here, or at least in new decisions that are made. It was never my intention to govern the Ark like some kind of dictator, so I'm happy to open decision-making to a supervisory board. I suggest we hold a vote within the next few days to elect thirteen board members. And the reason I called you all here is because I'd like you all to stand.'

He opened his hands to the group. 'You've all proven yourselves to be highly competent, perceptive, and courageous individuals. I can't govern the Ark without your help, so I implore you all to put yourselves forward. Does anyone have any objections?'

Mac looked around the table, but no one spoke up.

'I see no reason why anyone would vote against any of you, especially with my own word of recommendation, so I suggest we proceed with our first informal board meeting. I have a few items on the agenda, but we can open the floor for other subjects too.'

By the time they left the smoking room an hour and a half later, Mac was beginning to feel like he was in a dream again. His conception of the following weeks and months was changing. He would have to get used to the entrapment and the many limitations of the Ark, but the horrors he'd imagined this place to harbour did not seem so daunting now. If Charlotte pulled through this round of chemo, there was hope of a relatively normal life. But he'd been wrong before.

Only time would tell in the end.

SAFF

'How do I look?'

Saff held her breath as her mother looked up her figure. 'Honey, you look… stunning.' She enveloped Saff in her arms, who leaned away to avoid smudging her makeup but hugged her back fiercely.

The borrowed dress was not what she'd had in mind when she'd dreamed about her wedding day, but none of this was. She'd wanted a long mermaid dress with a frilly skirt and a sequinned bodice. She'd wanted to get married at sunset in the gardens of some grand London palace, Kensington or Hampton Court. She'd wanted her childhood friends and her grandparents there.

'What have you done with my daughter?' her mother said.

'Stop,' Saff said, giving her a light push and wiping at her eye with a knuckle. 'My makeup's not waterproof.'

'I'm sorry. I'm just so proud of you.'

Saff sat back down in her dresser chair, checked her makeup in the mirror. Would Rory find her beautiful? Perhaps she should have done her makeup plainer after all.

'Have you talked to Dad?' she asked.

Her mother sat down on the bed. 'We spoke this morning.'

'And?'

'He told me he's having sessions with the psychiatrist. He says he's reading a lot,' her mother laughed. 'I want to believe he can change, but I don't know. It's too early to say.'

Saff nodded, swallowed. 'You don't mind him walking me down the aisle?'

'Of course not, love. He's your father, and despite his flaws, he loves you. You need a good relationship with him, regardless.'

'Okay.' Saff examined her curls in the mirror. Jesus, one of them was falling out already. She looked around for the straighteners.

The front door opened and closed. A rap came on the bedroom door.

Her mother opened it as Saff was fixing her curl. Her father stepped in.

'Wow,' he said. He stared at her, a smile bleeding into his face. 'You look beautiful.'

'Thanks. Is Rory ready?'

'Yeah. They're all ready for you.'

The butterflies flittered in her bloated stomach.

It was too soon. She was not ready herself. She hadn't had time to… but no, there was nothing left to do.

'Okay.' She got to her feet and headed for the door.

Her father led her out of the apartment and down the corridor. She tried to focus on her breathing, but everything felt as tight as a vice, as though she were wearing a Victorian corset instead of a pink evening dress.

They stopped outside the chapel door, and her father turned to her.

'I know these aren't circumstances you ever anticipated, but I couldn't be happier to give you away. He's a good man. You have my blessing a thousand times over.'

'Thank you.' She hugged him for the first time since she'd slipped out of the Ark, probably for the first time in years. 'And thank you for coming after me. For helping get him back.'

'My pleasure,' he said, and when they withdrew, he wiped a tear away. 'Come on then.' He held out his arm. 'Let's get you married.'

She took his arm, and together, they walked into the chapel.

The room was packed, and they were all looking at her. People stood in front of each pew, and those with no seat filled the space at the back of the room. The chapel probably hadn't been designed to accommodate all of the Ark's residents at once.

On the raised platform, standing in front of the altar, was Rory. He beamed down at her, wearing a black shirt and trousers. She wanted to run up the aisle to him, but she had to walk slowly, acknowledge everyone else. Some of them she knew fairly well by now, and she knew most of the others' names.

When they reached the altar, her father released her arm and slipped into the front pew.

She stepped up to the stage to face Rory. She wanted to kiss him then, but that was not proper, was it? Instead, she threw her arms around him, drank the smell of his aftershave.

'You look incredible,' he said into her ear.

'Don't be ridiculous,' she said.

She looked down at the congregation and butterflies swam again. Her mother found her place in the pews.

Mary stepped up to the stage beside them, clutching a bible.

'Okay, please take your seats, everyone.' A ruffle of clothes. 'As you know, we are gathered here today to celebrate the matrimony of Saffron and Rory.'

She met Rory's eye, and a nervous giggle escaped her.

Everything faded away, and for a moment, it was just them. It didn't matter that they were trapped half a mile underground with no hope of ever seeing daylight again. For a moment, everything she needed was right there.

HARRIS

The meeting room door opened, jolting Harris out of a liminal sleep. Campbell stopped in the doorway.

'I thought you'd gone. Everyone else has.'

Harris shook his head. 'Not yet. There's something I need to do.'

Campbell frowned, nodded. Harris had the impression he didn't want to know what it was, didn't want to be reminded of the impossibility. 'Will I see you in New York?'

'No. If I make it out of here, I'll find my wife in Detroit.'

Campbell nodded again. He crossed the room to the window, lifted his bag from a chair and slung it over his shoulder. 'I guess this is goodbye then.'

'Yeah.' Harris got to his feet, shook Campbell's hand, then threw his arms around him.

A wavering breath escaped Campbell into his ear as he hugged him back fiercely.

'Thank you,' Campbell said as they withdrew. 'For everything.'

'Of course. Take care of yourself, man.'

Campbell nodded, staring emptily out of the window. 'And you.' He walked out and closed the door gently.

Harris stared at the closed door for a moment before washing his face with empty hands. He'd slept a few hours the night before, but his dreams had been plagued by dark, primitive images. He was still so tired, he wasn't himself. The medical school professor with his wife and his dog and his house was but a dream itself now.

The sky was growing darker. He had three hours of daylight left, four at the most. When night fell, it would steal morning away with it. The hosts had broken through the Swiss border late last night. Any remaining military and peacekeepers were leaving the medical school that afternoon to defend the highways.

Harris stretched, sat down again, and tried to focus on his book. He'd read a few pages when a knock came at the door.

'Come in.'

Police Chief Haberlin stepped inside, produced a manila envelope from his jacket, and handed it to Harris.

'We have orders to kill the hosts before we leave, but I can give you…' he frowned at his watch. 'Two hours.'

'That's great. Thank you.'

Haberlin nodded. 'I hope you know what you're doing, Professor.'

'Yeah,' Harris said. 'Me too.'

Haberlin paused, searching for something else to say, then made for the door. 'Good luck,' he said before closing the door.

Harris stared at the envelope for a second before snatching it up and hurrying to the lab next door.

He slipped on a pair of latex gloves and emptied the envelope over the counter. Out spilled a variety of off-white crystals in baggies, plastic-wrapped dried mushrooms, and a booklet of paper blotters printed with the image of the Mad Hatter from Disney's *Alice in Wonderland*.

He filled a petri dish with clean water and dropped the tabs into it. He'd give them about twenty, maybe thirty minutes to dissolve. After that, he'd only need a few minutes to test.

He covered the dish and went into the office. He dialled Laura's mobile, but the line would not connect.

She's fine, he told himself. There were no confirmed cases of the virus State-side.

He took out a Camel - the last of his pack - considered going outside to smoke it, but decided no one would care. The medical school would be empty within hours and perhaps filled with hosts after that. He shuddered at the thought, threw open a window, and smoked his cigarette.

When he was finished, he checked his watch, returned to the lab. He called it at twenty-five minutes, lifted the LSD tabs out of the water, and siphoned the liquid into a syringe.

As he carried it down to the lab where the hosts were kept, he wondered, indifferently, whether he'd gone crazy. Perhaps he was simply so sleep-deprived that his wild dreams had started to bleed into waking consciousness.

This was the end of the road. The progress they'd made counted for nothing. The virus was simply too powerful to fight. He could only hope that the States were safe. They had more guns per capita than any other nation. That had to count for something. Probably force was the only way to fight it after all. This last attempt was… a joke, but he had to try it anyway. Weaker drugs had subdued the hosts' more primitive impulses, dampened their limbic stimulation, but there were no pharmaceuticals powerful enough to light up the cortex like psychedelics.

When he'd been fifteen, he'd taken a high dose of psilocybin with a couple of friends. The things he'd experienced that night had changed him forever. The boy, filled with bitterness and rage at his own existence, had dissolved into the ether, and when he'd found his body again, he'd been a different person. Within weeks, he'd stopped fist-fighting at school, stopped drinking and smoking himself into a coma each weekend, and set his sights on studying psychology at college. And then he'd met Laura, and everything else had fallen into place like some multi-dimensional jigsaw. It were as though he'd been sleepwalking for fifteen years.

He passed the soldiers guarding the door and stepped into the lab. As the door closed behind him, his ears pinned to the silence.

A low groaning echoed across the room.

He strapped the helmet onto his head and lowered the night-vision goggles over his eyes. The room blinked into existence, the vibrant, negative world. It struck him then: he'd dreamed in this same green filter last night, but the content eluded him.

He walked slowly to the two remaining hosts, still strapped and handcuffed to the trolleys.

IV and EEG wires came off them like alien tendrils.

The male host stared at him with bared teeth, its whole face contorted in rage. It looked exhausted, hanging on by a thread. The female host in the trolley beside it was dead. Her heart rate on the electrocardiogram had flatlined.

'Just you and me left then,' Harris said. His own voice was thin and hollow. The host gave a clicking wail in response, forced against its restraints.

'Yeah, I know,' he said. He looked into the host's eyes, burning like white dwarfs in its pale green face, before reaching for its cannula and inserting the needle. He slowly pushed the plunger and watched the LSD-infused water snake through its IV.

He set the syringe down and stepped back, drew Laura's crucifix out of his shirt and pressed it to his lips.

The host only stared into the darkness, to a spot just to the right of Harris. Its eyelids pulled slowly shut, as though in sleep.

On his laptop screen, the beta waves transformed into theta, and then alpha.

The host opened his eyes and looked right at Harris. His heart was racing in his ears as he struggled to find his voice.

'Can you hear me?'

The man blinked. His brow furrowed.

302

'What's your name?'

The man stared emptily for a moment before his face contorted in pain. The noise which escaped him was a whimper. An ice-cold cloud washed over Harris.

'My name's Richard. Richard Harris. Can you understand me?'

The man parted his lips, frowned, as though trying to remember how to speak after a stroke. He breathed deeply, and then muttered something in French.

'What?' Harris stumbled back to find the light switch, tore off the night-vision helmet.

The man squeezed his eyes shut, wincing, but he did not cry out.

'Do you speak English?' Harris said.

The man closed his eyes and did not open them again. Just as Harris thought he'd lost the man, he spoke again.

'Is it… over?'

Harris was so stunned, he could not find his reply. The EEG displayed sharp, towering brainwaves: gamma waves.

'Kill me. Please.' The man opened his eyes and a tear rolled down his cheek. 'Don't make me go back.'

'It's okay. It's over.' Harris's face grew hot, and his own eyes stung with tears. 'It's over.'

Printed in Poland
by Amazon Fulfillment
Poland Sp. z o.o., Wrocław